Strange Beasts and Unnatural Monsters

George T. ...

Strange Beasts and Unnatural Monsters

SELECTED AND WITH AN INTRODUCTION

by Philip Van Doren Stern

A FAWCETT CREST BOOK

Fawcett Publications, Inc., Greenwich, Conn.
Member of American Book Publishers Council, Inc.

A Fawcett Crest Book
reprinted by arrangement with Philip Van Doren Stern

Library of Congress Catalog Card Number: 68-29492

First Fawcett Crest Printing, August 1968

Published by Fawcett World Library
67 West 44th Street, New York, N.Y. 10036
Printed in the United States of America

ACKNOWLEDGMENTS

"The Nature of the Evidence" by May Sinclair. Copyright 1923, 1951 by H. L. Sinclair and W. McNiele. Reprinted by permission.

"Slime" by Joseph Payne Brennan. Copyright 1953 by Weird Tales and reprinted by permission of Arkham House and Scott Meredith Literary Agency, Inc.

"The Garden of Paris" by Eric Williams. Copyright © 1965 by John Carnell for Weird Shadows from Beyond and reprinted by permission of the author.

"Doomsday Deferred" by Will F. Jenkins. Copyright 1949, Curtis Publishing Company. Reprinted by permission.

"The Cocoon" by J. B. L. Goodwin. Copyright 1946 by Story Magazine, Inc. Reprinted by permission.

"Aepyornis Island" by H. G. Wells. Copyright 1895 by George Philip Wells and Francis Richard Wells. Reprinted by permission.

"The Terror of Blue John Gap" by Arthur Conan Doyle. Copyright 1910 by Arthur Conan Doyle. Reprinted by permission of the Estate of Sir Arthur Conan Doyle.

"The Birds" by Daphne du Maurier. Copyright 1952 by Daphne du Maurier, from the book, Kiss Me Again, Stranger by Daphne du Maurier. Reprinted by permission of Doubleday and Company, Inc.

"The Kill" by Peter Fleming. Copyright 1942 by Peter Fleming, from A Story to Tell. Reprinted by permission.

"Mrs. Amworth" by E. F. Benson. Copyright 1922 by Kenneth Stewart Patrick McDowell. Reprinted by permission.

"Skeleton" by Ray Bradbury. Copyright 1945 by Ray Bradbury. Reprinted by permission of the Harold Matson Company.

"The Elephant Man" by Frederick Treves. Copyright the Executors of the Estate of Sir Frderick Treves. First published in 1923.

Table of Contents

INTRODUCTION by Philip Van Doren Stern   **9**

THE NATURE OF THE EVIDENCE   **17**
  by May Sinclair

  "There had been, behind that shut door, some experience, some terrible and exquisite contact."

SLIME by Joseph Payne Brennan   **27**

  "The black mantle . . . groped greedily and endlessly through the mud, eating and never sleeping, never resting."

THE GARDEN OF PARIS by Eric Williams   **49**

  "The root came free and took the end off my finger."

DOOMSDAY DEFERRED by Will F. Jenkins   **66**

  "I have heard the squealing of pigs at slaughtering time. . . . This was not that sort of noise. It was worse, much worse."

THE COCOON by John B. L. Goodwin   **76**

  "Something . . . had wormed its way beneath the sheet and was resting like a sticky pulp upon Denny's mouth."

ÆPYORNIS ISLAND by H. G. Wells **91**

"Here was this extinct animal mooning about my island . . . and I hatched him."

THE TERROR OF BLUE JOHN GAP **102**
by A. Conan Doyle

"There was some creature there . . . which could see in the dark. . . . Had it caught the scent of me?"

THE BIRDS by Daphne du Maurier **117**

"With each dive, with each attack, they became bolder. And they had no thought of themselves."

THE JUDGE'S HOUSE by Bram Stoker **150**

"He saw the great rat drop from the rope . . . and sit there glaring at him."

THE KILL by Peter Fleming **167**

"Whatever did it was . . . more powerful and cunning than a dog. . . . Their throats had been torn out."

MRS. AMWORTH by E. F. Benson **177**

"It is not human: it is an incarnate fiend."

SKELETON by Ray Bradbury **191**

"This thing inside, this invader, this horror, was supporting his arms, legs and head!"

THE ELEPHANT MAN **205**
by Sir Frederick Treves

"There stood . . . the most disgusting specimen of humanity I have every seen."

Strange Beasts and Unnatural Monsters

INTRODUCTION

Man's association with animals goes back to his earliest beginnings, for he evolved into human form among beasts that contested with him for territory, food, and survival. The carnivores preyed upon him, while he in turn killed anything he could eat. Like all denizens of the wilderness, he began each day with nothing and never knew what his next meal might be. When he slaughtered a warm-blooded victim, he dined well, but he often had to be satisfied with grubs, insects, or things that crawl.

For thousands of generations, killing or being killed was so natural to prehistoric man that sudden death was an everyday affair. As a walking nomad he could own nothing except the few simple objects he could carry. But he had the world's most highly developed brain, skillful fingers, and the ability to combine thought and dexterity to invent new devices. Unlike the less intelligent animals around him, he learned and slowly improved his lot.

Eventually, he made a hunting companion of the dog, which was the first wild beast to be domesticated. The dog's keen sense of smell, swift feet, piercing bark, and sharp teeth were of great help in the daily chase. He was also an excellent sentry. When your sleeping pet suddenly awakens, pricks his ears, and utters a low growl to warn you that something is approaching, he is reenacting a role he learned in fire-lit caves and rawhide tents, for he is still attuned to times when constant alertness and instant action were needed for survival.

After man recruited the dog as an ally, he learned to plant seeds and gather crops that could be stored for the winter. He also found out that certain animals besides the dog could be captured, tamed, and made to serve him. The hunter settled down; the nomad became a villager; the villager, a townsman; and with the discovery of metal and the invention of writing, the townsman became a city dweller. Civilization began, and as it developed and spread, man saw less and less of the creatures he had grown up with.

Finally, when machines replaced muscles as sources of power, man no longer needed the beasts he had used for their strength. They, and animals that supplied food, were banished to remote farms and mountain pastures. Only a few pets were permitted to stay in the city home. They are the last remaining symbols of a close association that has endured for thousands of years.

Throughout those ages man realized that some animals had senses far keener than his own. But only in recent times has he learned that a few are endowed with powers he does not have at all. He found out that dolphins and bats can locate solid objects by sending out sounds and receiving their echoes back; he discovered the fact that fish can "feel" the presence of underwater obstacles in lateral-line organs that respond to minute changes in pressure; and that birds, snakes, and insects have perceptive abilities which human beings do not possess. Wonder succeeded wonder as man learned more and more about the creatures that share his world. It is a pity that he came to respect their ultrahuman senses so late.

In medieval times, when man was still close enough to animals to think that some of them had supernatural powers, he compiled a black bestiary that contained such mythical monsters as the basilisk and the cockatrice, which were so fearful to behold that the very glance of them was believed to be fatal; the Chimera, the griffin, and the sphinx, which were ingenious composites; the roc, a bird so big that it could devour elephants; and the dragon, which came in all shapes and sizes. Others less monstrous were the phoenix, a winged creature that consumed itself in fire and then arose from its purified ashes; the caladrius, a white bird that could foretell the course of illness by averting its head from a patient who was going to die; and, last of all, the immortal unicorn that still dwells in the green pastures embroidered on medieval tapestries.

Other imaginary creatures crowd the pages of these bestiaries. A few survive in realistic sculptured portraits to remind us of the time when they were thought to be as real as barnyard calves.

In various places man became so impressed with the idea that animals had great powers that he made some of them into totems and gods. From Egypt to North America, he enshrined all kinds of beasts as minor deities. Perhaps their once potent images have dark powers still.

Did these grotesque creatures come from recollections of the real monsters that roamed the earth in primeval times? No, that cannot be, for the last of the mighty dinosaurs became extinct at least seventy million years before man first appeared on the earth. But their huge fossilized bones and multitoothed jaws may have provided the basic ideas for large mythical beasts. The Chinese, who live in a land where the remains of dinosaurs are fairly common, could very well have made dragons out of ordinary lizards simply by clothing the enormous fossil skulls with imagined flesh. Other people in other countries where big fossils are found could have had similar inspirations for local breeds of the ubiquitous dragon.

The great reptiles ruled the earth for more than a hundred million years and then became extinct at the end of the Cretaceous period. We say that they are gone, but they have not all been safely entombed in ancient rocks. Their descendants—crocodiles, turtles, lizards, and snakes—are smaller, but they perpetuate reptilian forms that most people abhor.

At least one modern lizard retains respectable size, for the komondo dragon, which was discovered on the island of Sunda in 1912, attains a length of nine feet. And a genuine relic from Triassic times lives on unchanged. This is the tuatara, a two-foot-long betailed tetrapod with a third pineal eye on the top of its head. Known since 1830, this rare creature is carefully protected by the New Zealand government on the offshore islands that are its natural habitat.

Recent years have seen another presumed fossil come dramatically to life. Near the east coast of South Africa, in December 1938, a trawlnet dragged up a large fish with paddle-like fins, a short, stubby tail, and big coarse scales. Scientists identified it as a coelacanth, which they had believed to be extinct for seventy million years. Later catches provided more details about its obsolete anatomy. Perhaps other survivors from remote ages are still among us; perhaps they too will someday swim into our ken. But they may not be so easily taken as the coelacanth was.

The oceans of the world are so vast and deep that they must harbor many forms of life which are as yet unknown. Recent explorations of the dark abysses, made possible by technically advanced equipment, have shown us that some very strange creatures do live down there. Most of them are small, but hidden away in an underwater lair may be monsters as terrible as any aquatic dinosaur.

Huge size is an important factor in inducing fear. We unconcernedly stamp out the life of a tiny insect that would cause us to flee in panic if it were enlarged a few hundred times. African elephants, grizzly bears, tigers, lions, gorillas, sharks, and boa constrictors are dangerous because they are big, strong, and ferocious when aroused.

Myths and legends are filled with creatures that were far more deadful than these, and there is good reason to believe that some of them were not wholly imaginary. The giant kraken, that was said to seize and hold a ship while it devoured the men on board, stained the water black when it surfaced. This inky discharge is typical of the armed cephalopods, so the kraken was probably a huge deep-sea squid that was built up into even larger dimensions by the terrified sailors who saw one approach their ship. Sea serpents have been reported in so many places by people who claim to have seen them clearly that it is hard to dismiss the possibility of their existence. A number of observers are sure that they have glimpsed Scotland's Loch Ness monster, and now another large swimming creature that sticks its head out of the water is supposed to inhabit Montana's Flathead Lake.

Living wild men, half human and half beast, are said to be at large in the more remote areas of the world. The best-known of them is the Abominable Snowman of the higher Himalayas. His alleged footprints have been photographed, and odd-looking scalps described as having been taken from these Yetis are preserved in Tibetan monasteries.

The Abominable Snowmen are supposed to be real—and must therefore be vulnerable. Far worse are spectral monsters, for there can be no defense against things that are more insubstantial than mist, more tenuous than a shaft of moonlight, more deadly than an unseen poisonous gas that clutches at the throat as it kills. An extensive body of literature has grown up around these shadow-shapes. They are all monsters, but they are not all beasts; some have the semblance of human form.

There are six basic kinds of stories about:
1. Invisible things whose presence can only be sensed
2. Shapeless masses of jelly or protoplasm
3. Small, nasty creatures that ordinarily make mass attacks
4. Large, dangerous, mythical monsters that are more powerful than anything that lives
5. Ordinarily friendly animals that suddenly revolt against man
6. Man himself when he temporarily assumes the form of a beast

And there are, of course, all sorts of variations and combinations of these basic themes.

Most horrible of all are the protean creatures in the sixth category, for they once were men. The others are more primitive, so less is expected of them. But a fellow being who falls from grace to wallow in mud and gore is truly frightening.

The idea of having men become beasts is very old. Yet in its origin, the were-animal was a pitiable thing, for he

13

came from a time when an offender could be driven out of his community and left to fend for himself as best he could. To stay alive, the outcast had to forage in the fields or raid outlying farms for food. Naturally, all good householders feared and hated him. They used his furtive figure to frighten children into obedience and finally convinced themselves that the shadowy outlaw was not a man but a wild beast.

The notion spread quickly. In Europe, where the wolf was the most feared predator, such creatures were called werewolves; in Japan, werefoxes; in Malaysia, weretigers; in Africa, wereleopards; in South America, werejaguars; in North America (among the Indians), bear-walkers—and so on throughout the world. The fact that the captured or slain body of one of these suspected man-monsters was always human simply proved that a were-creature could change his shape quickly.

This gave rise to the idea that men and beasts may be interchangeable—and perhaps in certain ways they are. We are all haunted by our ancient past when the first crude hominoids emerged from animalian stock. The formula is simple: beast plus time became man. Can this be reversed? And in accelerated time?

The monsters still inside us cannot always be kept immured. They appear in dreams and nightmares and plague the disordered mind even in daylight hours. Man and beast, when linked together in an unholy alliance, can release madness upon the world. Try to banish these ancestral demons as we will, we can never be rid of them entirely. Their primal laughter mocks our noblest thoughts.

Even a small child has a full share of this dark heritage. A four-year-old can evoke such creatures by scrawling their shapes on paper and then describe them with winning innocence by saying: "That's a cloben, and this is a shayben. But this one's the worst. It's a snorl with a long snout, and it creeps along the floor to catch you."*

*This is a verbatim quote.

Imaginary beasts? Yes, but that does not mean that they are not real to their young creator.

We are all so steeped in the lore of monsters that they penetrate our inmost defenses. At midnight, even in a seemingly secure city apartment, there may be the sound of hooves in the corridor—or, worse still, the scraping of scales upon the floor.

Who knows what may be lurking beyond the door to the hall? And which door is it, the substantial one of wood or steel or its unsubstantial counterpart that swings upon the hinges of the mind?

What is breathing so hard behind it? What dread creature is loose from the midnight zoo where all the monsters of the universe, real and unreal, are ordinarily confined? And who has let it out, its keeper—or you?

Or are you the keeper of that haunted zoo? You will soon know, for at this moment you are at the gate. Beyond the portal, vaguely seen shapes are stirring fitfully under the misshapen trees. And now a shriek that no living thing could ever utter is echoed by a hundred rasping throats.

But you must go forward, for you opened the gate when you raised the cover of this book. Its pages lead to strange precincts, to territory that will be dangerous to explore. Watch your footing; take care! All the beasts in this menagerie are not shut up in cages. Out of the dark a huge monster may suddenly loom up; out of the air a horde of vicious little hellbirds may come darting, swooping, shrilling at you. And what is that probing substance, rising, falling, and determinedly flowing around your ankles with a cold and clammy touch? Beyond it is a horde of slithering, slinking, writhing, creeping, twisting vile grotesqueries that slobber as they come. Even the ground beneath you is not safe because something may heave up the soil to confront you with its hideousness.

You are inside the dark menagerie now. Or is it inside you? Expect anything to happen—for it probably will. You can be sure only of this: that all these monsters, large and small, are contending for the same privilege—the privilege of frightening you.

They may succeed.

PHILIP VAN DOREN STERN

The Nature of the Evidence

by May Sinclair

This is the story Marston told me. He didn't want to tell it. I had to tear it from him bit by bit. I've pieced the bits together in their time order, and explained things here and there, but the facts are the facts he gave me. There's nothing that I didn't get out of him somehow.

Out of *him*—you'll admit my source is unimpeachable. Edward Marston, the great K.C., and the author of an admirable work on *The Logic of Evidence*. You should have read the chapters on "What Evidence Is and What It Is Not." You may say he lied; but if you knew Marston you'd know he wouldn't lie, for the simple reason that he's incapable of inventing anything. So that, if you ask me whether I believe this tale, all I can say is, I believe the things happened, because he said they happened and because they happened to him. As for what they *were*—well, I don't pretend to explain it, neither would he.

You know he was married twice. He adored his first wife, Rosamund, and Rosamund adored him. I suppose they were completely happy. She was fifteen years younger than he, and beautiful. I wish I could make you see how beautiful. Her eyes and mouth had the same sort of bow, full and wide-sweeping, and they stared out of her face with the same grave, contemplative innocence. Her mouth was finished off at each corner with the loveliest little molding, rounded like the pistil of a flower. She wore her hair in a solid gold fringe over her forehead, like a child's, and a big coil at the back. When it was let down it hung in a heavy cable to her waist. Marston used to tease her about it. She had a trick of tossing back the rope in the night when it was hot under her, and it would fall smack across his face and hurt him.

17

There was a pathos about her that I can't describe—a curious, pure, sweet beauty, like a child's; perfect, and perfectly immature; so immature that you couldn't conceive its lasting—like that—any more than childhood lasts. Marston used to say it made him nervous. He was afraid of waking up in the morning and finding that it had changed in the night. And her beauty was so much a part of herself that you couldn't think of her without it. Somehow you felt that if it went she must go too.

Well, she went first.

For a year afterwards Marston existed dangerously, always on the edge of a breakdown. If he didn't go over altogether it was because his work saved him. He had no consoling theories. He was one of those bigoted materialists of the nineteenth-century type who believe that consciousness is a purely physiological function, and that when your body's dead, *you're* dead. He saw no reason to suppose the contrary. "When you consider," he used to say, "the nature of the evidence!"

It's as well to bear this in mind, so as to realize that he hadn't any bias or anticipation. Rosamund survived for him only in his memory. And in his memory he was still in love with her. At the same time he used to discuss quite cynically the chances of his marrying again.

It seems that on their honeymoon they had gone into that. Rosamund said she hated to think of his being lonely and miserable, supposing she died before he did. She would like him to marry again. If, she stipulated, he married the right woman.

He had put it to her: "And if I marry the wrong one?"

And she had said, That would be different. She couldn't bear that.

He remembered all this afterwards; but there was nothing in it to make him suppose, at the time, that she would take action.

We talked it over, he and I, one night.

"I suppose," he said, "I shall have to marry again. It's a physical necessity. But it won't be anything more. I shan't marry the sort of woman who'll expect anything more. I won't put another woman in Rosamund's place. There'll be no unfaithfulness about it."

And there wasn't. Soon after that first year he married Pauline Silver.

She was a daughter of old Justice Parker, who was a

friend of Marston's people. He hadn't seen the girl till she came home from India after her divorce.

Yes, there'd been a divorce. Silver had behaved very decently. He'd let her bring it against *him,* to save her. But there were some queer stories going about. They didn't get round to Marston, because he was so mixed up with her people; and if they had he wouldn't have believed them. He'd made up his mind he'd marry Pauline the first minute he'd seen her. She was handsome; the hard, black, white and vermilion kind, with a little aristocratic nose and a lascivious mouth.

It was, as he had meant it to be, nothing but physical infatuation on both sides. No question of Pauline's taking Rosamund's place.

Marston had a big case on at the time.

They were in such a hurry that they couldn't wait till it was over; and as it kept him in London they agreed to put off their honeymoon till the autumn; and he took her straight to his own house in Curzon Street.

This, he admitted afterwards, was the part he hated. The Curzon Street house was associated with Rosamund; especially their bedroom—Rosamund's bedroom—and his library. The library was the room Rosamund liked best, because it was his room. She had her place in the corner by the hearth, and they were always alone there together in the evenings when his work was done, and when it wasn't done she would still sit with him, keeping quiet in her corner with a book.

Luckily for Marston, at the first sight of the library Pauline took a dislike to it.

I can hear her. "Br-rr-rh! There's something beastly about this room, Edward. I can't think how you can sit in it."

And Edward, a little caustic:

"*You* needn't, if you don't like it."

"I certainly shan't."

She stood there—I can see her—on the hearthrug by Rosamund's chair, looking uncommonly handsome and lascivious. He was going to take her in his arms and kiss her vermilion mouth, when, he said, something stopped him. Stopped him clean, as if it had risen up and stepped between them. He supposed it was the memory of Rosamund, vivid in the place that had been hers.

You see it was just that place, of silent, intimate communion, that Pauline would never take. And the rich, coarse, contented creature didn't even want to take it. He saw that he would be left alone there, all right, with his memory.

19

But the bedroom was another matter. That, Pauline had made it understood from the beginning, she would have to have. Indeed, there was no other he could well have offered her. The drawing room covered the whole of the first floor. The bedrooms above were cramped, and this one had been formed by throwing the two front rooms into one. It looked south, and the bathroom opened out of it at the back. Marston's small northern room had a door on the narrow landing at right angles to his wife's door. He could hardly expect her to sleep there, still less in any of the tight boxes on the top floor. He said he wished he had sold the Curzon Street house.

But Pauline was enchanted with the wide, three-windowed piece that was to be hers. It had been exquisitely furnished for poor little Rosamund; all seventeenth-century walnut wood, Bokhara rugs, thick silk curtains, deep blue with purple linings, and a big, rich bed covered with a purple counterpane embroidered in blue.

One thing Marston insisted on: that *he* should sleep on Rosamund's side of the bed, and Pauline in his own old place. He didn't want to see Pauline's body where Rosamund's had been. Of course he had to lie about it and pretend he had always slept on the side next the window.

I can see Pauline going about in that room, looking at everything; looking at herself, her black, white and vermilion, in the glass that had held Rosamund's pure rose and gold; opening the wardrobe where Rosamund's dresses used to hang, sniffing up the delicate, flower scent of Rosamund, not caring, covering it with her own thick trail.

And Marston (who cared abominably)—I can see him getting more miserable and at the same time more excited as the wedding evening went on. He took her to the play to fill up the time, or perhaps to get her out of Rosamund's rooms; God knows. I can see them sitting in the stalls, bored and restless, starting up and going out before the thing was half over, and coming back to that house in Curzon Street before eleven o'clock.

It wasn't much past eleven when he went to her room.

I told you her door was at right angles to his, and the landing was narrow, so that anybody standing by Pauline's door must have been seen the minute he opened his. He hadn't even to cross the landing to get to her.

Well, Marston swears that there was nothing there when he opened his own door; but when he came to Pauline's he

20

saw Rosamund standing up before it; and, he said, *"She wouldn't let me in."*

Her arms were stretched out, barring the passage. Oh yes, he saw her face, Rosamund's face; I gathered that it was utterly sweet, and utterly inexorable. He couldn't pass her.

So he turned into his own room, backing, he says, so that he could keep looking at her. And when he stood on the threshold of his own door she wasn't there.

No, he wasn't frightened. He couldn't tell me what he felt; but he left his door open all night because he couldn't bear to shut it on her. And he made no other attempt to go in to Pauline; he was so convinced that the phantasm of Rosamund would come again and stop him.

I don't know what sort of excuse he made to Pauline the next morning. He said she was very stiff and sulky all day; and no wonder. He was still infatuated with her, and I don't think that the phantasm of Rosamund had put him off Pauline in the least. In fact, he persuaded himself that the thing was nothing but a hallucination, due, no doubt, to his excitement.

Anyhow, he didn't expect to see it at the door again the next night.

Yes. It was there. Only, this time, he said, it drew aside to let him pass. It smiled at him, as if it were saying, "Go in, if you must; you'll see what'll happen."

He had no sense that it had followed him into the room; he felt certain that, this time, it would let him be.

It was when he approached Pauline's bed, which had been Rosamund's bed, that she appeared again, standing between it and him, and stretching out her arms to keep him back.

All that Pauline could see was her bridegroom backing and backing, then standing there, fixed, and the look on his face. That in itself was enough to frighten her.

She said, "What's the matter with you, Edward?"

He didn't move.

"What are you standing there for? Why don't you come to bed?"

Then Marston seems to have lost his head and blurted it out:

"I can't. I can't."

"Can't what?" said Pauline from the bed.

"Can't sleep with you. She won't let me."

"She?"

"Rosamund. My wife. She's there."

"What on earth are you talking about?"

21

"She's there, I tell you. She won't let me. She's pushing me back."

He says Pauline must have thought he was drunk or something. Remember, she *saw* nothing but Edward, his face, and his mysterious attitude. He must have looked very drunk.

She sat up in bed, with her hard, black eyes blazing away at him, and told him to leave the room that minute. Which he did.

The next day she had it out with him. I gathered that she kept on talking about the "state" he was in.

"You came to my room, Edward, in a *disgraceful* state."

I suppose Marston said he was sorry; but he couldn't help it; he wasn't drunk. He stuck to it that Rosamund was there. He had seen her. And Pauline said, if he wasn't drunk then he must be mad, and he said meekly, "Perhaps I *am* mad."

That set her off, and she broke out in a fury. He was no more mad than she was; but he didn't care for her; and he was making ridiculous excuses; shamming, to put her off. There was some other woman.

Marston asked her what on earth she supposed he'd married her for. Then she burst out crying and said she didn't know.

Then he seems to have made it up with Pauline. He managed to make her believe he wasn't lying, that he really had seen something, and between them they arrived at a rational explanation of the appearance. He had been overworking. Rosamund's phantasm was nothing but a hallucination of his exhausted brain.

This theory carried him on till bedtime. Then, he says, he began to wonder what would happen, what Rosamund's phantasm would do next. Each morning his passion for Pauline had come back again, increased by frustration, and it worked itself up crescendo, towards night. Supposing he *had* seen Rosamund. He might see her again. He had become suddenly subject to hallucinations. But as long as you *knew* you were hallucinated you were all right.

So what they agreed to do that night was by way of precaution, in case the thing came again. It might even be sufficient in itself to prevent his seeing anything.

Instead of going in to Pauline he was to get into the room before she did, and she was to come to him there. That, they said, would break the spell. To make him feel even safer he meant to be in bed before Pauline came.

Well, he got into the room all right.

22

It was when he tried to get into bed that—he saw her (I mean Rosamund).

She was lying there, in his place next the window, her own place, lying in her immature childlike beauty and sleeping, the firm full bow of her mouth softened by sleep. She was perfect in every detail, the lashes of her shut eyelids golden on her white cheeks, the solid gold of her square fringe shining, and the great braided golden rope of her hair flung back on the pillow.

He knelt down by the bed and pressed his forehead into the bedclothes, close to her side. He declared he could feel her breathe.

He stayed there for the twenty minutes Pauline took to undress and come to him. He says the minutes stretched out like hours. Pauline found him still kneeling with his face pressed into the bedclothes. When he got up he staggered.

She asked him what he was doing and why he wasn't in bed. And he said, "It's no use. I can't. I can't."

But somehow he couldn't tell her that Rosamund was there. Rosamund was too sacred; he couldn't talk about her. He only said:

"You'd better sleep in my room tonight."

He was staring down at the place in the bed where he still saw Rosamund. Pauline couldn't have seen anything but the bedclothes, the sheet smoothed above an invisible breast, and the hollow in the pillow. She said she'd do nothing of the sort. She wasn't going to be frightened out of her own room. He could do as he liked.

He couldn't leave them there; he couldn't leave Pauline with Rosamund, and he couldn't leave Rosamund with Pauline. So he sat up in a chair with his back turned to the bed. No. He didn't make any attempt to go back. He says he knew she was still lying there, guarding his place, which was her place. The odd thing is that he wasn't in the least disturbed or frightened or surprised. He took the whole thing as a matter of course. And presently he dozed off into a sleep.

A scream woke him and the sound of a violent body leaping out of the bed and thudding onto its feet. He switched on the light and saw the bedclothes flung back and Pauline standing on the floor with her mouth open.

He went to her and held her. She was cold to the touch and shaking with terror, and her jaws dropped as if she were palsied.

She said, "Edward, there's something in the bed."

He glanced again at the bed. It was empty.

"There isn't," he said. "Look."

He stripped the bed to the footrail, so that she could see.

"There *was* something."

"Do you see it?"

"No. I felt it."

She told him. First something had come swinging, smack across her face. A thick, heavy rope of woman's hair. It had waked her. Then she had put out her hands and felt the body. A woman's body, soft and horrible; her fingers had sunk in the shallow breasts. Then she had screamed and jumped.

And she couldn't stay in the room. The room, she said, was "beastly."

She slept in Marston's room, in his small single bed, and he sat up with her all night, on a chair.

She believed now that he had really seen something, and she remembered that the library was beastly, too. Haunted by something. She supposed that was what she had felt. Very well. Two rooms in the house were haunted; their bedroom and the library. They would just have to avoid those two rooms. She had made up her mind, you see, that it was nothing but a case of an ordinary haunted house; the sort of thing you're always hearing about and never believe in till it happens to yourself. Marston didn't like to point out to her that the house hadn't been haunted till she came into it.

The following night, the fourth night, she was to sleep in the spare room on the top floor, next to the servants, and Marston in his own room.

But Marston didn't sleep. He kept on wondering whether he would or would not go up to Pauline's room. That made him horribly restless, and instead of undressing and going to bed, he sat up on a chair with a book. He wasn't nervous; but he had a queer feeling that something was going to happen, and that he must be ready for it, and that he'd better be dressed.

It must have been soon after midnight when he heard the doorknob turning very slowly and softly.

The door opened behind him and Pauline came in, moving without a sound, and stood before him. It gave him a shock; for he had been thinking of Rosamund, and when he heard the doorknob turn it was the phantasm of Rosamund that he expected to see coming in. He says, for the first minute, it was this appearance of Pauline that struck him as the uncanny and unnatural thing.

24

She had nothing, absolutely nothing on but a transparent white chiffony sort of dressing gown. She was trying to undo it. He could see her hands shaking as her fingers fumbled with the fastenings.

He got up suddenly, and they just stood there before each other, saying nothing, staring at each other. He was fascinated by her, by the sheer glamor of her body, gleaming white through the thin stuff, and by the movement of her fingers. I think I've said she was a beautiful woman, and her beauty at that moment was overpowering.

And still he stared at her without saying anything. It sounds as if their silence lasted quite a long time, but in reality it couldn't have been more than some fraction of a second.

Then she began. "Oh, Edward, for God's sake *say* something. Oughtn't I to have come?"

And she went on without waiting for an answer. "Are you thinking of *her?* Because, if—if you are, I'm not going to let her drive you away from me. . . . I'm not going to. . . . She'll keep on coming as long as we don't—Can't you see that this is the way to stop it . . . ? When you take me in your arms."

She slipped off the loose sleeves of the chiffon thing and it fell to her feet. Marston says he heard a queer sound, something between a groan and a grunt, and was amazed to find that it came from himself.

He hadn't touched her yet—mind you, it went quicker than it takes to tell, it was still an affair of the fraction of a second—they were holding out their arms to each other, when the door opened again without a sound, and, without visible passage, the phantasm was there. It came incredibly fast, and thin at first, like a shaft of light sliding between them. It didn't do anything; there was no beating of hands, only, as it took on its full form, its perfect likeness of flesh and blood, it made its presence felt like a push, a force, driving them asunder.

Pauline hadn't seen it yet. She thought it was Marston who was beating her back. She cried out: "Oh, don't, don't push me away!" She stooped below the phantasm's guard and clung to his knees, writhing and crying. For a moment it was a struggle between her moving flesh and that still, supernatural being.

And in that moment Marston realized that he hated Pauline. She was fighting Rosamund with her gross flesh and blood, taking a mean advantage of her embodied state to beat down the heavenly, discarnate thing.

He called to her to let go.

"It's not I," he shouted. "Can't you *see* her?"

Then, suddenly, she saw, and let go, and dropped, crouching on the floor and trying to cover herself. This time she had given no cry.

The phantasm gave way; it moved slowly towards the door, and as it went it looked back over its shoulder at Marston, it trailed a hand, signaling to him to come.

He went out after it, hardly aware of Pauline's naked body that still writhed there, clutching at his feet as they passed, and drew itself after him, like a worm, like a beast, along the floor.

She must have got up at once and followed them out onto the landing; for, as he went down the stairs behind the phantasm, he could see Pauline's face, distorted with lust and terror, peering at them above the stairhead. She saw them descend the last flight, and cross the hall at the bottom and go into the library. The door shut behind them.

Something happened in there. Marston never told me precisely what it was, and I didn't ask him. Anyhow, that finished it.

The next day Pauline ran away to her own people. She couldn't stay in Marston's house because it was haunted by Rosamund, and he wouldn't leave it for the same reason.

And she never came back; for she was not only afraid of Rosamund, she was afraid of Marston. And if she *had* come it wouldn't have been any good. Marston was convinced that, as often as he attempted to get to Pauline, something would stop him. Pauline certainly felt that if Rosamund were pushed to it, she might show herself in some still more sinister and terrifying form. She knew when she was beaten.

And there was more in it than that. I believe he tried to explain it to her; said he had married her on the assumption that Rosamund was dead, but that now he knew she was alive; she was, as he put it, "there." He tried to make her see that if he had Rosamund he couldn't have *her*. Rosamund's presence in the world annulled their contract.

You see I'm convinced that something *did* happen that night in the library. I say, he never told me precisely what it was, but he once let something out. We were discussing one of Pauline's love affairs (after the separation she gave him endless grounds for divorce).

"Poor Pauline," he said, "she thinks she's so passionate."

"Well," I said, "wasn't she?"

Then he burst out. "No. She doesn't know what passion is.

26

None of you know. You haven't the faintest conception. You'd have to get rid of your bodies first. *I* didn't know until——"

He stopped himself. I think he was going to say, "until Rosamund came back and showed me." For he leaned forward and whispered: "It isn't a localized affair at all.... If you only knew——"

So I don't think it was just faithfulness to a revived memory. I take it there had been, behind that shut door, some experience, some terrible and exquisite contact. More penetrating than sight or touch. More—more extensive: passion at all points of being.

Perhaps the supreme moment of it, the ecstasy, only came when her phantasm had disappeared.

He couldn't go back to Pauline after *that*.

Slime

by Joseph Payne Brennan

It was a great gray-black hood of horror moving over the floor of the sea. It slid through the soft ooze like a monstrous mantle of slime obscenely animated with questing life. It was by turns viscid and fluid. At times it flattened out and flowed through the carpet of mud like an inky pool; occasionally it paused, seeming to shrink in upon itself, and reared up out of the ooze until it resembled an irregular cone or a gigantic hood. Although it possessed no eyes, it had a marvelously developed sense of touch, and it possessed a sensitivity to minute vibrations which was almost akin to telepathy. It was plastic, essentially shapeless. It could shoot out long tentacles, until it bore a resemblance to a nightmare squid or a huge starfish; it could retract itself into a round flattened disc, or squeeze into an irregular hunched shape so that it looked like a black boulder sunk on the bottom of the sea.

It had prowled the black water endlessly. It had been formed when the earth and the seas were young; it was almost as old as the ocean itself. It moved through a night which had no beginning and no dissolution. The black sea basin where it lurked had been dark since the world began—

an environment only a little less inimical than the stupendous gulfs of interplanetary space.

It was animated by a single, unceasing, never-satisfied drive: a voracious, insatiable hunger. It could survive for months without food, but minutes after eating it was as ravenous as ever. Its appetite was appalling and incalculable.

On the icy ink-black floor of the sea the battle for survival was savage, hideous—and usually brief. But for the shape of moving slime there was no battle. It ate whatever came its way, regardless of size, shape or disposition. It absorbed microscopic plankton and giant squid with equal assurance. Had its surface been less fluid, it might have retained the circular scars left by the grappling suckers of the wildly threshing deep-water squid, or the jagged toothmarks of the anachronistic frillshark, but as it was, neither left any evidence of its absorption. When the lifting curtain of living slime swayed out of the mud and closed upon them, their fiercest death throes came to nothing.

The horror did not know fear. There was nothing to be afraid of. It ate whatever moved, or tried not to move, and it had never encountered anything which could in turn eat it. If a squid's sucker, or a shark's tooth, tore into the mass of its viscosity, the rent flowed in upon itself and immediately closed. If a segment was detached, it could be retrieved and absorbed back into the whole.

The black mantle reigned supreme in its savage world of slime and silence. It groped greedily and endlessly through the mud, eating and never sleeping, never resting. If it lay still, it was only to trap food which might otherwise be lost. If it rushed with terrifying speed across the slimy bottom, it was never to escape an enemy, but always to flop its hideous fluidity upon its sole and inevitable quarry—food.

It had evolved out of the muck and slime of the primitive sea floor, and it was as alien to ordinary terrestrial life as the weird denizens of some wild planet in a distant galaxy. It was an anachronistic experiment of nature compared to which the saber-toothed tiger, the woolly mammoth and even Tyranno-saurus, the slashing, murderous king of the great earth reptiles, were as tame, weak entities.

Had it not been for a vast volcanic upheaval on the bottom of the ocean basin, the black horror would have crept out its entire existence on the silent sea ooze without ever manifesting its hideous powers to mankind.

Fate, in the form of a violent subterranean explosion,

covering huge areas of the ocean's floor, hurled it out of its black slime world and sent it spinning towards the surface.

Had it been an ordinary deep-water fish, it never would have survived the experience. The explosion itself, or the drastic lessening of water pressure as it shot towards the surface, would have destroyed it. But it was no ordinary fish. Its viscosity, or plasticity, or whatever it was that constituted its essentially amoebic structure, permitted it to survive.

It reached the surface slightly stunned and flopped on the surging waters like a great blob of black blubber. Immense waves stirred up by the subterranean explosion swept it swiftly towards shore, and because it was somewhat stunned it did not try to resist the roaring mountains of water.

Along with scattered ash, pumice, and the puffed bodies of dead fish, the black horror was hurled towards a beach. The huge waves carried it more than a mile inland, far beyond the strip of sandy shore, and deposited it in the midst of a deep brackish swamp area.

As luck would have it, the submarine explosion and subsequent tidal wave took place at night, and therefore the slime horror was not immediately subjected to a new and hateful experience—light.

Although the midnight darkness of the storm-lashed swamp did not begin to compare with the stygian blackness of the sea bottom where even violet rays of the spectrum could not penetrate, the marsh darkness was nevertheless deep and intense.

As the water of the great wave receded, sluicing through the thorn jungle and back out to sea, the black horror clung to a mudbank surrounded by a rank growth of cattails. It was aware of the sudden, startling change in its environment, and for some time it lay motionless, concentrating its attention on obscure internal readjustment which the absence of crushing pressure and a surrounding cloak of frigid sea water demanded. Its adaptability was incredible and horrifying. It achieved in a few hours what an ordinary creature could have attained only through a process of gradual evolution. Three hours after the titanic wave flopped it onto the mudbank, it had undergone swift organic changes which left it relatively at ease in its new environment.

In fact, it felt lighter and more mobile than it ever had before in its sea basin existence.

As it flung out feelers and attuned itself to the minutest vibrations and emanations of the swamp area, its pristine hunger drive reasserted itself with overwhelming urgency.

And the tale which its sensory apparatus returned to the monstrous something which served it as a brain, excited it tremendously. It sensed at once that the swamp was filled with luscious tidbits of quivering food—more food, and food of a greater variety than it had ever encountered on the cold floor of the sea.

Its savage, incessant hunger seemed unbearable. Its slimy mass was swept by a shuddering wave of anticipation.

Sliding off the mud bank, it slithered over the cattails into an adjacent area consisting of deep black pools interspersed with waterlogged tussocks. Weed stalks stuck up out of the water and the decayed trunks of fallen trees floated half-submerged in the larger pools.

Ravenous with hunger, it sloshed into the bog area, flicking its tentacles about. Within minutes it had snatched up several fat frogs and a number of small fish. These, however, merely titillated its appetite. Its hunger turned into a kind of ecstatic fury. It commenced a systematic hunt, plunging to the bottom of each pool and quickly but carefully exploring every inch of its oozy bottom. The first creature of any size which it encountered was a muskrat. An immense curtain of adhesive slime suddenly swept out of the darkness, closed upon it—and squeezed.

Heartened and whetted by its find, the hood of horror rummaged the rank pools with renewed zeal. When it surfaced, it carefully probed the tussocks for anything that might have escaped it in the water. Once it snatched up a small bird nesting in some swamp grass. Occasionally it slithered up the crisscrossed trunks of fallen trees, bearing them down with its unspeakable slimy bulk, and hung briefly suspended like a great dripping curtain of black marsh mud.

It was approaching a somewhat less swampy and more deeply wooded area when it gradually became aware of a subtle change in its new environment. It paused, hesitating, and remained half in and half out of a small pond near the edge of the nearest trees.

Although it had absorbed twenty-five or thirty pounds of food in the form of frogs, fish, water snakes, the muskrat, and a few smaller creatures, its fierce hunger had not left it. Its monstrous appetite urged it on, and yet something held it anchored in the pond.

What it sensed, but could not literally see, was the rising sun spreading a gray light over the swamp. The horror had never encountered any illumination except that generated by the grotesque phosphorescent appendages of various deep-sea fishes. Natural light was totally unknown to it.

As the dawn light strengthened, breaking through the scattering storm clouds, the black slime monster fresh from the inky floor of the sea sensed that something utterly unknown was flooding in upon it. Light was hateful to it. It cast out quick feelers, hoping to catch and crush the light. But the more frenzied its efforts became, the more intense became the abhorred aura surrounding it.

At length, as the sun rose visibly above the trees, the horror, in baffled rage rather than in fear, grudgingly slid back into the pond and burrowed into the soft ooze of its bottom. There it remained while the sun shone and the small creatures of the swamp ventured forth on furtive errands.

A few miles away from Wharton's Swamp, in the small town of Clinton Center, Henry Hossing sleepily crawled out of the improvised alley shack which had afforded him a degree of shelter for the night and stumbled into the street. Passing a hand across his rheumy eyes, he scratched the stubble on his cheek and blinked listlessly at the rising sun. He had not slept well; the storm of the night before had kept him awake. Besides, he had gone to bed hungry, and that never agreed with him.

Glancing furtively along the street, he walked slouched forward, with his head bent down, and most of the time he kept his eyes on the walk or on the gutter in the hopes of spotting a chance coin.

Clinton Center had not been kind to him. The handouts were sparse, and only yesterday he had been warned out of town by one of the local policemen.

Grumbling to himself, he reached the end of the street and started to cross. Suddenly he stooped quickly and snatched up something from the edge of the pavement.

It was a crumpled green bill, and as he frantically unfolded it, a look of stupefied rapture spread across his bristly face. Ten dollars! More money than he had possessed at any one time in months!

Stowing it carefully in the one good pocket of his seedy gray jacket, he crossed the street with a swift stride. Instead of sweeping the sidewalks, his eyes now darted along the rows of stores and restaurants.

He paused at one restaurant, hesitated, and finally went on until he found another less pretentious one a few blocks away.

31

When he sat down, the counterman shook his head. "Get goin', bud. No free coffee today."

With a wide grin, the hobo produced his ten-dollar bill and spread it on the counter. "That covers a good breakfast here, pardner?"

The counterman seemed irritated. "Okay, okay. What'll you have?" He eyed the bill suspiciously.

Henry Hossing ordered orange juice, toast, ham and eggs, oatmeal, melon and coffee.

When it appeared, he ate every bit of it, ordered three additional cups of coffee, paid the check as if two-dollar breakfasts were customary with him, and then sauntered back to the street.

Shortly after noon, after his three-dollar lunch, he saw the liquor store. For a few minutes he stood across the street from it, fingering his five-dollar bill. Finally he crossed with an abstracted smile, entered and bought a quart of rye.

He hesitated on the sidewalk, debating whether or not he should return to the little shack in the side alley. After a minute or two of indecision, he decided against it and struck out instead for Wharton's Swamp. The local police were far less likely to disturb him there, and since the skies were clearing and the weather mild, there was little immediate need of shelter.

Angling off the highway which skirted the swamp several miles from town, he crossed a marshy meadow, pushed through a fringe of bush, and sat down under a sweet gum tree which bordered a deeply wooded area.

By late afternoon he had achieved a quite cheerful glow, and he had little inclination to return to Clinton Center. Rousing himself from reverie, he stumbled about collecting enough wood for a small fire and went back to his sylvan seat under the sweet gum.

He slept briefly as dusk descended, but finally bestirred himself again to build a fire, as deeper shadows fell over the swamp. Then he returned to his swiftly diminishing bottle. He was suspended in a warm net of inflamed fantasy when something abruptly broke the spell and brought him back to earth.

The flickering flames of his fire had dwindled down until now only a dim eerie glow illuminated the immediate area under the sweet gum. He saw nothing and at the moment heard nothing, and yet he was filled with a sudden and profound sense of lurking menace.

He stood up, staggering, leaned back against the sweet

gum and peered fearfully into the shadows. In the deep darkness beyond the waning arc of firelight he could distinguish nothing that had any discernible form or color.

Then he detected the stench and shuddered. In spite of the reek of cheap whiskey which clung around him, the smell was overpowering. It was heavy, fulsome, fetid, alien, and utterly repellent. It was vaguely fishlike, but otherwise beyond any known comparison.

As he stood trembling under the sweet gum, Henry Hossing thought of something dead which had lain for long ages at the bottom of the sea.

Filled with mounting alarm, he looked around for some wood which he might add to the dying fire. All he could find nearby, however, were a few twigs. He threw these on and the flames licked up briefly and subsided.

He listened and heard—or imagined he heard—an odd sort of slithering sound in the nearby bushes. It seemed to retreat slightly as the flames shot up.

Genuine terror took possession of him. He knew that he was in no condition to flee—and now he came to the horrifying conclusion that whatever unspeakable menace waited in the surrounding darkness was temporarily held at bay only by the failing gleam of his little fire.

Frantically he looked around for more wood. But there was none. None, that is, within the faint glow of firelight. And he dared not venture beyond.

He began to tremble uncontrollably. He tried to scream, but no sound came out of his tightened throat.

The ghastly stench became stronger, and now he was sure that he could hear a strange sliding, slithering sound in the black shadows beyond the remaining spark of firelight.

He stood frozen in absolute helpless panic as the tiny fire smoldered down into darkness.

At the last instant a charred bit of wood broke apart, sending up a few sparks, and in that flicker of final light he glimpsed the horror.

It had already glided out of the bushes, and now it rushed across the small clearing with nightmare speed. It was a final incarnation of all the fears, shuddering apprehensions, and bad dreams which Henry Hossing had ever known in his life. It was a fiend from the pit of Hell come to claim him at last.

A terrible ringing scream burst from his throat, but it was smothered before it was finished as the black shape of slime fastened upon him with irresistible force.

33

Giles Gowse—"Old Man" Gowse—got out of bed after eight hours of fitful tossing and intermittent nightmares and grouchily brewed coffee in the kitchen of his dilapidated farmhouse on the edge of Wharton's Swamp. Half the night, it seemed, the stench of stale seawater had permeated the house. His interrupted sleep had been full of foreboding, full of shadowy and evil portents.

Muttering to himself, he finished breakfast, took a milk pail from the pantry, and started for the barn where he kept his single cow.

As he approached the barn, the strange offensive odor which had plagued him during the night assailed his nostrils anew.

"Wharton's Swamp! That's what it is!" he told himself. And he shook his fist at it.

When he entered the barn the stench was stronger than ever. Scowling, he strode towards the rickety stall where he kept the cow, Sarey.

Then he stood still and stared. Sarey was gone. The stall was empty.

He reentered the barnyard. "Sarey!" he called.

Rushing back into the barn, he inspected the stall. The rancid reek of the sea was strong here, and now he noticed a kind of shine on the floor. Bending closer, he saw that it was a slick coat of glistening slime, as if some unspeakable creature covered with ooze had crept in and out of the stall.

This discovery, coupled with the weird disappearance of Sarey, was too much for his jangled nerves. With a wild yell he ran out of the barn and started for Clinton Center, two miles away.

His reception in the town enraged him. When he tried to tell people about the disappearance of his cow, Sarey, about the reek of sea and ooze in his barn the night before, they laughed at him. The more impolite ones, that is. Most of the others patiently heard him out—and then winked and touched their heads significantly when he was out of sight.

One man, the druggist, Jim Jelinson, seemed mildly interested. He said that as he was coming through his backyard from the garage late the previous evening, he had heard a fearful shriek somewhere in the distant darkness. It might, he averred, have come from the direction of Wharton's Swamp. But it had not been repeated and eventually he had dismissed it from his mind.

When Old Man Gowse started for home late in the afternoon he was filled with sullen, resentful bitterness. They thought he was crazy, eh? Well, Sarey *was* gone; they couldn't explain *that* away, could they? They explained the smell by saying it was dead fish cast up by the big wave which had washed into the swamp during the storm. Well— maybe. And the slime on his barn floor they said was snails. *Snails!* As if any he'd ever seen could cause that much slime!

As he was nearing home, he met Rupert Barnaby, his nearest neighbor. Rupert was carrying a rifle and he was accompanied by Jibbe, his hound.

Although there had been an element of bad blood between the two bachelor neighbors for some time, Old Man Gowse, much to Barnaby's surprise, nodded and stopped.

"Evenin' hunt, neighbor?"

Barnaby nodded. "Thought Jibbe might start up a coon. Moon later, likely."

"My cow's gone," Old Man Gowse said abruptly. "If you should see her—" He paused. "But I don't think you will. . . ."

Barnaby, bewildered, stared at him. "What you gettin' at?"

Old Man Gowse repeated what he had been telling all day in Clinton Center.

He shook his head when he finished, adding, "I wouldn't go huntin' in that swamp tonight fur—ten thousand dollars!"

Rupert Barnaby threw back his head and laughed. He was a big man, muscular, resourceful, and levelheaded—little given to even mild flights of the imagination.

"Gowse," he laughed, "no use you givin' me those spook stories! Your cow got loose and wandered off. Why, I ain't even seen a bobcat in that swamp for over a year!"

Old Man Gowse set his lips in a grim line. "Maybe," he said, as he turned away, "you'll see suthin' worse than a wildcat in that swamp tonight!"

Shaking his head, Barnaby took after his impatient hound. Old Man Gowse was getting queer all right. One of these days he'd probably go off altogether and have to be locked up.

Jibbe ran ahead, sniffing, darting from one ditch to another. As twilight closed in, Barnaby angled off the main road onto a twisting path which led into Wharton's Swamp.

He loved hunting. He would rather tramp through the brush than sit home in an easy chair. And even if an evening's foray turned up nothing, he didn't particularly mind. Actually he made out quite well; at least half his meat supply consisted of the rabbits, racoons, and occasional deer which he brought down in Wharton's Swamp.

When the moon rose, he was deep in the swamp. Twice Jibbe started off after rabbits, but both times he returned quickly, looking somewhat sheepish.

Something about his actions began to puzzle Barnaby. The dog seemed reluctant to move ahead; he hung directly in front of the hunter. Once Barnaby tripped over him and nearly fell headlong.

The hunter paused finally, frowning, and looked ahead. The swamp appeared no different than usual. True, a rather offensive stench hung over it, but that was merely the result of the big waves which had splashed far inland during the recent storm. Probably an accumulation of seaweed and the decaying bodies of some dead fish lay rotting in the stagnant pools of the swamp.

Barnaby spoke sharply to the dog. "What ails you, boy? Git, now! You trip me again, you'll get a boot!"

The dog started ahead some distance, but with an air of reluctance. He sniffed the clumps of marsh grass in a perfunctory manner and seemed to have lost interest in the hunt.

Barnaby grew exasperated. Even when they discovered the fresh track of a racoon in the soft mud near a little pool, Jibbe manifested only slight interest.

He did run on ahead a little further, however, and Barnaby began to hope that, as they closed in, he would regain his customary enthusiasm.

In this he was mistaken. As they approached a thickly wooded area, latticed with tree thorns and covered with a heavy growth of cattails, the dog suddenly crouched in the shadows and refused to budge.

Barnaby was sure that the racoon had taken refuge in the nearby thickets. The dog's unheard-of conduct infuriated him.

After a number of sharp cuffs, Jibbe arose stiffly and moved ahead, the hair on his neck bristled up like a lion's mane.

Swearing to himself, Barnaby pushed into the darkened thickets after him.

It was quite black under the trees, in spite of the moonlight, and he moved cautiously in order to avoid stepping into a pool.

Suddenly, with a frantic yelp of terror, Jibbe literally darted between his legs and shot out of the thickets. He ran on, howling weirdly as he went.

For the first time that evening Barnaby experienced a

thrill of fear. In all his previous experience, Jibbe had never turned tail. On one occasion he had even plunged in after a sizeable bear.

Scowling into the deep darkness, Barnaby could see nothing. There were no baleful eyes glaring at him.

As his own eyes tried to penetrate the surrounding blackness, he recalled Old Man Gowse's warning with a bitter grimace. If the old fool happened to spot Jibbe streaking out of the swamp, Barnaby would never hear the end of it.

The thought of this angered him. He pushed ahead now with a feeling of sullen rage for whatever had terrified the dog. A good rifle shot would solve the mystery.

All at once he stopped and listened. From the darkness immediately ahead, he detected an odd sound, as if a large bulk were being dragged over the cattails.

He hesitated, unable to see anything, stoutly resisting an idiotic impulse to flee. The black darkness and the slimy stench of stagnant pools here in the thickets seemed to be suffocating him.

His heart began to pound as the slithering noise came closer. Every instinct told him to turn and run, but a kind of desperate stubbornness held him rooted to the spot.

The sound grew louder, and suddenly he was positive that something deadly and formidable was rushing towards him through the thickets with accelerated speed.

Throwing up his rifle, he pointed at the direction of the sound and fired.

In the brief flash of the rifle he saw something black and enormous and glistening, like a great flapping hood, break through the final thicket. It seemed to be *rolling* towards him, and it was moving with nightmare swiftness.

He wanted to scream and run, but even as the horror rushed forward, he understood that flight at this point would be futile. Even though the blood seemed to have congealed in his veins, he held the rifle pointed up and kept on firing.

The shots had no more visible effect than so many pebbles launched from a slingshot. At the last instant his nerve broke and he tried to escape, but the monstrous hood lunged upon him, flapped over him, and squeezed, and his attempt at a scream turned into a tiny gurgle in his throat.

Old Man Gowse got up early, after another uneasy night, and walked out to inspect the barnyard area. Nothing further seemed amiss, but there was still no sign of Sarey. And that detestable odor arose from the direction of Wharton's Swamp when the wind was right.

After breakfast, Gowse set out for Rupert Barnaby's place, a mile or so distant along the road. He wasn't sure himself what he expected to find.

When he reached Barnaby's small but neat frame house, all was quiet. Too quiet. Usually Barnaby was up and about soon after sunrise.

On a sudden impulse, Gowse walked up the path and rapped on the front door. He waited and there was no reply. He knocked again, and after another pause, stepped off the porch.

Jibbe, Barnaby's hound, slunk around the side of the house. Ordinarily he would bound about and bark. But today he stood motionless—or nearly so—he was trembling—and stared at Gowse. The dog had a cowed, frightened, guilty air which was entirely alien to him.

"Where's Rup?" Gowse called to him. "Go get Rup!"

Instead of starting off, the dog threw back his head and emitted an eerie, long-drawn howl.

Gowse shivered. With a backward glance at the silent house, he started off down the road.

..Now maybe they'd listen to him, he thought grimly. The day before they had laughed about the disappearance of Sarey. Maybe they wouldn't laugh so easily when he told them that Rupert Barnaby had gone into Wharton's Swamp with his dog—and that the dog had come back alone!

When Police Chief Miles Underbeck saw Old Man Gowse come into headquarters in Clinton Center, he sat back and sighed heavily. He was busy this morning and undoubtedly Old Man Gowse was coming in to inquire about the infernal cow of his that had wandered off.

The old eccentric had a new and startling report, however. He claimed that Rupert Barnaby was missing. He'd gone into the swamp the night before, Gowse insisted, and had not returned.

When Chief Underbeck questioned him closely, Gowse admitted that he wasn't *positive* Barnaby hadn't returned. It was barely possible that he had returned home very early in the morning and then left again before Gowse arrived.

But Gowse fixed his flashing eyes on the chief and shook his head. "He never came out, I tell ye! That dog of his knows! Howled, he did, like a dog howls for the dead!

38

Whatever come took Sarey—got Barnaby in the swamp last night!"

Chief Underbeck was not an excitable man. Gowse's burst of melodrama irritated him and left him unimpressed.

Somewhat gruffly he promised to look into the matter if Barnaby had not turned up by evening. Barnaby, he pointed out, knew the swamp better than anyone else in the county. And he was perfectly capable of taking care of himself. Probably, the chief suggested, he had sent the dog home and gone elsewhere after finishing his hunt the evening before. The chances were he'd be back by suppertime.

Old Man Gowse shook his head with a kind of fatalistic skepticism. Vouching that events would soon prove his fears well founded, he shambled grouchily out of the station.

The day passed and there was no sign of Rupert Barnaby. At six o'clock, Old Man Gowse grimly marched into the Crown, Clinton Center's second-rung hotel, and registered for a room. At seven o'clock Chief Underbeck dispatched a prowl car to Barnaby's place. He waited impatiently for its return, drumming on the desk, disinterestedly shuffling through a sheaf of reports which had accumulated during the day.

The prowl car returned shortly before eight. Sergeant Grimes made his report. "Nobody there, sir. Place locked up tight. Searched the grounds. All we saw was Barnaby's dog. Howled and ran off as if the devil were on his tail!"

Chief Underbeck was troubled. If Barnaby *was* missing, a search should be started at once. But it was already getting dark, and portions of Wharton's Swamp were very nearly impassable even during the day. Besides, there was no proof that Barnaby had not gone off for a visit, perhaps to nearby Stantonville, for instance, to call on a crony and stay overnight.

By nine o'clock he had decided to postpone any action till morning. A search now would probably be futile in any case. The swamp offered too many obstacles. If Barnaby had not turned up by morning, and there was no report that he had been seen elsewhere, a systematic search of the marsh could begin.

Not long after he had arrived at this decision, and as he was somewhat wearily preparing to leave headquarters and go home, a new and genuinely alarming interruption took place.

Shortly before nine thirty, a car braked to a sudden stop outside headquarters. An elderly man hurried in, supporting by the arm a sobbing, hysterical young girl. Her skirt and stockings were torn and there were a number of scratches on her face.

After assisting her to a chair, the man turned to Chief Underbeck and the other officers who gathered around.

"Picked her up on the highway out near Wharton's Swamp. Screaming at the top of her lungs!" He wiped his forehead. "She ran right in front of my car. Missed her by a miracle. She was so crazy with fear I couldn't make sense out of what she said. Seems like something grabbed her boyfriend in the bushes out there. Anyway, I got her in the car without much trouble and I guess I broke a speed law getting here."

Chief Underbeck surveyed the man keenly. He was obviously shaken himself, and since he did not appear to be concealing anything, the chief turned to the girl.

He spoke soothingly, doing his best to reassure her, and at length she composed herself sufficiently to tell her story.

Her name was Dolores Rell and she lived in nearby Stantonville. Earlier in the evening she had gone riding with her fiancé, Jason Bukmeist of Clinton Center. As Jason was driving along the highway adjacent to Wharton's Swamp, she had remarked that the early evening moonlight looked very romantic over the marsh. Jason had stopped the car, and after they had surveyed the scene for some minutes, he suggested that, since the evening was warm, a brief "stroll in the moonlight" might be fun.

Dolores had been reluctant to leave the car, but at length had been persuaded to take a short walk along the edge of the marsh where the terrain was relatively firm.

As the couple were walking along under the trees, perhaps twenty yards or so from the car, Dolores became aware of an unpleasant odor and wanted to turn back. Jason, however, told her she only imagined it and insisted on going farther. As the trees grew closer together, they walked Indian file, Jason taking the lead.

Suddenly, she said, they both heard something swishing through the brush towards them. Jason told her not to be frightened, that it was probably someone's cow. As it came closer, however, it seemed to be moving with incredible speed. And it didn't seem to be making the kind of noise a cow would make.

At the last second Jason whirled with a cry of fear and told her to run. Before she could move, she saw a monstrous something rushing under the trees in the dim moonlight. For an instant she stood rooted with horror; then she turned and

40

ran. She thought she heard Jason running behind her. She couldn't be sure. But immediately after she heard him scream.

In spite of her terror, she turned and looked behind her.

At this point in her story she became hysterical again, and several minutes passed before she could go on.

She could not describe exactly what she had seen as she looked over her shoulder. The thing which she had glimpsed rushing under the trees had caught up with Jason. It almost completely covered him. All she could see of him was his agonized face and part of one arm, low near the ground, as if the thing were squatting astride him. She could not say what it was. It was black, formless, bestial and yet not bestial. It was the dark gliding kind of indescribable horror which she had shuddered at when she was a little girl alone in the nursery at night.

She shuddered now and covered her eyes as she tried to picture what she had seen. "O God—*the darkness came alive! The darkness came alive!*"

Somehow, she went on presently, she had stumbled through the trees into the road. She was so terrified she hardly noticed the approaching car. There could be no doubt that Dolores Rell was in the grip of a genuine terror. Chief Underbeck acted with alacrity. After the white-faced girl had been driven to a nearby hospital for treatment of her scratches and the administration of a sedative, Underbeck rounded up all available men on the force, equipped them with shotguns, rifles, and flashlights, hurried them into four prowl cars, and started off for Wharton's Swamp.

Jason Bukmeist's car was found where he had parked it. It had not been disturbed. A search of the nearby swamp area, conducted in the glare of flashlights, proved fruitless. Whatever had attacked Bukmeist had apparently carried him off into the farthest recesses of the sprawling swamp.

After two futile hours of brush breaking and marsh sloshing, Chief Underbeck wearily rounded up his men and called off the hunt until morning.

As the first faint streaks of dawn appeared in the sky over Wharton's Swamp, the search began again. Reinforcements, including civilian volunteers from Clinton Center, had arrived, and a systematic combing of the entire swamp commenced.

By noon, the search had proved fruitless—or nearly so. One of the searchers brought in a battered hat and a rye whiskey bottle which he had discovered on the edge of the

41

marsh under a sweet gum tree. The shapeless felt hat was old and worn, but it was dry. It had, therefore, apparently been discarded in the swamp since the storm of a few days ago. The whiskey bottle looked new; in fact, a few drops of rye remained in it. The searcher reported that the remains of a small campfire were also found under the sweet gum.

In the hope that this evidence might have some bearing on the disappearance of Jason Bukmeist, Chief Underbeck ordered a canvass of every liquor store in Clinton Center in an attempt to learn the names of everyone who had recently purchased a bottle of the particular brand of rye found under the tree.

The search went on, and midafternoon brought another, more ominous discovery. A diligent searcher, investigating a trampled area in a large growth of cattails, picked a rifle out of the mud.

After the slime and dirt had been wiped away, two of the searchers vouched that it belonged to Rupert Barnaby. One of them had hunted with him and remembered a bit of scrollwork on the rifle stock.

While Chief Underbeck was weighing this unpalatable bit of evidence, a report of the liquor store canvass in Clinton Center arrived. Every recent purchaser of a quart bottle of the particular brand in question had been investigated. Only one could not be located—a tramp who had hung around the town for several days and had been ordered out.

By evening most of the exhausted searching party were convinced that the tramp, probably in a state of homicidal viciousness brought on by drink, had murdered both Rupert Barnaby and Jason and secreted their bodies in one of the deep pools of the swamp. The chances were the murderer was still sleeping off the effects of drink somewhere in the tangled thickets of the marsh.

Most of the searchers regarded Dolores Rell's melodramatic story with a great deal of skepticism. In the dim moonlight, they pointed out, a frenzied, wild-eyed tramp bent on imminent murder might very well have resembled some kind of monster. And the girl's hysteria had probably magnified what she had seen.

As night closed over the dismal morass, Chief Underbeck reluctantly suspended the hunt. In view of the fact that the murderer probably still lurked in the woods, however, he decided to establish a system of night-long patrols along the highway which paralleled the swamp. If the quarry lay hidden in the treacherous tangle of trees and brush, he would not be able to escape onto the highway without running into one of the patrols. The only other means of egress from the swamp lay miles across the mire where the open sea washed against a reedy beach. And it was quite unlikely that the fugitive would even attempt escape in that direction.

The patrols were established in three-hour shifts, two men to a patrol, both heavily armed, and both equipped with powerful searchlights. They were ordered to investigate every sound or movement which they detected in the brush bordering the highway. After a single command to halt, they were to shoot to kill. Any curious motorists who stopped to inquire about the hunt were to be swiftly waved on their way, after being warned not to give rides to anyone and to report all hitchhikers.

Fred Storr and Luke Matson, on the midnight to three o'clock patrol, passed an uneventful two hours on their particular stretch of the highway. Matson finally sat down on a fallen tree stump a few yards from the edge of the road.

"Legs givin' out," he commented wryly, resting his rifle on the stump. "Might as well sit a few minutes."

Fred Storr lingered nearby. "Guess so, Luke. Don't look like——" Suddenly he scowled into the black fringes of the swamp. "You hear something, Luke?"

Luke listened, twisting around on the stump. "Well, maybe," he said finally, "kind of a little scratchy sound like."

He got up, retrieving his rifle.

"Let's take a look," Fred suggested in a low voice. He stepped over the stump and Luke followed him towards the tangle of brush which marked the border of the swamp jungle.

Several yards farther along they stopped again. The sound became more audible. It was a kind of slithering, scraping sound, such as might be produced by a heavy body dragging itself over uneven ground.

"Sounds like—a snake," Luke ventured. "A damn big snake!"

"We'll get a little closer," Fred whispered. "You be ready with that gun when I switch on my light!"

They moved ahead a few more yards. Then a powerful yellow ray stabbed into the thickets ahead as Fred switched on his flashlight. The ray seached the darkness, probing in one direction and then another.

Luke lowered his rifle a little, frowning. "Don't see a thing," he said. "Nothing but a big pool of black scum up ahead there."

Before Fred had time to reply, the pool of black scum reared up into horrible life. In one hideous second it hunched itself into an unspeakable glistening hood and rolled forward with fearful speed.

Luke Matson screamed and fired simultaneously as the monstrous scarf of slime shot forward. A moment later it swayed above him. He fired again and the thing fell upon him.

In avoiding the initial rush of the horror, Fred Storr lost his footing. He fell headlong—and turned just in time to witness a sight which slowed the blood in his veins.

The monster had pounced upon Luke Matson. Now, as Fred watched, literally paralyzed with horror, it spread itself over and around the form of Luke until he was completely enveloped. The faint writhing of his limbs could still be seen. Then the thing squeezed, swelling into a hood and flattening itself again, and the writhing ceased.

As soon as the thing lifted and swung forward in his direction, Fred Storr, goaded by frantic fear, overcame the paralysis of horror which had frozen him.

Grabbing the rifle which had fallen beside him, he aimed it at the shape of living slime and started firing. Pure terror possessed him as he saw that the shots were having no effect. The thing lunged towards him, to all visible appearances entirely oblivious to the rifle slugs tearing into its loathsome viscid mass.

Acting out of some instinct which he himself could not have named, Fred Storr dropped the rifle and seized his flashlight, playing its powerful beam directly upon the on-rushing horror.

The thing stopped, scant feet away, and appeared to hesitate. It slid quickly aside at an angle, but he followed it immediately with the cone of light. It backed up finally and flattened out, as if trying by that means to avoid the light, but he trained the beam on it steadily, sensing with every primitive fiber which he possessed that the yellow shaft of light was the one thing which held off hideous death.

Now there were shouts in the nearby darkness and other lights began stabbing the shadows. Members of the adjacent patrols, alarmed by the sound of rifle fire, had come running to investigate.

Suddenly the nameless horror squirmed quickly out of the flashlight's beam and rushed away in the darkness.

In the leaden light of early dawn Chief Underbeck climbed

into a police car waiting on the highway near Wharton's Swamp and headed back for Clinton Center. He had made a decision and he was grimly determined to act on it at once.

When he reached headquarters, he made two telephone calls in quick succession, one to the governor of the state and the other to the commander of the nearby Camp Evans Military Reservation.

The horror in Wharton's Swamp—he had decided—could not be coped with by the limited men and resources at his command.

Rupert Barnaby, Jason Bukmeist, and Luke Matson had without any doubt perished in the swamp. The anonymous tramp, it now began to appear, far from being the murderer, had been only one more victim. And Fred Storr—well, he hadn't disappeared. But the other patrol members had found him sitting on the ground near the edge of the swamp in the clutches of a mind-warping fear which had, temporarily at least, reduced him to near idiocy. Hours after he had been taken home and put to bed, he had refused to loosen his grip on a flashlight which he squeezed in one hand. When they switched the flashlight off, he screamed, and they had to switch it on again. His story was so wildly melodramatic it could scarcely be accepted by rational minds. And yet—they had said as much about Dolores Rell's hysterical account. And Fred Storr was no excitable young girl; he had a reputation for levelheadedness, stolidity, and verbal honesty which was touched with understatement rather than exaggeration. As Chief Underbeck arose and walked out to his car in order to start back to Wharton's Swamp, he noticed Old Man Gowse coming down the block.

With a sudden thrill of horror he remembered the eccentric's missing cow. Before the old man came abreast, he slammed the car door and issued crisp directions to the waiting driver. As the car sped away, he glanced in the rearview mirror.

Old Man Gowse stood grimly motionless on the walk in front of Police Headquarters.

"Old Man Cassandra," Chief Underbeck muttered. The driver shot a swift glance at him and stepped on the gas.

Less than two hours after Chief Underbeck arrived back at Wharton's Swamp, the adjacent highway was crowded with cars—state police patrol cars, cars of the local curious, and Army trucks from Camp Evans.

Promptly at nine o'clock over three hundred soldiers, police, and citizen volunteers, all armed, swung into the swamp to begin a careful search.

Shortly before dusk most of them had arrived at the sea on the far side of the swamp. Their exhaustive efforts had netted nothing. One soldier, noticing fierce eyes glaring out of a tree, had bagged an owl, and one of the state policemen had flushed a young bobcat. Someone else had stepped on a copperhead and been treated for snakebite. But there was no sign of a monster, a murderous tramp, nor any of the missing men.

In the face of mounting skepticism, Chief Underbeck stood firm. Pointing out that, so far as they knew to date, the murderer prowled only at night, he ordered that after a four-hour rest and meal period the search should continue.

A number of helicopters which had hovered over the area during the afternoon landed on the strip of shore, bringing food and supplies. At Chief Underbeck's insistence, barriers were set up on the beach. Guards were stationed along the entire length of the highway; powerful searchlights were brought up. Another truck from Camp Evans arrived with a portable machine gun and several flamethrowers.

By eleven o'clock that night the stage was set. The beach barriers were in place, guards were at station, and huge searchlights, erected near the highway, swept the dismal marsh with probing cones of light.

At eleven fifteen the night patrols, each consisting of ten strongly-armed men, struck into the swamp again.

Ravenous with hunger, the hood of horror reared out of the mud at the bottom of a rancid pool and rose towards the surface. Flopping ashore in the darkness, it slid quickly away over the clumps of scattered swamp grass. It was impelled, as always, by a savage and enormous hunger.

Although hunting in its new environment had been good, its immense appetite knew no appeasement. The more food it consumed, the more it seemed to require.

As it rushed off, alert to the minute vibrations which indicated food, it became aware of various disturbing emanations. Although it was the time of darkness in this strange world, the darkness at this usual hunting period was oddly pierced by the monster's hated enemy—light. The food vibrations were stronger than the shape of slime had ever experienced. They were on all sides, powerful, purposeful, moving in many directions all through the lower layers of puzzling, light-riven darkness.

Lifting out of the ooze, the hood of horror flowed up a latticework of gnarled swamp snags and hung motionless, while drops of muddy water rolled off its glistening surface and dripped below. The thing's sensory apparatus told it that the maddening streaks of lack of darkness were everywhere.

Even as it hung suspended on the snags like a great filthy carpet coated with slime, a terrible touch of light slashed through the surrounding darkness and burned against it.

It immediately loosened its hold on the snags and fell back into the ooze with a mighty *plop*. Nearby, the vibrations suddenly increased in intensity. The maddening streamers of light shot through the darkness on all sides.

Baffled and savage, the thing plunged into the ooze and propelled itself in the opposite direction.

But this proved to be only a temporary respite. The vibrations redoubled in intensity. The darkness almost disappeared, riven and pierced by bolts and rivers of light.

For the first time in its incalculable existence, the thing experienced something vaguely akin to fear. The light could not be snatched up and squeezed and smothered to death. It was an alien enemy against which the hood of horror had learned only one defence—flight, hiding.

And now as its world of darkness was torn apart by sudden floods and streamers of light, the monster instinctively sought the refuge afforded by that vast black cradle from which it had climbed.

Flinging itself through the swamp, it headed back for sea.

The guard patrols stationed along the beach, roused by the sound of gunfire and urgent shouts of warning from the interior of the swamp, stood or knelt with ready weapons as the clamor swiftly approached the sea.

The dismal reedy beach lay fully exposed in the harsh glare of searchlights. Waves rolled in towards shore, splashing white crests of foam far up the sands. In the searchlights' illumination the dark waters glistened with an oily iridescence.

The shrill cries increased. The watchers tensed, waiting. And suddenly across the long dreary flats clotted with weed stalks and sunken drifts there burst into view a nightmare shape which froze the shore patrols in their tracks.

A thing of slimy blackness, a thing which had no essential shape, no discernible earthly features, rushed through the thorn thickets and onto the flats. It was a shape of utter darkness, one second a great flapping hood, the next a black viscid pool of living ooze which flowed upon itself, sliding forward with incredible speed.

47

Some of the guards remained rooted where they stood, too overcome with horror to pull the triggers of their weapons. Others broke the spell of terror and began firing. Bullets from half a dozen rifles tore into the black monster speeding across the mud flats.

As the thing neared the end of the flats and approached the first sand dunes of the open beach, the patrol guards who had flushed it from the swamp broke into the open.

One of them paused, bellowing at the beach guards. "It's heading for sea! For God's sake don't let it escape!"

The beach guards redoubled their firing, suddenly realizing with a kind of sick horror that the monster was apparently unaffected by the rifle slugs. Without a single pause, it rolled through the last fringe of cattails and flopped onto the sands.

As in a hideous nightmare, the guards saw it flap over the nearest sand dune and slide towards the sea. A moment later, however, they remembered the barbed wire beach barrier which Chief Underbeck had stubbornly insisted on their erecting.

Gaining heart, they closed in, running over the dunes towards the spot where the black horror would strike the wire.

Someone in the lead yelled in sudden triumph. "It's caught! It's stuck on the wire!"

The searchlights concentrated swaths of light on the barrier.

The thing had reached the barbed wire fence and apparently flung itself against the twisted strands. Now it appeared to be hopelessly caught; it twisted and flopped and squirmed like some unspeakable giant jellyfish snared in a fisherman's net.

The guards ran forward, sure of their victory. All at once, however, the guard in the lead screamed a wild warning. "It's squeezing through! It's getting away!"

In the glare of light they saw with consternation that the monster appeared to be *flowing* through the wire, like a blob of liquescent ooze.

Ahead lay a few yards of downward slanting beach and, beyond that, rolling breakers of the open sea.

There was a collective gasp of horrified dismay as the monster, with a quick forward lurch, squeezed through the barrier. It tilted there briefly, twisting, as if a few last threads of itself might still be entangled in the wire.

As it moved to disengage itself and rush down the wet sand into the black sea, one of the guards hurled himself

48

forward until he was almost abreast of the barrier. Sliding to his knees, he aimed at the escaping hood of horror.

A second later a great searing spout of flame shot from his weapon and burst in a smoky red blossom against the thing on the opposite side of the wire.

Black oily smoke billowed into the night. A ghastly stench flowed over the beach. The guards saw a flaming mass of horror grope away from the barrier. The soldier who aimed the flamethrower held it remorselessly steady.

There was a hideous bubbling, hissing sound. Vast gouts of thick, greasy smoke swirled into the night air. The indescribable stench became almost unbearable.

When the soldier finally shut off the flamethrower, there was nothing in sight except the white-hot glowing wires of the barrier and a big patch of blackened sand.

With good reason the mantle of slime had hated light, for its ultimate source was fire—the final unknown enemy which even the black hood could not drag down and devour.

The Garden of Paris

by Eric Williams

The messenger distributing mail to the various Ministerial offices occupying the top floor of the Palais de Chaillot, Paris, reached into the bag hanging from his shoulder and extracted one last bundle. It was a thick packet of odd-shaped and colored envelopes, all torn open, in varying degrees of impatience, and all with two words scrawled across each "Delacroix-Chaillot." The messenger gave his habitual groan of disgust and plodded to the end of the corridor where he ascended a short flight of stone steps that let out of one wall and led to a redwood door upon a small landing. A card tacked to the door announced "Monsieur Delacroix UNO." The messenger opened the door and said in an irritated voice, "Good morning, Mademoiselle Lamaroux, early as usual." The office was small, its ceiling low, its two windows made to look small by virtue of the overhanging eaves just above them, and the whole effect of cramp exaggerated by two large, old-fashioned desks and equally as dated filing cabinets that occupied all but various narrow lanes on the floor.

Mademoiselle took the proffered bundle with the barest of smiles. She did not deign to answer the implied criticism which had been put in one form or another almost daily for the past ten years. How could she explain that she came early through love for her boss? She had loved him for twenty years, but ten years ago being by chance early in the office, she had arranged all the letters in alphabetic order of sender's name and this had pleased him very much. Since then, she had done him this ridiculous service each morning at the cost of twenty minutes of her own time per day. She knew that now if she omitted to do this gratuitous act he would be most ill pleased and think her remiss. Not that her love could ever be assuaged or even revealed since Monsieur Delacroix was a most respectable man and had been married fifteen years. But the habit of love died hard in her breast and every day she allowed Monsieur Delacroix to be a king in his office, speaking only when she sensed he required talk, making his coffee, cleaning his desk, not moving while he thought, and being altogether an inferior being.

Monsieur Delacroix held a peculiar position in UNO. To his office were sent each day all those letters which UNO, by virtue of its idealistic nature, attracts from thousands of idealists who insist they have a scheme or information that must be acted upon for the good of Mankind. These writers are a persistent race and pester the various offices of UNO year in and year out with their letters. Mixed with these ravings, and often indistinguishable to the unpracticed eye, is the occasional far-fetched but pregnant scheme and the anonymous warning with real information. Paris set Monsieur Delacroix up in a remote office, out of reach of the more insistent evangelists and appointed him to answer the cranks and sift out the gold from the brass. He did this job thoroughly and better than most. His mind was so uncomplicated and literal in its appraisal of things that he had much in common with the people who wrote the letters he was given to answer, and was thus able to sense unbridled sincerity when he read it and to discard it. Whenever, on the other hand, he encountered the flavor of sincerity plus knowledge, he investigated.

This morning, after the unvarying succession of actions and words that accompanied his entry and passage across the office each day, he picked up the pile of letters, placed them in the middle of the blotting pad before him, saying, without really listening for an answer, "Anything interesting, mademoiselle?" He was already intent upon opening the first letter which was written by a M. Abime. He read: "Once again I have to report that I heard a scream from the grounds of the Jardin des Plantes. This was at three during the morning of September 6th. On looking from my window I saw, as on other occasions, lights shining through the trees of the grounds. I am convinced that we have here in the heart of Paris a cell of the sinister 'Union d'exécution' set up by Moscow and of which I have sent you many details. I pray you to hasten to eradicate this nauseatious limb of . . ."

Monsieur Delacroix did not read on: his inner ear had caught something. Across the top of the letter was written "Please answer. This character has written us and the police fifty odd letters over the past five years. There is nothing in it. Put him off. Vesta extension 7211."

Monsieur Delacroix picked up the phone and asked for Monsieur Vesta's number.

"Hallo!" said a high-pitched, genial voice.

Monsieur Delacroix introduced himself. "I would like to see some of those other letters," he said, "and if you have it, the report of the investigation. I don't feel I can answer properly without a bit more background."

"Certainly, certainly. I have a complete file here, police correspondence and everything. I'll send it along. Only for heaven's sake, get him off my neck. I'll be getting nightmares if I read many more of these things about screams in the night!"

Two days later Monsieur Delacroix felt himself in a position to write to Monsieur Abime. Vesta had not exaggerated; there *were* fifty letters in the file, plus correspondence between UNO and the police requesting investigation of the matter and a long report adding up to very little except that these letters always came at or near full moon, and as no murders were actually committed in the grounds of the Jardin des Plantes, it could only be assumed that Monsieur Abime was affected by the full moon.

Monsieur Delacroix dictated a police letter expressing interest and suggesting that both he and Monsieur Abime should keep vigil together at the next full moon in eight days' time in the hope of hearing screams issuing from the Jardin des Plantes. His suggestion was accepted by return post.

In the intervening weekend, Monsieur Delacroix took his family to the Jardin des Plantes to get a clear picture in his

51

mind of the layout of this park *cum* zoo *cum* botanical school *cum* museum. He himself had not been to the Jardin since his teens, when he remembered taking a young lady to see the monkeys, but his children knew the place well and unerringly led their parents to the most sensational of the animals, and then at their father's request, to the labyrinth adjacent to Rue Geoffroy St. Hilaire where Monsieur Abime had his flat.

They climbed the spiral track around the tree-covered hillock that comprised the labyrinth, but were unable to reach the derelict gazebo on the crest as the path had been railed off by the authorities. Monsieur Delacroix stood for some moments at this highest permissible point surveying the probable scene of Monsieur Abime's reported screams. The place was quite wild and tangled in shrubbery. The paths were edged with high iron-rod fences that precluded any possibility of sightseers leaving the path, although Monsieur Delacroix could see no reason to protect what seemed such a dreary, untidy wilderness. Below, through the trees, he could see the administration buildings on the left and the hothouses on the right. Beyond the administration buildings would be the zoo, and beyond the hothouses the formal beds of the botanical gardens; fifty or so meters behind him was the wall of the Jardin with the noise of occasional traffic echoing from the tall, concrete-fronted buildings overlooking the Jardin from the other side of the street. This corner of the Jardin seemed old and forgotten and drear as if the vitality of the soil had been used up.

"I feel cold," complained Madame Delacroix. "I don't like this place. What are you up to, standing there like Napoleon watching Moscow?"

Monsieur Delacroix in no way resembled Napoleon at Moscow except perhaps that he, too, was suddenly cold. He took Madame Delacroix's arm and briskly walked her down to the sunlight at the foot of the mound.

"I shall be watching the hill from across the road next Wednesday night," he told her. "I wished to see it at close hand before then. I must say I'm disappointed in the place."

Madame Delacroix gave her husband a penetrating look, but simply said: "You will be careful, dear!"

To which Monsieur Delacroix replied, "Let's go into the cactus house; I'm chilled. It's as cold as a morgue under those trees."

Being early September, it was quite dark when Monsieur

Delacroix rang the bell which announced him to Monsieur Abime's apartment. There was a long pause, and then the tall wooden door opened and a shadowy figure in the dim-lit vestibule asked Monsieur Delacroix to enter.

"We have no concierge," apologized Monsieur Abime, leading the way into an elevator just large enough to accommodate them both. "My place is on the top floor." The elevator rose with obvious effort to the fourth floor. Monsieur Abime had left the door of his apartment open and showed Monsieur Delacroix directly into the well-lit lounge.

"This building is very quiet," observed Monsieur Delacroix. "I presume they were offices we passed on the lower floors." He studied Monsieur Abime for signs of full moon madness as he said this, but there was nothing peculiar about Monsieur Abime's visage except its pallor. His eyes were gentle, there were no tics about his mouth.

"Yes," confirmed Monsieur Abime. "It is very quiet. At two or three in the morning you can hear every bit of chatter from the zoo. I believe I am the only resident in the whole street."

"No," said Monsieur Delacroix, "there *are* other residents, but as it happens none of them sleep overlooking the Jardin. The point was checked by the police."

"Let me show you my bedroom," said Monsieur Abime, rising. "You will be able to see the view I have."

He opened a door leading to another room which was lined with books, even between the two tall windows overlooking the street. There was a bed and a table, but no wardrobe.

Monsieur Delacroix saw all this in the light from the inner room, then Monsieur Abime shut the door and there was darkness except from the pale light of the street lights forty feet below.

Monsieur Abime threw open one set of the door-like windows. There was a narrow balcony outside. It seemed to Monsieur Delacroix as he carefully leaned out of the window, that the leaves of the trees in the Jardin were a mere arm's length away.

"The moon will not be full until about ten A.M.," said Monsieur Abime. "Until then, I think I had better tell you all I know about the Union d'exécution."

"Where is the nearest entrance to the Jardin," asked Monsieur Delacroix, deliberately ignoring Monsieur Abime's suggestion.

Monsieur Abime pointed a little way to the left. "Just

53

there on the corner of Rue Cuvier. There's another about a hundred meters down Rue Cuvier."

"And to the right?"

"Oh, right up at the far end of the Zoological Museum where this street joins Rue Buffon. I have a large-scale map next door which shows all the entrances to the Jardin."

The two men retired to the lounge where, with the map open on the table and a glass of brandy each, they speculated upon the probable source of the light Monsieur Abime claimed to have seen whenever there were screams from the Jardin. In this way Monsieur Delacroix prevented Monsieur Abime from airing his particular obsession for some time, and finally, there was only time for a brief outline before it was necessary for the silent vigil to begin.

They returned to the dark bedroom, carrying chairs, and sat at the open windows.

An occasional car hurtled down the street below, but as ten A.M. came and went, all noise of human life died out leaving only faint, sporadic noises from the zoo. Monsieur Abime sat motionless at his window. Monsieur Delacroix dozed and woke and dozed and woke in the warm air, his eyes fixed on the dark trees on the other side of the street. The sky seemed pale-blue with the light of the moon now standing vertically above, but below the trees was intense black.

Suddenly Delacroix realized that he was looking at several spots of yellow light through the trees and that Abime was gesticulating violently at him. Immediately Monsieur Delacroix shook off sleep and concentrated his attention. The light seemed to float indeterminately in a line somewhere in the direction of the cactus house, but it was impossible to know whether it was a moving light or the effect of swaying boughs in front of a stationary light.

Suddenly a most appalling shriek tore Monsieur Delacroix's nerves to cringing pieces. It exploded like a magnesium flare of sound on the silent night. Delacroix involuntarily turned away in horror. Almost immediately the shriek became muffled and then ceased.

Monsieur Abime was on his feet in triumph.

"There!" he called. "That's it! You heard that."

"Quick," said Delacroix, "let us get down to Rue Cuvier; we may see someone come from the Jardin."

The elevator descended quicker than it ascended, but it still seemed funereal to Delacroix. He burst from the building and ran down the street towards the junction with Rue

Cuvier. Abime hurried behind. As they came to the junction a small car drew away from the front of the entrance heading their way accelerating fast. Monsieur Delacroix teetered on the curb between heroic excitement and caution, and in a second the car had roared past and away.

"Don't worry," said Monsieur Abime, "I got his number."

They returned to the flat and as a good public servant Monsieur Delacroix forthwith reported the scream over the telephone to the police. He was told by a voice already committed to disbelief that the matter would be investigated.

"You did not say anything about the car?" commented Monsieur Abime, his pale face just the faintest bit flushed with excitement.

"They will not find a corpse, will they?" explained Monsieur Delacroix. "It would be infringing on a citizen's privacy to give his name uselessly to the police."

Monsieur Abime nodded silently and remained watching Monsieur Delacroix.

"It will take no more than an hour for me to secure the car-owner's name tomorrow," said Monsieur Delacroix, thinking as he stood. "It is quite certain that he or she is connected in some way with the scream—and I am sure that people do not scream like that unless they are being killed in some horrible way. The police have failed to find any sign of violence before, therefore this person is very cunning and we shall have to be equally as cunning to catch him. We must secrete ourselves in the grounds at the next full moon and watch. Are you willing to do this?"

Monsieur Abime paled again.

"You don't realize how ferocious the Union d'exécution is!" he appealed.

Monsieur Delacroix compressed his lips in exasperation.

"You may be assured, Monsieur Abime," he said, "that there is no cell of the Union d'exécution in Paris. This has been checked and checked again by our police and Interpol. There is nothing. Your fears in this respect are groundless. Whatever it is we are dealing with here, it is not political assassination. Please use your head. The regularity of these—whatever they are—indicates only mania. We shall be perfectly safe if we stay together and hidden."

Monsieur Abime was unconvinced, but resigned to the fact of his own involvement. Monsieur Delacroix departed at three A.M. with a promise of rendezvous in a lunar month's time.

The car, a little corrugated iron, hunchbacked Citroën,

was owned by Monsieur Philippe Medan, of Rue Lecourbe. Mademoiselle Lamaroux, who was good at this sort of thing, soon ascertained that he was a bachelor, aged thirty-seven, living with his mother, that he had played a gallant part in the Paris uprising of 1944, had trained in botany—without notable results—and was now employed at the Jardin des Plantes specializing in cactus plants. He had written a few papers for scientific journals and one small book for the amateur on cactus-growing. From the telephone operator in the Jardin des Plantes administration building, Mademoiselle, playing the part of a young woman interested in Monsieur Philippe, learnt that he was a solitary kind of fellow who did a lot of voluntary overtime at the Jardin; that he had no lady friends, that he was known in the Jardin as "Sandy," and that he had a little office of his own just near the back door of the building.

With this smattering of knowledge Monsieur Delacroix passed an afternoon in the Jardin, and by casual gossip with various persons working among the flower beds, he was able to get the "cactus authority" pointed out to him without the necessity of addressing him personally. Medan was a swarthy-faced block of a man, probably with Corsican blood, deliberate in his walk like some tired peasant, and with a ridged brow that gave him a brooding look. He looked more like fifty than thirty-seven, there was no animation in his step. Life seemed to have beaten him. "Nevertheless," thought Monsieur Delacroix, "judging by those shoulders you're as solid and strong as an ox."

Medan entered the tropical house with his private key and a few minutes later Monsieur Delacroix saw him through the glass erecting a ladder to examine the summit of a tall palm. "I wonder what you're up to," mused Monsieur Delacroix as he walked away. "Do you climb the trees and scream at the full moon? You look like an ape." Monsieur Delacroix stopped in his tracks. The possible connection with animals had not occurred to him before. Could it be that murder was committed and then the body thrown to the lions so that no remains were found? It certainly seemed a possible explanation of the one mysterious thing about this business—where did the bodies go if there had been fifty murders? Of course— meat for the animals! By dawn, all evidence chewed and licked up, clean as a whistle!

Monsieur Delacroix returned to his office a little aghast at his explanation, but triumphant.

Full moon in October fell on the first of the month. September had continued mild until two days previous, and then had ensued a steady, strong wind from the north pushing all summer air out of the streets. The sun fought through on both days about midday, but soon retired exhausted. The citizens of Paris now hurled their cars along the cobbled boulevards with a different kind of abandon, with a hurrying grimness as if they felt the breath of winter close behind. Mademoiselle Lamaroux appeared in the office garbed in a thick woollen two-piece suit and numerous accessory garments to ensure protection from the blasts.

Madame Delacroix categorically forbade her husband to spend the night in the Jardin des Plantes (not that she knew the true reason for his proposed vigil) "at your time of life—you must be mad!"

"My dear, I shall be wrapped up warm and we shall be in a sheltered place. After all, it will not be all night."

"Paul, you are not to go!"

Monsieur Delacroix expressed the overpowering flux of UNO affairs by a shrug.

"I must. But I shall be careful," he said miserably.

As he crouched with Monsieur Abime in the lee of the brick wall at the rear of the hothouses, Monsieur Delacroix knew his wife to be correct in calling him mad. It was as black and as cold as space beneath the trees, and his knees and shoulders ached with what felt like deposits of ice crystals. Monsieur Abime groaned softly every now and again and prayed for a cigarette. From their "hide" they could observe the path that passed between the Australian and cactus houses and forked left to the labyrinth and right to the administration building. The nearest loop of the path circling the hillock was a mere five or six yards away, and in the light of the full moon filtering through the trees from high above, Monsieur Delacroix was sure they would be able to definitely identify any person climbing the labyrinth.

"It's midnight," breathed Monsieur Abime.

Monsieur Delacroix nodded wearily, then clutched his companion's arm. In the distance was the faint crunching and squeaking of a wheelbarrow being wheeled over the stony paths. Someone was coming from the gate by the conciergeries on Rue Cuvier. The noise became more distinct and presently they could hear a peculiar mumble of conversation accompanying the harsh cracking of grit. The wheelbarrow was pushed to the foot of the path ascending into the labyrinth and here the pusher rested. In the quiet Monsieur Delacroix felt sure the mumbler said, "Port your helm," but the voice was so quiet and slurred that he could not believe his ears.

Monsieur Abime breathed into Delacroix's ear, "That's a drunk talking to himself!"

"Or a maniac!" answered Monsieur Delacroix in similar fashion.

The squeaks began again. The two watchers fixed their eyes upon the dappled path and presently a black shape moved in the blackness and became a forward-leaning figure pushing a wheelbarrow in which lay the rag-doll limp shape of another man. As the pair passed the "hide," the limp shape raised its head and began cursing in a nonsensical way, only to collapse back almost immediately. The pair passed onwards into the shadows.

"Did you see his face?" asked Delacroix softly.

"No, it was in shadow."

The noise of the barrow stopped, and there was the distant noise of a key rattling on iron as a keyhole was searched for.

"He's going through the gate at the top," said Monsieur Abime. "Shall I go after him?"

"Wait," commanded Monsieur Delacroix.

After a few indistinct noises, they heard the barrow returning, the slam of the gate, and then a helter-skelter skidding as the pusher rushed back along his tracks. He was past Monsieur Delacroix and Abime before they could see his face.

"I'm going up to see what he's done to that drunk," said Monsieur Abime. "You stay here, I won't be a minute."

At that precise moment a ghastly scream from above seemed to clamp a ring round their hearts. It finished on one last uprising yell of horror. Monsieur Abime was the first to recover. He athletically clambered over the iron railings onto the path and disappeared towards the summit. Monsieur Delacroix also negotiated the railings but clumsily and stood trembling on the path. Suddenly he was aware that the lights of the cactus house had been switched on. This was no strange, floating light. He could see the tracery of iron struts forming the skeleton of the greenhouse silhouetted against the lights inside. The murderer was performing his customary ritual. Where was Abime?

There came a second scream, more shattering than the first, since it began with the call "help" but gargled into a shriek of incoherent horror and pain.

Monsieur Delacroix hurled himself up the path towards the

58

gazebo on the summit. As he ran up to the gate near the summit, he heard a tremendous thrashing going on among the shrubbery surrounding the gazebo. The spiral nature of the path still made it necessary for him to make another half turn of the hill before coming to the level top upon which the gazebo stood, and it was this which saved Monsieur Delacroix's life. Panting around this stretch of weed-grown path, with the terrifying vegetable noise going on only a yard to his right, fear had time to give him caution. He stopped and peered into the dappled light around the gazebo. He saw the half-severed body of Monsieur Abime hanging in the myriad toothed jaws of a gigantic snake. The tube of the snake's body was already distended where it had begun to ingest Monsieur Abime, and it convulsed with the prodigious effort of crushing the bones in his limbs.

Monsieur Delacroix nearly fainted. He reeled back into the bushes, then sick and panic-stricken rushed down the spiral path to the lighted beacon of the cactus house. Blindly he dragged open the heavy, iron-framed door of the greenhouse, and fell into the heat and light. Philippe Medan was on his knees before one of the tree-like cacti. "Help!" rattled Monsieur Delacroix, staggering: "In the labyrinth. Oh God! Monster."

Philippe Medan stood up, his face twisted with emotion. He had some kind of short gardening tool in his hand. With this he struck Monsieur Delacroix across the head. "Fool!" he shouted. He struck Monsieur Delacroix again and again with his full bull-like strength. Too late Monsieur Delacroix realized his folly. He collapsed unconscious upon the concrete floor.

When consciousness had pushed its way up to the surface through layers of pain and sickness, Monsieur Delacroix found himself propped against one of the walls of the greenhouse with his ankles tied together and his arms tied behind his back. Medan was busy at the base of the cactus tree, working with the flitting motions of a barber around a rich client. He had a pad on which he wrote figures after consulting certain spots on the trunk of the cactus and he also had a syringe which he plunged into the plant to draw off liquid. Between these motions, he circled the trunk fingering the scale-like spines and exhibiting nervous anticipation, as if he expected some miraculous metamorphosis to take place at any moment. Suddenly he stood back, almost falling over Monsieur Delacroix's legs.

"Ah!" he exclaimed. He stretched his arms up towards the crest of the cactus like a pagan priest welcoming the sun.

Monsieur Delacroix was amazed to see the triangular scales forming the bark near the summit of the cactus trunk, lifting and falling back as if puffs of air agitated them from within. This motion quickly spread down the trunk until the twenty-foot column was covered with rhythmic pulses of movement.

"This time!" appealed Medan to the quivering plant. He clenched his fists and visibly willed the plant to do something. Suddenly there was a noise like tearing cloth and the dirty green of the bark parted at the summit and from the yard-long split welled out a most stupendous blossom of tightly packed petals. Simultaneously Monsieur Delacroix breathed in such a powerful perfume that his eyes closed in a paroxysm of delight. The flower burst open in a stunning flamboyance of red and yellow, rustling like a silken umbrella being opened.

Medan fell to his knees at Delacroix's side.

"What do you think of my lovely?" he breathed.

"It's incredible!" answered Delacroix sincerely.

"Worth killing for," amplified Medan with enthusiasm.

Delacroix remained silent, not knowing what to answer.

The flower gave out dense waves of perfume so disturbing to the senses, that Monsieur Delacroix felt the onset of that fever-like disorientation that comes with drugging.

"She must feed," shouted Medan, "so I kill for her." Without looking at Monsieur Delacroix, Medan went on, "You know what she is? She's a survivor from the Miocene. I reared her myself from a seed." He laughed. "That's *one* thing we have to thank the war for—dropping a block-buster so that it blew the insides out of a hill in which a seed had been imprisoned for forty million years. I found her sprouting there on the side of the crater—near the corpse of a cow." He laughed uproariously.

"I recognized a stranger and I potted her. Even then her root was a size. It took me five years to realize that she was unique on this earth. I went back and investigated the place where I had found Selina." Medan checked momentarily at the realization that he had revealed his secret name for the plant. "There was a railway tunnel through the hill, and this bomb had pierced the covering of rock and exploded in the tunnel, literally blowing out the heart of the hill—it was all pure Miocene stuff. That and the resemblance to some fossil pieces that can be found in most museums convinced me. She was a prehistoric fern." Medan closed his eyes and breathed deeply of the scent which filled the greenhouse. He smiled evilly with his eyes still closed.

60

"She likes blood," he said. "I found that out one day when I was repotting her. She has a tubular root that is mobile along its length and toothed all the way along inside—like a barracuda's mouth, and as I lifted her out of the old pot, the root came free and took the end off my finger. She loved it! She grew six inches overnight. After that I got the idea, and fed her mice and things of that size. There was no holding her. It became impossible to keep her potted in my apartment, so I moved her into here—surreptitiously, you understand, and by the time she was a big girl, people thought she had been here all the time."

Medan laughed convulsively at that. Tears ran down his face.

"Of course, she tried to have her root free for hunting in the greenhouse, but I had to discourage that. I kept burying the root until she was forced to burrow under the walls and outside. I lost her for several years after that—the root, I mean—until one night she caught a tramp who had gone into the gazebo for a sleep. I was washing her down at the time and I heard the screaming, then she seemed to come alive under my hands. I realized the connection at once and before the noise had stopped I found out where her root was. The meal transfigured her. She bloomed like you see her. For the first time in her life she bloomed. What an amazing sight! What an incredible phenomenon! Flower for two to three hours, and then an explosion of seed. I collected every one of those seeds—and on every subsequent occasion on which I have been able to make her bloom. Millions of seeds I have. Sacks of them. Every one potentially a beauty like my Selina. Soon I shall embark on my pilgrimage of planting them all over Europe. The Miocene shall be born again!"

Monsieur Delacroix, who had been listening to Medan and watching the plant in a semi-coma, was suddenly speared through by the realization that Medan could not tell him all this and allow him to live.

Medan seemed to be recalled from his dream too. He turned his head and looked at Monsieur Delacroix. "She has never had *three* bodies in one night," he whispered. "I wonder what she will do."

"No!" croaked Monsieur Delacroix.

Medan fetched the wheelbarrow, and despite his wriggling, bundled Monsieur Delacroix into it. He stuffed a handkerchief into Monsieur Delacroix's mouth and secured the plug with some scrim.

"We must hurry," he told Monsieur Delacroix. "Once the flower drops she will not feed until another full moon."

Monsieur Delacroix was too horror-struck to reflect on the humor of Medan's use of the word "we." Come what may, he was going to the most ghastly death conceivable. There was no hope of help—Abime no more now than fertilizer for the plant, as was the hapless drunk before him. Only his wife knew of his intention to watch in the labyrinth—and she would be now deeply asleep. Tears sprang to Monsieur Delacroix's eyes as he said good-bye to his wife. Medan wheeled him through the gate left open in Delacroix's frantic escape. They began the last dozen or so yards of ascent. The moonlight was still as strong in the open and the shadows as black beneath the bushes. Monsieur Delacroix became almost demented in his writhings as they came to the end of the path at the edge of the small clearing around the gazebo. If he had not been gagged he would have shrieked his fear of that terrible mouth lurking somewhere in the bushes, but all that came from him were vague mumbles.

"Selina!" called Medan coaxingly. He stamped on the grass. "She can't hear, you understand," he explained to Delacroix. "She is sensitive to vibrations in the ground. Selina! Selina!"

There was a rustle in the bracken to one side of the gazebo, and then with a rush the great mouth reared up into the moonlight weaving from side to side like some stupendous cobra. "Ah!" shouted Medan in adoration, and pushed the wheelbarrow nearer. The blind mouth swished over Delacroix missing his recumbent body by a few inches. He had a momentary look right down that fibrous tube and saw the glint of hundreds of spines moving with a wavelike motion into the blackness.

The tube was growing longer with every second, smoothly expanding from the hole under the gazebo. It waved high into the air right above the two men seeming to yearn at the bright moon overhead. Medan stamped his foot again. The mouth seemed to look downwards. Its ghastly, thorn-lined maw gaped wider and then it dived down, mouth fully extended and swallowed Medan completely. Delacroix, rigid with terror, was knocked from the wheelbarrow by the convulsions of the plant. He rolled into the bushes near the entrance to the path and watched in horror the bulge of Medan pass downwards into the earth. The mouth lay prone on the ground in satiation, and then slowly contracted back into its burrow.

Delacroix writhed to his knees and with the strength of panic, gained his bound feet, and hopped from the clearing. He moved in huge staggering hops round the spiral to the gate, then fell on the wider public path and rolled. His senses became blurred and eventually left him. He lay senseless, bound hand and foot halfway to the foot of the mound.

Just after dawn, one of the gardeners passing near the labyrinth on his way to look at the tropical house furnace, heard Monsieur Delacroix groan. Monsieur Delacroix was very feeble with cold and cramp and not very intelligible. The gardener spread his thick coat over Delacroix, then went off to phone the police and ambulance. The gardener returned with a bottle of brandy and a pair of secateurs. He cut the innumerable strands of string that bound Monsieur Delacroix's wrists and ankles, then helped him to sit up and drink from the bottle. Both the restored circulation and the brandy were agony and Monsieur Delacroix fainted again.

An hour later, in a private room in a nearby hospital he was able to tell his story to a policeman. The man had him repeat the story, asking only short questions from time to time. He then went off and to Monsieur Delacroix's consternation Madame Delacroix was then admitted. The ensuing scene was astonishing for the mixture of tenderness and temper. Monsieur Delacroix was forced to admit his own imbecility in undertaking to sit up all night in the Jardin at this time in the year. At length he was asked to tell what had happened. Madame Delacroix looked at him with increasing bewilderment. "Are you joking, Paul?" she interrupted. "No, my dear," he replied, "what I tell you is true." Madame Delacroix burst out crying. "Oh, my poor Paul!" she sobbed. The nurse came in and administered a potent sleeping draught, then led Madame away. As he slipped into sleep, Monsieur Delacroix realized with dismay that neither his wife nor the policeman had believed him.

There was another visit the next day from a more superior police officer, accompanied by a doctor, who sat listening intently to everything that passed Monsieur Delacroix's lips but only made comment with his eyes. Monsieur Delacroix found himself watching the doctor when making his replies and endeavoring to make his story less spectacular, but there is little that can be done to make a man-eating plant appear mundane.

The police officer stood up and retrieved his cap from the bedside table.

"It is an astonishing story, monsieur," he said. "The only part we have been able to confirm so far is that Philippe Medan has not been seen since the evening on which you claim the events took place, although his car has been found in Rue Cuvier outside the Jardin. Also, we have not been able to find Monsieur Abime, but he appears to have been a man of somewhat peculiar ways and may have taken it into his mind to go off. Never fear, monsieur, we shall investigate every aspect of your account until we arrive at the truth."

Monsieur Delacroix was rather put out by this ambiguous statement.

"Have you found no blood by the gazebo!" he exclaimed despairingly.

"No, monsieur," replied the officer briskly. "Now, please excuse us. We shall return again."

The ensuing week was the most depressing Monsieur Delacroix remembered spending. He was most courteously imprisoned in the hospital, despite all his vehement assurances that he was well. They were, apparently, afraid of "shock." The doctor lectured Monsieur Delacroix on the mysterious unpredictability and dreadfulness of "shock." "At your age, you are more prone to aftereffects than at any age," he affirmed. "It would be—we shall not say suicidal, but most certainly extremely dangerous—for you to resume your normal life until the body has had a chance to adjust."

"Is it shock or mania you are afraid of," asked Monsieur Delacroix with a bitterness that was most unusual for him. "Never have I heard of a physically well man being detained in the hospital at government expense just in case he should experience a reaction. If I had been assaulted by a thief instead of a mad botanist I have no doubt but that I should have been released the first day. You believe I am mad and that I have made away with two men."

The doctor moved to the door.

"The police are checking your story for truth. I am only interested in you as a medical patient, and I know you are unwell. Please try to rest. Good day."

"Unwell," the euphemism did not deceive Monsieur Delacroix.

He questioned Madame Delacroix closely about her conversation with the police and with the matron of the ward. He persisted in an attempt to make her admit that she herself thought him mad, until she exhausted the number of ways of saying "no" and cut short her visit in exasperation.

Monsieur Delacroix spent one day lying on his back in silent despair, examining all the signs of madness within his mind. He spoke to no one and drank only one cup of coffee the whole day.

Eventually the police officer reappeared, accompanied once more by the doctor. The door was fastened behind them. The officer would not sit down and stood stiffly beside the bed with his light-gray eyes pinning Monsieur Delacroix to the pillow.

"We have completed our investigations," he announced. "We have found the bodies of Monsieur Abime and Medan."

From the corner of his eyes Monsieur Delacroix could see the face of the doctor fixed rigid like a staring under-colored tailor's dummy. His heart seemed to turn over. He knew that the bodies had been found in circumstances that incriminated him. His mind suffered a sudden confusion of thoughts that centered upon the certainty that, after all, he *was* mad, and the whole terrible night was an illusion thrown up by his guilty mind to drown out the actual crime. What had he done!

"Are you all right, monsieur?" queried the doctor in concern. He took Monsieur Delacroix's wrist.

The police officer remained silent, keeping his unwavering eyes on Monsieur Delacroix while the doctor counted out the pulse.

"A drink of water," said the doctor, and helped Monsieur Delacroix to take it.

"Go on," croaked Monsieur Delacroix.

"It took time because we had to obtain permission from the directorate of the Jardin for our every move," said the officer. "But we dug up the gazebo. We found the tube. I was there when we found it. Monsieur, you must have had a terrifying experience."

"Oh!" said Monsieur Delacroix, closing his eyes. His relief was so intense that tears ran from beneath his lids.

"Fortunately the thing was inert and did not attack us. We obtained permission and dug up the cactus described by yourself. The remains of both men were found in a sac at the base of the plant. It is thought that some chemical that Medan kept about himself as a protection from the plant poisoned it. The plant was already beginning to decay when we dug it up."

"Oh!" sighed Monsieur Delacroix. He looked at the police officer through the distorting lenses of his tears. "That was a terrible experience for you."

"One gets used to such things," said the officer grimly.

"So I'm not mad," murmured Monsieur Delacroix. "Am I free?"

"Of course, monsieur!" answered the officer. "You have not been a prisoner. Of course you are free."

Monsieur Delacroix looked at the doctor, who shrugged as he stood up. "I think you may go."

The two men left. The nurse opened the door and ushered in Monsieur Delacroix's full family. The youngest child bore a giant bouquet of flowers.

Monsieur Delacroix shrieked and fell back onto the bed.

The doctor reentered almost immediately.

"That's better," he observed with satisfaction as he stooped over the trembling Delacroix. "Didn't I tell you about the dangers of shock?"

Doomsday Deferred

by Will F. Jenkins

If I were sensible, I'd say that somebody else told me this story, and then cast doubts on his veracity. But I saw it all. I was part of it. I have an invoice of a shipment I made from Brazil, with a notation on it, "José Ribiera's stuff." The shipment went through. The invoice, I noticed only today, has a mashed *soldado* ant sticking to the page. There is nothing unusual about it as a specimen. On the face of things, every element is irritatingly commonplace. But if I were sensible, I wouldn't tell it this way.

It began in Milhão, where José Ribiera came to me. Milhão is in Brazil, but from it the Andes can be seen against the sky at sunset. It is a town the jungle unfortunately did not finish burying when the rubber boom collapsed. It is so far up the Amazon basin that its principal contacts with the outer world are smugglers and fugitives from Peruvian justice who come across the mountains, and nobody at all goes there except for his sins. I don't know what took José Ribiera there. I went because one of the three known specimens of *Morpho andiensis* was captured nearby by Böhler in 1911, and a lunatic millionaire in Chicago was willing to pay for a try at a fourth for his collection.

I got there after a river steamer refused to go any farther, and after four days more in a canoe with paddlers who had lived on or near river water all their lives without once taking a bath in it. When I got to Milhão, I wished myself back in the canoe. It's that sort of place.

But that's where José Ribiera was, and in back-country Brazil there is a remarkable superstition that *os senhores norteamericanos* are honest men. I do not explain it. I simply record it. And just as I was getting settled in a particularly noisome inn, José knocked on my door and came in. He was a small brown man, and he was scared all the way down deep inside. He tried to hide that. The thing I noticed first was that he was clean. He was barefoot, but his tattered duck garments were immaculate, and the rest of him had been washed, and recently. In a town like Milhão, that was startling.

"*Senhor*," said José in a sort of apologetic desperation, "you are a *senhor norteamericano*. I—I beg your aid."

I grunted. Being an American is embarrassing, sometimes and in some places. José closed the door behind him and fumbled inside his garments. His eyes anxious, he pulled out a small cloth bundle. He opened it with shaking fingers. And I blinked. The lamplight glittered and glinted on the most amazing mass of tiny gold nuggets I'd ever seen. I hadn't a doubt it was gold, but even at first glance I wondered how on earth it had been gathered. There was no flour gold at all—that fine powder which is the largest part of any placer yield. Most of it was gravelly particles of pinhead size. There was no nugget larger than a half pea. There must have been five pounds of it altogether, though, and it was a rather remarkable spectacle.

"*Senhor*," said José tensely, "I beg that you will help me turn this into cattle! It is a matter of life or death."

I hardened my expression. Of course, in thick jungle like that around Milhão, a cow or a bull would be as much out of place as an Eskimo, but that wasn't the point. I had business of my own in Milhão. If I started gold buying or cattle dealing out of amiability, my own affairs would suffer. So I said in polite regret, "I am not a businessman, *senhor*, do not deal in gold or cattle either. To buy cattle, you should go down to São Pedro"—that was four days' paddle downstream, or considering the current perhaps three—"and take this gold to a banker. He will give you money for it if you

67

can prove that it is yours. You can then buy cattle if you wish."

José looked at me desperately. Certainly half the population of Milhão—and positively the Peruvian-refugee half— would have cut his throat for a fraction of his hoard. He almost panted: "But, *senhor!* This would be enough to buy cattle in São Pedro and send them here, would it not?"

I agreed that at a guess it should buy all the cattle in São Pedro, twice over, and hire the town's wheezy steam launch to tow them upriver besides. José looked sick with relief. But, I said, one should buy his livestock himself, so he ought to go to São Pedro in person. And I could not see what good cattle would be in the jungle anyhow.

"Yet—it would buy cattle!" said José, gulping. "That is what I told—my friends. But I cannot go farther than Milhão, *senhor*. I cannot go to São Pedro. Yet I must—I need to buy cattle for—my friends! It is life and death! How can I do this, *senhor?*"

Naturally, I considered that he exaggerated the emergency.

"I am not a businessman," I repeated. "I would not be able to help you." Then at the terrified look in his eyes I explained, "I am here after butterflies."

He couldn't understand that. He began to stammer, pleading. So I explained.

"There is a rich man," I said wryly, "who wishes to possess a certain butterfly. I have pictures of it. I am sent to find it. I can pay one thousand milreis for one butterfly of a certain sort. But I have no authority to do other business, such as the purchase of gold or cattle."

José looked extraordinarily despairing. He looked numbed by the loss of hope. So, merely to say or do something, I showed him a color photograph of the specimen of *Morpho andiensis* which is in the Goriot collection in Paris. Bug collectors were in despair about it during the war. They were sure the Nazis would manage to seize it. Then José's eyes lighted hopefully.

"Senhor!" he said urgently. "Perhaps my—friends can find you such a butterfly! Will you pay for such a butterfly in cattle sent here from São Pedro, *senhor?*"

I said rather blankly that I would, but—— Then I was talking to myself. José had bolted out of my room, leaving maybe five pounds of gravelly gold nuggets in my hands. That was not usual.

I went after him, but he'd disappeared. So I hid his small

fortune in the bottom of my collection kit. A few drops of formaldehyde, spilled before closing up a kit of collection bottles and insects, is very effective in chasing away pilferers. I make use of it regularly.

Next morning I asked about José. My queries were greeted with shrugs. He was a very low person. He did not live in Milhão, but had a clearing, a homestead, some miles upstream, where he lived with his wife. They had one child. He was suspected of much evil. He had bought pigs, and taken them to his clearing and behold he had no pigs there! His wife was very pretty, and a Peruvian had gone swaggering to pay court to her, and he had never come back. It is notable, as I think of it, that up to this time no ant of any sort has come into my story. Butterflies, but no ants. Especially not *soldados*—army ants. It is queer.

I learned nothing useful about José, but I had come to Milhão on business, so I stated it publicly. I wished a certain butterfly, I said. I would pay one thousand milreis for a perfect specimen. I would show a picture of what I wanted to any interested person, and I would show how to make a butterfly net and how to use it, and how to handle butterflies without injuring them. But I wanted only one kind, and it must not be squashed.

The inhabitants of Milhao became happily convinced that I was insane, and that it might be profitable insanity for them. Each person leaped to the nearest butterfly and blandly brought it to me. I spent a whole day explaining to bright-eyed people that matching the picture of *Morpho andiensis* required more than that the number of legs and wings should be the same. But, I repeated, I would pay one thousand milreis for a butterfly exactly like the picture. I had plenty of margin for profit and loss, at that. The last time a *Morpho andiensis* was sold, it brought $25,000 at auction. I'd a lot rather have the money, myself.

José Ribiera came back. His expression was tense beyond belief. He plucked at my arm and said, *"Senhor,"* and I grabbed him and dragged him to my inn.

I hauled out his treasure. "Here!" I said angrily. "This is not mine! Take it!"

He paid no attention. He trembled. *"Senhor,"* he said, and swallowed. "My friends—my friends do not think they can catch the butterfly you seek. But if you will tell them——" He wrinkled his brows. *"Senhor,* before a butterfly is born, is it a little soft nut with a worm in it?"

That could pass for a description of a cocoon. José's

friends—he was said not to have any—were close observers. I said so. José seemed to grasp at hope as at a straw.

"My—friends will find you the nut which produces the butterfly," he said urgently, "if you tell them which kind it is and what it looks like."

I blinked. Just three specimens of *Morpho andiensis* had ever been captured, so far as was known. All were adult insects. Of course nobody knew what the cocoon was like. For that matter, any naturalist can name a hundred species— and in the Amazon valley alone—of which only the adult forms have been named. But who would hunt for cocoons in jungle like that outside of Milhão?

"My friend," I said skeptically, "there are thousands of different such things. I will buy five of each different kind you can discover, and I will pay one milreis apiece. But only five of each kind, remember!"

I didn't think he'd even try, of course. I meant to insist that he take back his gold nuggets. But again he was gone before I could stop him. I had an uncomfortable impression that when I made my offer, his face lighted as if he'd been given a reprieve from a death sentence. In the light of later events, I think he had.

I angrily made up my mind to take his gold back to him next day. It was a responsibility. Besides, one gets interested in a man—especially of the half-breed class—who can unfeignedly ignore five pounds of gold. I arranged to be paddled up to his clearing next morning.

It was on the river, of course. There are no footpaths in Amazon-basin jungle. The river flowing past Milhão is a broad deep stream perhaps two hundred yards wide. Its width seems less because of the jungle walls on either side. And the jungle is daunting. It is trees and vines and lianas as seen from the stream, but it is more than that. Smells come out, and you can't identify them. Sounds come out, and you can't interpret them. You cut your way into its mass, and you see nothing. You come out, and you have learned nothing. You cannot affect it. It ignores you. It made me feel insignificant.

My paddlers would have taken me right on past José's clearing without seeing it, if he hadn't been on the river-bank. He shouted. He'd been fishing, and now that I think, there were no fish near him, but there were some picked-clean fish skeletons. And I think the ground was very dark about him when we first saw him, and quite normal when we

70

approached. I know he was sweating, but he looked terribly hopeful at the sight of me.

I left my two paddlers to smoke and slumber in the canoe. I followed José into the jungle. It was like walking in a tunnel of lucent green light. Everywhere there were tree trunks and vines and leaves, but green light overlay everything. I saw a purple butterfly with crimson wing tips, floating abstractedly in the jungle as if in an undersea grotto.

Then the path widened, and there was José's dwelling. It was a perfect proof that man does not need civilization to live in comfort. Save for cotton garments, an iron pot and a machete, there was literally nothing in the clearing or the house which was not of and from the jungle, to be replaced merely by stretching out one's hand. To a man who lives like this, gold has no value. While he keeps his wants at this level, he can have no temptations. My thoughts at the moment were almost sentimental.

I beamed politely at José's wife. She was a pretty young girl with beautifully regular features. But, disturbingly, her eyes were as panic-filled as José's. She spoke, but she seemed tremblingly absorbed in the contemplation of some crawling horror. The two of them seemed to live with terror. It was too odd to be quite believable. But their child—a brown-skinned three-year-old quite innocent of clothing—was unaffected. He stared at me, wide-eyed.

"Senhor," said José in a trembling voice, "here are the things you desire, the small nuts with worms in them."

His wife had woven a basket of flat green strands. He put it before me. And I looked into it tolerantly, expecting nothing. But I saw the sort of thing that simply does not happen. I saw a half bushel of cocoons!

José had acquired them somehow in less than twenty-four hours. Some were miniature capsules of silk which would yield little butterflies of wingspread no greater than a mosquito's. Some were sturdy fat cocoons of stout brown silk. There were cocoons which cunningly mimicked the look of bird droppings, and cocoons cleverly concealed in twisted leaves. Some were green—I swear it—and would pass for buds upon some unnamed vine. And——

It was simply, starkly impossible. I was stupefied. The Amazon basin has been collected, after a fashion, but the pupa and cocoon of any reasonably rare species is at least twenty times more rare than the adult insect. And these cocoons were fresh! They were alive! I could not believe it, but I could not doubt it. My hands shook as I turned them over.

I said, "This is excellent, José! I will pay for all of them at the rate agreed on—one milreis each. I will send them to São Pedro today, and their price will be spent for cattle and the bringing of the cattle here. I promise it!"

José did not relax. I saw him wipe sweat off his face.

"I—beg you to command haste, *senhor*," he said thinly.

I almost did not hear. I carried that basket of cocoons back to the riverbank. I practically crooned over it all the way back to Milhão. I forgot altogether about returning the gold pellets. And I began to work frenziedly at the inn.

I made sure, of course, that the men who would cart the parcel would know that it contained only valueless objects like cocoons. Then I slipped in the parcel of José's gold. I wrote a letter to the one man in São Pedro who, if God was good, might have sense enough to attend to the affair for me. And I was almost idiotically elated.

While I was making out the invoice that would carry my shipment by refrigerated air express from the nearest airport it could be got to, a large ant walked across my paper. One takes insects very casually in back-country Brazil. I mashed him, without noticing what he was. I went blissfully to start the parcel off. I had a shipment that would make history among bug collectors. It was something that simply could not be done!

The fact of the impossibility hit me after the canoe with the parcel started downstream. How the devil those cocoons had been gathered——

The problem loomed larger as I thought. In less than one day, José had collected a half bushel of cocoons, of at least one hundred different species of moths and butterflies. It could not be done! The information to make it possible did not exist! Yet it had happened. How?

The question would not down. I had to find out. I bought a pig for a present and had myself ferried up to the clearing again. My paddlers pulled me upstream with languid strokes. The pig made irritated noises in the bottom of the canoe. Now I am sorry about that pig. I would apologize to its ghost if opportunity offered. But I didn't know.

I landed on the narrow beach and shouted. Presently José came through the tunnel of foliage that led to his house. He thanked me, dry-throated, for the pig. I told him I had ordered cattle sent up from São Pedro. I told him humorously that every ounce of meat on the hoof the town contained would soon be on the way behind a wheezing steam launch. José swallowed and nodded numbly. He still looked like someone who contemplated pure horror.

We got the pig to the house. José's wife sat and rocked her child, her eyes sick with fear. I probably should have felt embarrassed in the presence of such tragedy, even if I could not guess at its cause. But instead, I thought about the questions I wanted to ask. José sat down dully beside me.

I was oblivious of the atmosphere of doom. I said blandly, "Your friends are capable naturalists, José. I am much pleased. Many of the 'little nuts' they gathered are quite new to me. I would like to meet such students of the ways of nature."

José's teeth clicked. His wife caught her breath. She looked at me with an oddly despairing irony. It puzzled me. I looked at José, sharply. And then the hair stood up on my head. My heart tried to stop. Because a large ant walked on José's shoulder, and I saw what kind of ant it was.

"My God!" I said shrilly. "*Soldados!* Army ants!"

I acted through pure instinct. I snatched up the baby from its mother's arms and raced for the river. One does not think at such times. The *soldado* ant, the army ant, the driver ant, is the absolute and undisputed monarch of all jungles everywhere. He travels by millions of millions, and nothing can stand against him. He is ravening ferocity and inexhaustible number. Even man abandons his settlements when the army ant marches in, and returns only after he has left—to find every bit of flesh devoured to the last morsel, from the earwigs in the thatch to a horse that may have been tethered too firmly to break away. The army ant on the march can and does kill anything alive, by tearing the flesh from it in tiny bites, regardless of defense. So—I grabbed the child and ran.

José Ribiera screamed at me, *"No! Senhor! No!"*

He sat still and he screamed. I'd never heard such undiluted horror in any man's voice.

I stopped. I don't know why. I was stunned to see José and his wife sitting frozen where I'd left them. I was more stunned, I think, to see the tiny clearing and the house unchanged. The army ant moves usually on a solid front. The ground is covered with a glistening, shifting horde. The air is filled with tiny clickings of limbs and mandibles. Ants swarm up every tree and shrub. Caterpillars, worms, bird nestlings, snakes, monkeys unable to flee—anything living becomes buried under a mass of ferociously rending small forms which tear off the living flesh in shreds until only white bones are left.

But José sat still, his throat working convulsively. I had seen *soldados* on him. But there were no *soldados*. After a moment José got to his feet and came stumbling toward me. He looked like a dead man. He could not speak.

"But look!" I cried. My voice was high-pitched. "I saw *soldado* ants! I saw them!"

José gulped by pure effort of will. I put down the child. He ran back to his mother.

"*S-sí*. Yes," said José, as if his lips were very stiff and his throat without moisture. "But they are—special *soldados*. They are—pets. Yes. They are tame. They are my—friends. They—do tricks, *senhor*. I will show you!"

He held out his hand and made sucking noises with his mouth. What followed is not to be believed. An ant—a large ant, an inch or more long—walked calmly out of his sleeve and onto his outstretched hand. It perched there passively while the hand quivered like an aspen leaf.

"But yes!" said José hysterically. "He does tricks, *senhor*! Observe! He will stand on his head!"

Now, this I saw, but I do not believe it. The ant did something so that it seemed to stand on its head. Then it turned and crawled tranquilly over his hand and wrist and up his sleeve again.

There was silence, or as much silence as the jungle ever holds. My own throat went dry. And what I have said is insanity, but this is much worse. I felt Something waiting to see what I would do. It was, unquestionably, the most horrible sensation I had ever felt. I do not know how to describe it. What I felt was—not a personality, but a mind. I had a ghastly feeling that Something was looking at me from thousands of pairs of eyes, that it was all around me.

I shared, for an instant, what that Something saw and thought. I was surrounded by a mind which waited to see what I would do. It would act upon my action. But it was not a sophisticated mind. It was murderous, but innocent. It was merciless, but naïve.

That is what I felt. The feeling doubtless has a natural explanation which reduces it to nonsense, but at the moment I believed it. I acted on my belief. I am glad I did.

"Ah, I see!" I said in apparent amazement. "That is clever, José! It is remarkable to train an ant! I was absurd to be alarmed. But—your cattle will be on the way, José! They should get here very soon! There will be many of them!"

Then I felt that the mind would let me go. And I went.

My canoe was a quarter mile downstream when one of the paddlers lifted his blade from the water and held it there, listening. The other stopped and listened too. There was a noise in the jungle. It was mercifully far away, but it sounded like a pig. I have heard the squealing of pigs at slaughtering time, when instinct tells them of the deadly intent of men and they try punily to fight. This was not that sort of noise. It was worse; much worse.

I make a hopeless spectacle of myself in the canoe. Now, of course, I can see that, from this time on, my actions were not those of a reasoning human being. I did not think with proper scientific skepticism. It suddenly seemed to me that Norton's theory of mass consciousness among social insects was very plausible. Bees, says Norton, are not only units in an organization. They are units of an organism. The hive or the swarm is a creature—one creature—says Norton. Each insect is a body cell only, just as the corpuscles in our bloodstream are individuals and yet only parts of us. We can destroy a part of our body if the welfare of the whole organism requires it, though we destroy many cells. The swarm or the hive can sacrifice its members for the hive's defense. Each bee is a mobile body cell. Its consciousness is a part of the whole intelligence, which is that of the group. The group is the actual creature. And ants, says Norton, show the fact more clearly still; the ability of the creature which is an ant colony to sacrifice a part of itself for the whole.... He gives illustrations of what he means. His book is not accepted by naturalists, generally, but there in the canoe, going downriver from José's clearing, I believed it utterly.

I believed that an army-ant army was as much a single creature as a sponge. I believed that the Something in José's jungle clearing—its body cells were *soldado* ants—had discovered that other creatures perceived and thought as it did. Nothing more was needed to explain everything. An army-ant creature, without physical linkages, could know what its own members saw and knew and felt. It should need only to open its mind to perceive what other creatures saw and knew and felt.

The frightening thing was that when it could interpret such unantish sensations, it could find its prey with a terrible infallibility. It could flow through the jungle in a streaming, crawling tide of billions of tiny stridulating bodies. It could know the whereabouts and thoughts of every living thing around it. Nothing could avoid it, as nothing could withstand it. And if it came upon a man, it could know his thoughts too. It could perceive in his mind vast horizons beyond its former ken. It could know of food—animal food—in quantities never before imagined. It could, intelligently, try to arrange to secure that food.

It had.

But if so much was true, there was something else it could do. The thought made the blood seem to cake in my veins. I began frantically to thrust away the idea. The Something in José's clearing hadn't discovered it yet. But pure terror of the discovery had me drenched in sweat when I got back to Milhão.

The Cocoon

by John B. L. Goodwin

Whereas downstairs his father had a room the walls of which were studded with trophies of his aggressive quests: heads of ibex, chamois, eland, keitloa, peccary, and ounce, upstairs Denny had pinned upon his playroom walls the fragile bodies of swallowtails, nymphs, fritillaries, meadow browns and anglewings.

Although his father had maneuvered expeditions, experienced privation, waded through jungles, climbed upon crags for his specimens, Denny had blithely gathered his within the fields and gardens close to home. It was likely that his father's day as a collector was over; Denny's had just begun.

Denny was eleven and his father forty-six and the house in which they lived was a hundred or more years old though no one could be exact about it. Mr. Peatybog, the postmaster in the shriveled village, said as how he could recall when the circular window on the second-story landing hadn't been there and Mrs. Bliss said she knew that at one time what was now the kitchen had been a taproom because her father had told her about it. The heart of the house, as Denny's father put it, was very old but people had altered it and added on and covered up. Denny's father had added the room where his heads were hung, but Denny's playroom must have been the original attic because where the rafters of its high, abrupt

76

ceiling were visible the nails in them were square-headed and here and there the timbers were still held together with wooden pegs.

But the playroom, where Denny also slept, appeared to the casual glance anything but old. The floor was carpeted in blue, and curtains were yellow and the bedspread blue and white. The wallpaper, which his mother had chosen for him before she left, was yellow willow trees on a pale blue ground and to an alien eye the butterflies pinned on the walls seemed part of the design. It had been a long time since Denny's father had been up in the room and although he knew that his son's collection of Lepidoptera, as he called them, was pinned upon the walls he did not know and therefore could not reprimand his son for the damage they had done the pretty wallpaper. Under each specimen a putty-colored blot was spreading over the blue paper. It was the oil exuding from the drying bodies of the dead insects.

In one corner of the room was a chintz-covered chest in which lay the remains of Denny's earlier loves: battered trains and sections of track, an old transformer, batteries covered with cavernlike crystals of zinc salts, trucks, and windmills no longer recognizable as much more than haphazard, wooden arrangements of fitted blocks and sticks, books crumpled and torn with Denny's name or current dream scrawled aggressively in crayon across the print and pictures, a gyroscope, a rubber ball, its cracked paint making a mosaic of antique red and gold around its sphere, and somewhere at the bottom weighed down with tin and lead and wood more than any corpse with earth and grass, lay a bear, a monkey, and a boy doll with a scar across one cheek where Denny had kicked it with a skate. In another corner the symbols of his present were proudly displayed. The butterfly net leaned against the wall, and close to the floor on a wooden box turned upside down stood Denny's cyanide bottle, tweezers, and pins, the last shining as dangerously bright as minute surgical instruments in their packet of black paper.

After almost a year of collecting butterflies, Denny had found that a certain equivocal quality could be added to his pursuit if he were to collect not only the butterflies but also the earlier stages of their mutations. By cramming milk bottles, shoe boxes, and whatever other receptacle the house might offer with caterpillars and pupae he was, in the case of those that survived, able to participate in a sort of alchemy. Intently he would squat on his haunches and gaze into the receptacles, studying the laborious transformations, the caterpillar shedding skin, the exudation that is used to hitch its shroudlike chrysalid to twigs or undersides of leaves, and then the final unpredictable attainment of the imago. It was like opening a surprise package, for as yet Denny had not learned to tell what color, size, or shape worm would turn into a dog's head sulphur, mourning cloak, or tiger swallowtail.

As late summer approached, Denny insisted that the servant girl refrain from opening the windows wide in order to air out his room. The sudden change in temperature, he said, would disturb the caterpillars and pupae. Even though the girl reported to his father that Denny's room smelled unhealthily from all the bugs and things, the man did no more than mention it to Denny in an offhand manner. Denny grunted to show that he had heard and did no more about it, and as his father was writing a book on his jungles and crags and beasts, he had really very little concern about what went on upstairs.

So it was that an acrid smell of decaying vegetable matter resolving itself into insect flesh pervaded Denny's bright attic room and the oily blotches on the walls beneath his specimens spread over so slightly, discoloring the paper more and more.

In a book, *Butterflies You Ought to Know Better,* which an aunt had sent him for Christmas, Denny read that a suitable "castle" for a caterpillar could be made by placing a lamp chimney, closed at the top, upon a flowerpot filled with earth. He prepared this enclosure, purchasing the lamp chimney from the village store with his own money. It was such an elegant contrivance and yet so magical that he decided to save it for an especially unusual specimen. It was not until a late afternoon in October that Denny found one worthy of the "castle."

He was exploring a copse between two fields. Because of the stoniness of its ground it had never been cultivated and lay like a sword between the fertility of the fields on either side. Denny had never trespassed on it before and dared to now only because of his growing self-confidence in his power over nature. A month ago he would have shied away from the area entirely, even taking the precaution to circumvent the two fields enclosing it. But he felt a little now the way he thought God must feel when, abject within its glass and cardboard world, the life he watched took form, changed, and ceased. Protected from unpleasant touch or any unpredictable action, Denny watched the metamorphosis from worm to chrysalid to miraculously vibrant petal. It lay within his power to sever abruptly the magical chain of their evolution at any point he chose. In a little way he *was* a little like God. It was this conceit that now gave him the courage to climb over the stones of the old wall and enter the half acre of dense woodland.

The autumn sun, already low, ogled the brittle landscape like some improbable jack-o'-lantern hanging in the west. What birds were still in that country spoke in the rasping tone of the herd; the more mellifluous and prosperous had already gone south. Although the leaves on the trees displayed the incautious yellows of senility and ochres of decay, the underbrush such as cat briar and wild grape were mostly green. Armed with his forceps and his omnipotence, Denny explored each living leaf and twig.

Brambles tore his stockings and scratched his knees but, except for vulgar tent caterpillars in the wild cherry trees, Denny's efforts went unrewarded. It was dusk when, searching among the speculatively shaped leaves of a sassafras, Denny found a specimen beyond his most arrogant expectations. At first sight, due in part to the twilight, it looked more like some shriveled dragon than a caterpillar. Between it and the twig a filament stretched and this, added to the fact that when Denny touched it gingerly he could feel its puffy flesh contract the way caterpillars do, convinced him that it was no freak of nature or if it was it was a caterpillar freak and therefore nothing to fear. Tearing it cautiously with his tweezers from the twig, he put the monster in the Diamond Match box he always carried with him and, running breathlessly, blind to briar and brambles, Denny headed home.

It was suppertime when he got there and his father was already at the table, his left hand turning the pages of a book while with his right hand he ladled soup into his mouth. Denny had clattered up the stairs before his father was aware of his presence.

"You're late, son," he said in the moment between two printed sentences and two spoonfuls of soup.

"I know, Father," Denny replied without stopping, "but I got something."

Another sentence and another spoonful.

"How many times have I told you to be explicit? *Something* can be anything from a captive balloon to a case of mumps."

From the second landing Denny called down, "It's just *something*. I don't know what it is."

His father mumbled, and by the time he had finished a paragraph and scooped up the last nugget of meat out of his soup and had addressed his son with the words, "Whatever it is it will wait until you have your supper," Denny was peering at it through the glass of the lamp chimney.

Even in the bright electric glare it was reptilian. It was large for a caterpillar, between four and five inches long Denny guessed, and was a muddy purple color, its underside a yellowish black. At either extremity it bore a series of three horny protuberances of a vermilion shade; they were curved sharply inward and stiff little hairs grew from them. From its mouth there protruded a set of small grasping claws like those of a crustacean. Its skin was wrinkled like that of a tortoise and the abdominal segments were sharply defined. The feet lacked the usual suction-like apparatuses caterpillars have but were scaly and shaped like tiny claws.

It was indeed worthy of its "castle." It was not to be found in any of the illustrated books Denny had. He would guard it and keep it a secret and finally, when he presented its metamorphosis into a winged thing to the world, his father's renown as the captor of extraordinary beasts would pale beside his own. The only thing he could guess at, and that because of its size, was that it was the larva of a moth rather than that of a butterfly.

He was still peering at it when the servant girl brought up a tray. "Here," she said, "if you're such a busy little gentleman that you can't spare time for supper like an ordinary boy. If I had my way you'd go hungry." She set the tray down on the table. "Pugh!" she added. "The smell of this room is something awful. What have you got there now?" And she was about to peer over Denny's shoulder.

"Get out!" he shrieked, turning on her. "Get out!"

"I'm not so sure I will if you speak like that."

He arose and in his fury pushed her hulk out the door, slamming it and locking it after her.

She started to say something on the other side, but what it was Denny never knew or cared, for his own voice screaming, "And stay out!" sent the young girl scurrying down the stairs to his father.

It was typical of the man that he merely commiserated with the girl, agreed with her on the urgency of some sort of discipline for his son, and then, settling back to his pipe and his manuscript, dismissed the matter from his mind.

The following day Denny told the girl that henceforth she

was not to enter his room, neither to make the bed nor to clean.

"We shall see about that," she said, "though it would be a pleasure such as I never hoped for this side of heaven were I never to enter that horrid smelling room again."

Again his father was approached and this time he reluctantly called his son to him.

"Ethel tells me something about you not wanting her to go into your room," he said, peering over his glasses.

"I'd rather she didn't, Father," Denny replied, humble as pie. "You see, she doesn't understand about caterpillars and cocoons and things and she messes everything up."

"But who will see to the making of your bed and dusting and such?"

"I will," asserted Denny. "There's no reason why if I don't want anyone to go into my room I shouldn't have to make up for it somehow, like making my own bed and clearing up."

"Spoken like a soldier, son," the father said. "I know the way you feel and if you're willing to pay the price in responsibility I see no reason why you shouldn't have your wish. But," and he pointed a paper knife of walrus tusk at the boy, "if it isn't kept neat and tidy we'll have to rescind the privilege; remember that."

His father, grateful that the interview had not been as tedious as he had anticipated, told his son he could go. From then on Denny always kept the key to his room in his pocket.

Because caterpillars cease to eat prior to their chrysalis stage and Denny's caterpillar refused to eat whatever assortment of leaves he tried to tempt it with, Denny knew that it had definitely been preparing its cocoon when he had plucked it from the sassafras branch. It was very restless, almost convulsive now, and within the lamp chimney it humped itself aimlessly from twig to twig, its scaly little claws searching for something to settle upon. After a day of such meanderings the caterpillar settled upon a particular crotch of the twig and commenced to spin its cocoon. By the end of twenty-four hours the silken alembic was complete.

Though there was now nothing for Denny to observe, he still squatted for hours on end staring at the cocoon that hung like some parasitic growth from the sassafras twig. His concentration upon the shape was so great as he sat hunched over it, that his eyes seemed to tear the silken shroud apart and to be intimately exploring the secret that was taking place within.

Now Denny spent less and less of the days out in the open searching for the more common types of chrysalid with which he was acquainted. Such were for him as garnets would be to a connoisseur of emeralds. His lean, tanned face became puffy and the palms of his hands were pale and moist.

The winter months dragged on and Denny was as listlessly impatient as what was inside the cocoon. His room was cold and airless, for a constant low temperature must be kept if the cocoon was to lie dormant until spring. His bed was seldom made and the floor was thick with dust and mud. Once a week the girl left the broom and dustpan along with the clean sheets outside his door, but Denny took only the sheets into his room where they would collect into a stack on the floor for weeks at a time. His father took no notice of his condition other than to write a postscript to what was otherwise a legal and splenetic letter to his wife that their son looked peaked and upon receiving an apprehensive reply he casually asked Denny if he was feeling all right. The boy's affirmative though noncommittal answer seemed to satisfy him and, dropping a card to his wife to the effect that their son professed to be in sound health, he considered himself released from any further responsibility.

When April was about gone Denny moved his treasure close to the window where the sun would induce the dormant thing within it into life. In a few days Denny was sure that it was struggling for release, for the cocoon seemed to dance up and down idiotically upon its thread. All that night he kept vigil, his red and swollen eyes focused on the cocoon as upon some hypnotic object. His father ate breakfast alone and by nine o'clock showed enough concern to send the servant girl up to see if everything was all right. She hurried back to report that his son was at least still alive enough to be rude to her. The father mumbled something in reply about the boy's mother having shirked her responsibilities. The girl said that if it pleased him, she would like to give notice. She was very willing to enumerate the reasons why, but the man dismissed her casually with the request that she stay until she found someone to take her place.

At ten Denny was positive that the cocoon was about to break; by ten thirty there was no longer any doubt in his mind. Somewhat before eleven the eclosion took place. There was a convulsive movement inside and the cocoon opened at

82

the top with the faint rustle of silk. The feathery antennae and the two forelegs issued forth, the legs clutching the cocoon in order to hoist the body through the narrow aperture. The furry and distended abdomen, upon which were hinged the crumpled wings, was drawn out with effort. Immediately the creature commenced awkwardly to climb the twig from which the cocoon was suspended. Denny watched the procedure in a trance. Having gained the tip of the branch and unable to proceed farther, the insect rested, its wings hanging moist and heavy from its bloated body. The abdomen with each pulsation shrank visibly and gradually, very gradually, the antennae unfurled and the wings expanded with the juices pumped into them from the body.

Within an hour the metamorphosis of many months was complete. The beast, its wings still slightly damp though fully spread, fluttered gently before the eyes of the boy. Though escaped from its cocoon, it lay imprisoned still behind the glass.

Denny's pallor was suddenly flushed. He grasped the lamp chimney as if he would hold the insect to him. This was his miracle, his alone. He watched with a possessive awe as the creature flexed its wings, although it was still too weak to attempt flight. Surely this specimen before him was unique. The wings were easily ten inches across and their color was so subtly graduated that it was impossible to say where black turned to purple and purple to green and green back to black. The only definite delineations were a crablike simulacrum centered on each hind wing and upon each fore wing, the imitation of an open mouth with teeth bared. Both the crabs and the mouths were chalked in white and vermilion.

By noon Denny was hungry, yet so overcome with nervous exhaustion that he almost decided to forego the midday meal. Aware, however, that an absence from two meals running would surely precipitate an intrusion by his father with the servant girl as proxy, he reluctantly left his room and went downstairs to face his father over luncheon.

Despite his compliance, the father was immediately aware of the transformation in his son.

"Spring seems to have put new life into the lad," he said, turning over the page of a book. "You're like your mother in that respect and in that respect only, thank God. She never did so well in cold weather."

It was the first time he had mentioned the mother to the son since he had been forced to explain her departure obliquely some five years before. The boy was shocked. But as the opportunity had arisen, he hastily decided to follow up the mention of his mother. It was unseemly that he should disclose any sentiment, so he hesitated and calculated before putting his question. "Why doesn't she write or send me presents?" he asked.

His father's pause made him almost unbearably aware of the man's chagrin in having opened the subject. He didn't look up at the boy as he answered. "Because legally she is not allowed to."

The remainder of the meal was passed in silent and mutual embarrassment.

Denny returned to his room as soon as he could respectfully quit the table, and while unlocking the door for an awful moment the possibility that the moth might have escaped, might never really have been there, scorched Denny's mind. But it was there, almost as he had left it, only now it had changed its position; the spread of its wings being nearly horizontal and in this position Denny realized that the lamp chimney was too narrow to allow it free movement.

There was no receptacle in the room any larger and in Denny's mind there paraded the various jars, the vases, and other vessels in the house that had from time to time in the past served as enclosures for his specimens. None of them was large enough. Without sufficient room, the moth as soon as it attempted flight would in no time at all damage its wings. In a kind of frenzy Denny racked his brains for the memory of some container that would satisfy his need. Like a ferret his thoughts suddenly pounced on what had eluded them. In his father's room a huge crystal tobacco jar with a lid of repoussé silver stood on an ebony taboret beneath the smirking head of a tiger.

There was no time to lose; for within five hours after emerging from the cocoon a moth will try its wings in flight. Breathlessly Denny bounded down the stairs and for a moment only hesitated before he knocked upon his father's door.

"Yes?" his father asked querulously, and Denny turned the knob and walked in.

"Father——" he began, but he had not as yet caught his breath.

"Speak up, boy, and stop shaking. Why, even confronted by a rogue elephant I never shook so."

"I want to b-b-borrow something," the boy managed to stammer.

"Be more explicit! Be more explicit! What do you want? A

ticket to Fall River? A hundred-dollar bill? A dose of ipecac? The last would seem the most logical to judge from your looks."

Hating his father as he had never hated him before, the boy spoke up. "I want to borrow your tobacco jar."

"Which one?" the father parried. "The elephant foot the President gave me? The Benares brass? The Dutch pottery one? The music box?"

The boy could bear this bantering no longer. "I want that one." And he pointed directly where it stood half full of tobacco.

"What for?" his father asked.

The boy's bravura was suddenly extinguished.

"Speak up. If you make an extraordinary request you must be ready to back it up with a motive."

"I want it for a specimen."

"What's wrong with all the containers you have already appropriated from the kitchen, pantry, and parlor?"

Denny would not say they were not big enough. It might arouse sufficient interest within his father so that he would insist on seeing for himself what this monster was. Denny had a vision of his father grabbing the moth and hastening to impale it upon the study wall, adding it to his other conquests.

"They won't do," Denny said.

"Why won't they do?"

"They just won't."

"Be explicit!" his father thundered at him.

"I want to put some stuff in it that won't fit in the others."

"You will stand where you are without moving until you can tell me what you mean by 'stuff.'" His father laid down his glasses and settled back in his chair to underscore the fact that he was prepared to wait all day if need be.

"Chrysalids and dirt and sticks and food for them," the boy mumbled.

The man stared at Denny as if he were an animal he had at bay.

"You intend to put *that* filth into *that* jar?"

Denny made no answer. His father continued.

"Are you by any chance aware that that jar was a gift from the Maharana of Udaipur? Have you any faintest conception of its intrinsic value aside from the sentimental one? And can you see from where you stand that, besides any other objections I might have, the jar is being employed for what it was intended for? And if for one moment you think I am going to remove my best tobacco from my best jar so that you can use it for a worm bowl you are, my lad, very much mistaken."

The man waited for the effect of his speech and then added, "Go and ask Ethel for a crock."

It was useless for Denny to attempt to explain that he wouldn't be able to see through a crock. Without a word he turned and walked out of the room, leaving the door open behind him.

His father called him back, but he paid no mind. As he reached the second landing Denny heard the door slam downstairs.

A half hour had been wasted and, as he had been sure it would, the moth, having gained control over itself, was in the first struggles of flight.

There was only one thing to do. Denny went to the corner where he kept his equipment. Returning, he lifted the lid from the lamp chimney and reaching inside with his forceps he clenched the moth with a certain brutality, though he took pains to avoid injury to its wings. Lifting it out, the beauty of so few hours, Denny once again felt his omnipotence. Without hesitation he plunged the moth into the cyanide jar and screwed down the lid.

The wings beat frantically with the effort that should have carried the moth on its first flight through the spring air. Breathless, Denny watched for fear the wings would be injured. The dusty abdomen throbbed faster and faster, the antennae twitched from side to side; with a spasm the abdomen formed a curve to meet the thorax. The eyes, still bearing the unenlightened glaze of birth, turned suddenly into the unknowing glaze of death. But in the moment that they turned Denny thought he saw his distorted image gleaming on their black, china surfaces as if in that instant the moth had stored his image in its memory.

Denny unscrewed the cap, plucked out the moth and, piercing its body with a pin from the black paper packet, he pinned the moth to the wall at the foot of his bed. He gave it a place of honor, centering it upon a yellow willow tree. From his bed he would see it first thing in the morning and last thing at night.

A few days and nights passed, and Denny, though still on edge, felt somewhat as a hero must returning from a labor. The untimely death of the moth had perhaps been fortuitous, because now in its death the creature was irrevocably his.

86

The meadows were already filled with cabbage butterflies, and Denny would go out with his net and catch them, but they were too common to preserve and so, having captured them, he would reach his hand into the net and squash them, wiping the mess in his palm off on the grass.

It was less than a week after the death of the moth when Denny was awakened in the night by a persistent beating on his windowpane. He jumped from bed, switched on the light, and peered outside. With the light on he could see nothing, and whatever it had been was gone. Realizing that though the light made anything outside invisible to him it would also act as a lure to whatever had tried to come in, he went back to bed leaving the light on and the window open. He tried to stay awake but soon fell back into sleep.

In the morning he looked about the room, but there was no sign of anything having entered. It must have been a June bug or possibly a luna moth though it had sounded too heavy for one, thought Denny. He went over to look at the moth on the wall, a morning ritual with him. Although he could not be sure, the dust of one wing seemed to be smudged and the oily stain from the body had soaked into the wallpaper considerably since the day before. He put his face close to the insect to inspect it more fully. Instinctively he drew back; the odor was unbearable.

The following night Denny left his window wide open and shortly before midnight he was awakened by a beating of wings upon his face. Terrified and not fully conscious, he hit out with his open hands. He touched something and it wasn't pleasant. It was yielding and at the same time viscid. And something scratched against the palm of his hand like a tiny spur or horn.

Leaping from bed, Denny switched on the light. There was nothing in the room. It must have been a bat and the distasteful thought made him shudder. Whatever it had been, it left a stench behind not unlike the stench of the spot on the wall. Denny slammed the window shut and went back to bed and tried to sleep.

In the morning his red-rimmed eyes inspecting the moth plainly saw that not only were the wings smudged but that the simulacra of crabs and mouths upon the wings seemed to have grown more definite. The oily spot had spread still farther and the smell was stronger.

That night Denny slept with his window closed, but in his dreams he was beset by horned and squashy things that pounded his flesh with their fragile wings, and awakening in fright he heard the same sound as he had heard the previous night; something beating against the windowpane. All night it beat against the closed window and Denny lay rigid and sleepless in his bed and the smell within the room grew into something almost tangible.

At dawn Denny arose and forced himself to look at the moth. He held his nose as he did so and with horror he saw the stain on the paper and the crabs and the mouths which now not only seemed more definite but also considerably enlarged.

For the first time in months Denny left his room and did not return to it until it was his bedtime. Even that hour he contrived to postpone a little by asking his father to read to him. It was the lesser of two evils.

The stench in the room was such that although Denny dared not leave the window open he was forced to leave the door from the landing into his room ajar. What was left of the light in the hall below, after it had wormed its way up and around the stairs, crawled exhaustedly into the room. For some perverse reason it shone most brightly upon the wall where the moth was transfixed. From his bed Denny could not take his eyes off it. Though they made no progress, the two crabs on the hind wings appeared to be attempting to climb up into the two mouths on the fore wings. The mouths seemed to be very open and ready for them.

That night no sooner had the beating of wings upon the window awakened Denny than it abruptly ceased. The light downstairs was out and the room was now in darkness. Curling himself up into a ball and pulling the sheet over his head, Denny at length went off to sleep.

Sometime shortly afterward something came through the door and half crawled and half fluttered to the bed. Denny awoke with a scream, but it was too muffled for either his father or Ethel to hear because what caused him to scream had wormed its way beneath the sheet and was resting like a sticky pulp upon Denny's mouth.

Floundering like a drowning person, the boy threw back the covers and managed to dislodge whatever had been upon his mouth. When he dared to, he reached out and turned on the light. There was nothing in the room, but upon his sheets there were smudges of glistening dust almost black, almost purple, almost green, but not quite any of them.

Denny went down to breakfast without looking at the moth.

"No wonder you look ghastly," his father said to him, "if

the smell in this house is half of what it must be in your room, it's a wonder you're not suffocated. What are you running up there? A potters' field for Lepidoptera? I'll give you until noon to get them out."

All day Denny left the window of his room wide open. It was the first of May and the sun was bright. As a sop to his father he brought down a box of duplicate specimens. He showed them to his father before disposing of them.

"Pugh!" said his father. "Dump them far away from the house."

That night Denny went to bed with both the door and window locked tight in spite of the smell. The moon was bright and shone all night unimpaired upon the wall. Denny could not keep his eyes off the moth.

By now both crabs and mouths were nearly as large as the wings themselves and the crabs were moving, Denny could swear. They appeared in relief, perhaps through some trick of chiaroscuro induced by the moonlight upon the dusty white and red markings. The claws seemed upon the verge of attacking the mouths, or were the so terribly white teeth of the mouths waiting to clamp down upon the crabs? Denny shuddered and closed his eyes.

Sleep came eventually, only to be broken in upon by the beating of wings against the windowpane. And no sooner had that ceased and Denny become less rigid than the thing was at the door beating urgently as though it must be let in. The only relief from the tap-tapping was an occasional, more solid thud against the panel of the door. It was, Denny guessed, caused by the soft and fleshy body of the thing.

If he survived the night Denny vowed he would destroy the thing upon the wall or, better than losing it entirely, he would give it to his father and he in turn would present it to some museum in Denny's name. Denny for a moment was able to forget the persistent rapping which had now returned to the window, for in his mind he saw a glass case with the moth in it and a little card below upon which was printed

Unique specimen Lepidoptera. Gift of Mr. Denny Longwood, Aged 12.

All through the night, first at the window, then at the door, the beating of the wings continued, relieved only by the occasional plop of the soft, heavy body.

Though having dozed for only an hour or two, with the bright light of day Denny felt his decision of the night before indefensible. The moth smelled; that was undeniable. The matter of the crab and mouthlike markings seeming to expand and become more intense in their color could probably be explained by somebody who knew about such things. As for the beating against the window and the door, it was probably as he had at first surmised, a bat or, if need be, two bats. The moth on the wall was dead, was his. He had hatched it and he knew the limitations of a moth dead or alive. He looked at it. The stain had spread so that now its diameter was as great as the spread of the wings. It was no longer exactly a stain, either. It looked as if a spoonful of dirty cereal had adhered to the wall; it was just about the color of mush. It will stop in time like the others; just as soon as the abdomen dries up, thought Denny.

At breakfast his father remarked that the smell as yet hadn't left the house, that it was in fact stronger if anything. Denny admitted it might take a day or two more before it was completely gone.

Before the meal was over his father told Denny that he was looking so badly that he had better see Dr. Phipps.

"How much do you weigh?" he asked.

Denny didn't know.

"You look," his father said, "all dried up like one of those pupae you had upstairs."

The moon shone bright again that night. In spite of his logic of the morning Denny felt sure that the movement of the white and vermilion crabs up to the white teeth and vermilion lips was more than just hallucination. And the beating of wings started at the window again. Then at the door. Then back to the window. And, in a way, worse than that the plop now and then of the body against the barrier. Though he tried to rise and look out when it was at the window, his limbs would not obey him. Hopelessly his eyes turned to the wall again. The crablike spots clicked their tiny claws together each time the wings struck against the windowpane. And each time the plump, squashy body went plop, the teeth snapped together between the thin-lipped mouths.

All at once the stench within the room became nauseating. There was nothing for Denny to do but make for the door while whatever it was still pounded at the window. As much as he feared and hated him, his father's cynical disbelief was to be preferred to this terror.

Denny refrained from switching on the light for fear that it would reveal his movements to the thing outside. Halfway across the room and shivering, he involuntarily turned his head and for a moment his feverish eyes saw what was outside before it disappeared.

Denny rushed for the door and unlocked it, but as he twisted the knob something beat against the other side of the door, pushing it open before Denny could shut the door against it.

When luncheon was over Ethel was sent upstairs to see what had happened. She was so hysterical when she came down that Denny's father went up to see for himself.

Denny lay in his pajamas on the floor just inside the door. The skin of his lonely and somewhat arrogant face was marred by the marks of something pincerlike and from his nose, eyes, ears, and mouth a network of viscid filaments stretched across his face and to the floor as though something had tried to bind his head up in them. His father had some trouble in lifting him up because the threads adhered so stubbornly to the nap of the blue carpet.

The body was feather light in the father's arms. The thought that the boy had certainly been underweight passed inanely through his father's mind.

As he carried his son out his eyes fell upon a spot on the wall at the foot of the bed. The pattern of a willow tree was completely obliterated by a creeping growth that looked like fungus. Still carrying his son, the man crossed over to it. A pin protruded from its center and it was from this spot, Mr. Longwood could tell, that the terrible smell came.

Æpyornis Island

by H. G. Wells

The man with the scarred face leant over the table and looked at my bundle.

"Orchids?" he asked.

"A few," I said.

"Cypripediums?" he said.

"Chiefly," said I.

"Anything new?—I thought not. *I* did these islands twenty-five—twenty-seven years ago. If you find anything new here—well, it's brand new. I didn't leave much."

"I'm not a collector," said I.

"I was young then," he went on. "Lord! how I used to fly around." He seemed to take my measure. "I was in the East Indies two years, and in Brazil seven. Then I went to Madagascar."

"I know a few explorers by name," I said anticipating a yarn. "Who did you collect for?"

"Dawsons. I wonder if you've heard the name of Butcher ever?"

"Butcher—Butcher?" The name seemed vaguely present in my memory; then I recalled *Butcher* v. *Dawson*. "Why!" said I, "you are the man who sued them for four years' salary—got cast away on a desert island——"

"Your servant," said the man with the scar, bowing. "Funny case, wasn't it? Here was me, making a little fortune on that island, doing nothing for it neither, and them quite unable to give me notice. It often used to amuse me thinking over it while I was there. I did calculations of it—big—all over the blessed atoll in ornamental figuring."

"How did it happen?" said I. "I don't rightly remember the case."

"Well—you've heard of the Æpyornis?"

"Rather. Andrews was telling me of a new species he was working on only a month or so ago. Just before I sailed. They've got a thigh bone, it seems, nearly a yard long. Monster the thing must have been!"

"I believe you," said the man with the scar. "It *was* a monster. Sinbad's roc was just a legend of 'em. But when did they find these bones?"

"Three or four years ago—'91 I fancy. Why?"

"Why?—Because *I* found 'em—Lord! it's nearly twenty years ago. If Dawsons hadn't been silly about that salary they might have made a perfect ring in 'em.—I couldn't help the infernal boat going adrift."

He paused. "I suppose it's the same place. A kind of swamp about ninety miles north of Antananarivo. Do you happen to know? You have to go to it along the coast by boats. You don't happen to remember, perhaps?"

"I don't. I fancy Andrews said something about a swamp."

"It must be the same. It's on the east coast. And somehow there's something in the water that keeps things from decaying. Like creosote it smells. It reminded me of Trinidad. Did they get any more eggs? Some of the eggs I found were a foot and a half long. The swamp goes circling round, you know, and cuts off this bit. It's mostly salt, too. Well— What a time I had of it! I found the things quite by accident. We went for eggs, me and two native chaps, in one of those rum canoes all tied together, and found the bones at the same time. We had a tent and provisions for four days, and we pitched on one of the firmer places. To think of it brings that odd tarry smell back even now. It's funny work. You go probing into the mud with iron rods, you know. Usually the egg gets smashed. I wonder how long it is since these Æpyornises really lived. The missionaries say the natives have legends about when they were alive, but I never heard any such stories myself. But certainly those eggs we got were as fresh as if they had been new-laid. Fresh! Carrying them down to the boat one of my nigger chaps dropped one on a rock and it smashed. How I lammed into the beggar! But sweet it was as if it was new-laid, not even smelly, and its mother dead these four hundred years perhaps. Said a centipede had bit him. However, I'm getting off the straight with the story. It had taken us all day to dig into the slush and get these eggs out unbroken, and we were all covered with beastly black mud, and naturally I was cross. So far as I knew they were the only eggs that had ever been got out not even cracked. I went afterward to see the ones they have at the Natural History Museum in London: all of them were cracked and just stuck together like a mosaic, and bits missing. Mine were perfect, and I meant to blow them when I got back. Naturally I was annoyed at the silly devil dropping three hours' work just on account of a centipede. I hit him about rather."

The man with the scar took out a clay pipe. I placed my pouch before him. He filled up absentmindedly.

"How about the others? Did you get those home? I don't remember——"

"That's the queer part of the story. I had three others. Perfectly fresh eggs. Well, we put 'em in the boat, and then I went up to the tent to make some coffee, leaving my two heathens down by the beach—the one fooling about with his sting and the other helping him. It never occurred to me that the beggars would take advantage of the peculiar position I was in to pick a quarrel. But I suppose the centipede poison and the kicking I'd given him had upset the one—he was always a cantankerous sort—and he persuaded the other.

"I remember I was sitting and smoking and boiling up the water over a spirit-lamp business I used to take on these expeditions. Incidentally I was admiring the swamp under the sunset. All black and blood red it was, in streaks—a beautiful sight. And up beyond, the land rose gray and hazy to the hills, and the sky behind them red, like a furnace mouth. And fifty yards behind the back of me was these blessed heathen— quite regardless of the tranquil air of things—plotting to cut off with the boat and leave me all alone with three day's provisions and a canvas tent, and nothing to drink whatsoever, beyond a little keg of water. I heard a kind of yelp behind me, and there they were in this canoe affair—it wasn't properly a boat—and perhaps twenty yards from land. I realized what was up in a moment. My gun was in the tent, and besides I had no bullets—only duck shot. They knew that. But I had a little revolver in my pocket and I pulled that out as I ran down to the beach.

" 'Come back!' says I, flourishing it.

"They jabbered something at me, and the man that broke the egg jeered. I aimed at the other—because he was unwounded and had the paddle, and I missed. They laughed. However, I wasn't beat. I knew I had to keep cool, and I tried him again and made him jump with the whang of it. The third time I got his head, and over he went, and the paddle with him. It was a precious lucky shot for a revolver. I reckon it was fifty yards. He went right under. I don't know if he was shot, or simply stunned and drowned. Then I began to shout to the other chap to come back, but he huddled up in the canoe and refused to answer. So I fired out my revolver at him and never got near him.

"I felt a precious fool, I can tell you. There I was on this rotten, black beach, flat swamp all behind me, and the flat sea, cold after the sunset, and just this black canoe drifting steadily out to sea. I tell you I damned Dawsons and Jamrachs and Museums and all the rest of it just to rights. I bawled to this nigger to come back, until my voice went up into a scream.

"There was nothing for it but to swim after him and take my luck with the sharks. So I opened my claspknife and put it in my mouth and took off my clothes and waded in. As soon as I was in the water I lost sight of the canoe, but I aimed, as I judged, to head it off. I hoped the man in it was too bad to navigate it, and that it would keep on drifting in the same direction. Presently it came up over the horizon again to the southwestward. The afterglow of sunset was well over now and the dim of night creeping up. The stars were coming through the blue. I swam like a champion, though my legs and arms were soon aching.

"However, I came up to him by the time the stars were fairly out. As it got darker I began to see all manner of glowing things in the water—phosphorescence, you know. At times it made me giddy. I hardly knew which was stars and which was phosphorescence, and whether I was swimming on my head or my heels. The canoe was as black as sin, and the ripple under the bows like liquid fire. I was naturally chary of clambering up into it. I was anxious to see what he was up to first. He seemed to be lying cuddled up in a lump in the bow, and the stern was all out of water. The thing kept turning round slowly as it drifted—kind of waltzing, don't you know. I went to the stern and pulled it down, expecting him to wake up. Then I began to clamber in with my knife in my hand, and ready for a rush. But he never stirred. So there I sat in the stern of the little canoe, drifting away over the calm phosphorescent sea, and with all the host of the stars above me, waiting for something to happen.

"After a long time I called him by name, but he never answered. I was too tired to take any risks by going along to him. So we sat there. I fancy I dozed once or twice. When the dawn came I saw he was as dead as a doornail and all puffed up and purple. My three eggs and the bones were lying in the middle of the canoe, and the keg of water and some coffee and biscuits wrapped in a Cape *Argus* by his feet, and a tin of methylated spirit underneath him. There was no paddle, nor in fact anything except the spirit tin that one could use as one, so I settled to drift until I was picked up. I held an inquest on him, brought in a verdict against some snake, scorpion, or centipede unknown, and sent him overboard.

"After that I had a drink of water and a few biscuits, and took a look round. I suppose a man low down as I was don't see very far; leastways, Madagascar was clean out of sight, and any trace of land at all. I saw a sail going southwestward—looked like a schooner, but her hull never came up. Presently the sun got high in the sky and began to beat down upon me. Lord!—it pretty near made my brains boil. I tried dipping my head in the sea, but after a while my eye fell on the Cape *Argus,* and I lay down flat in the canoe and spread this over me. Wonderful things these newspapers. I never read one through thoroughly before, but it's odd what you get up to when you're alone, as I was. I suppose I read that blessed old Cape *Argus* twenty times. The pitch in the canoe simply reeked with the heat and rose up into big blisters.

"I drifted ten days," said the man with the scar. "It's a

little thing in the telling, isn't it? Every day was like the last. Except in the morning and the evening I never kept a lookout even—the blaze was so infernal. I didn't see a sail after the first three days, and those I saw took no notice of me. About the sixth night a ship went by scarcely half a mile away from me, with all its lights ablaze and its ports open, looking like a big firefly. There was music aboard. I stood up and shouted and screamed at it. The second day I broached one of the Æpyornis eggs, scraped the shell away at the end bit by bit, and tried it, and I was glad to find it was good enough to eat. A bit flavory—not bad, I mean, but with something of the taste of a duck's egg. There was a kind of circular patch about six inches across on one side of the yolk, and with streaks of blood and a white mark like a ladder in it that I thought queer, but I didn't understand what this meant at the time, and I wasn't inclined to be particular. The eggs lasted me three days, with biscuits and a drink of water. I chewed coffee berries too—invigorating stuff. The second egg I opened about the eighth day. And it scared me."

The man with the scar paused. "Yes," he said—"developing.

"I daresay you find it hard to believe. *I* did, with the thing before me. There the egg had been, sunk in that cold black mud, perhaps three hundred years. But there was no mistaking it. There was the—what is it?—embryo, with its big head and curved back and its heart beating under its throat, and the yolk shriveled up and great membranes spreading inside of the shell and all over the yolk. Here was I hatching out the eggs of the biggest of all extinct birds, in a little canoe in the midst of the Indian Ocean. If old Dawson had known that! It was worth four years' salary. What do *you* think?

"However, I had to eat that precious thing up, every bit of it, before I sighted the reef, and some of the mouthfuls were beastly unpleasant. I left the third one alone. I held it up to the light, but the shell was too thick for me to get any notion of what might be happening inside; and though I fancied I heard blood pulsing, it might have been the rustle of my own ears, like what you listen to in a seashell.

"Then came the atoll. Came out of the sunrise, as it were, suddenly, close up to me. I drifted straight toward it until I was about half a mile from shore—not more, and then the current took a turn, and I had to paddle as hard as I could with my hands and bits of the Æpyornis shell to make the place. However, I got there. It was just a common atoll about four miles round, with a few trees growing and a spring in one place and the lagoon full of parrot fish. I took the egg ashore and put it in a good place well above the tide lines and in the sun, to give it all the chance I could, and pulled the canoe up safe, and loafed about prospecting. It's rum how dull an atoll is. When I was a kid I thought nothing could be finer or more adventurous than the Robinson Crusoe business, but that place was as monotonous as a book of sermons. I went round finding eatable things and generally thinking; but I tell you I was bored to death before the first day was out. It shows my luck—the very day I landed the weather changed. A thunderstorm went by to the north and flicked its wing over the island, and in the night there came a drencher and a howling wind slap over us. It wouldn't have taken much, you know, to upset that canoe.

"I was sleeping under the canoe, and the egg was luckily among the sand higher up the beach, and the first thing I remember was a sound like a hundred pebbles hitting the boat at once and a rush of water over my body. I'd been dreaming of Antananarivo, and I sat up and holloaed to Intoshi to ask her what the devil was up, and clawed out at the chair where the matches used to be. Then I remembered where I was. There were phosphorescent waves rolling up as if they meant to eat me, and all the rest of the night as black as pitch. The air was simply yelling. The clouds seemed down on your head almost, and the rain fell as if heaven was sinking and they were baling out the waters above the firmament. One great roller came writhing at me, like a fiery serpent, and I bolted. Then I thought of the canoe, and ran down to it as the water went hissing back again, but the thing had gone. I wondered about the egg then, and felt my way to it. It was all right and well out of reach of the maddest waves, so I sat down beside it and cuddled it for company. Lord! what a night that was!

"The storm was over before morning. There wasn't a rag of cloud left in the sky when the dawn came, and all along the beach there were bits of plank scattered—which was the disarticulated skeleton, so to speak, of my canoe. However, that gave me something to do, for, taking advantage of two of the trees being together, I rigged up a kind of storm shelter with these vestiges. And that day the egg hatched.

"Hatched, sir, when my head was pillowed on it and I was asleep. I heard a whack and felt a jar and sat up, and there was the end of the egg pecked out and a rum little brown head looking out at me. 'Lord!' I said, 'you're welcome,' and with a little difficulty he came out.

97

"He was a nice friendly little chap, at first about the size of a small hen—very much like most other young birds, only bigger. His plumage was a dirty brown to begin with, with a sort of gray scab that fell off it very soon, and scarcely feathers—a kind of downy hair. I can hardly express how pleased I was to see him. I tell you, Robinson Crusoe don't make near enough of his loneliness. But here was interesting company. He looked at me and winked his eye from the front backward like a hen, and gave a chirp and began to peck about at once, as though being hatched three hundred years too late was just nothing. 'Glad to see you, Man Friday!' says I, for I had naturally settled he was to be called Man Friday if ever he was hatched, as soon as ever I found the egg in the canoe had developed. I was a bit anxious about his feed, so I gave him a lump of raw parrot fish at once. He took it and opened his beak for more. I was glad of that, for, under the circumstances, if he'd been fanciful, I should have had to eat him after all.

"You'd be surprised what an interesting bird that Æpyornis chick was. He followed me about from the very beginning. He used to stand by me and watch while I fished in the lagoon and go shares in anything I caught. And he was sensible, too. There were nasty green warty things, like pickled gherkins, used to lie about on the beach, and he tried one of these and it upset him. He never even looked at any of them again.

"And he grew. You could almost see him grow. And as I was never much of a society man, his quiet, friendly ways suited me to a T. For nearly two years we were as happy as we could be on that island. I had no business worries, for I knew my salary was mounting up at Dawsons'. We would see a sail now and then, but nothing ever came near us. I amused myself too by decorating the island with designs worked in sea urchins and fancy shells of various kinds. I put ÆPYOR-NIS ISLAND all round the place very nearly, in big letters, like what you see done with colored stones at railway stations in the old country. And I used to lie watching the blessed bird stalking round and growing, growing, and think how I could make a living out of him by showing him about if ever I got taken off. After his first moult he began to get handsome, with a crest and a blue wattle, and a lot of green feathers at the behind of him. And then I used to puzzle whether Dawsons had any right to claim him or not. Stormy weather and in the rainy season we lay snug under the shelter I had made out of the old canoe, and I used to tell him lies about my friends at home. It was a kind of idyll, you might say. If only I had had some tobacco it would have been simply just like Heaven.

"It was about the end of the second year our little Paradise went wrong. Friday was then about fourteen feet high to the bill of him, with a big broad head like the end of a pickaxe, and two huge brown eyes with yellow rims set together like a man's—not out of sight of each other like a hen's. His plumage was fine—none of the half mourning style of your ostrich—more like a cassowary as far as color and texture go. And then it was he began to cock his comb at me and give himself airs and show signs of a nasty temper.

"At last came a time when my fishing had been rather unlucky and he began to hang about me in a queer, meditative way. I thought he might have been eating sea cucumbers or something, but it was really just discontent on his part. I was hungry too, and when at last I landed a fish I wanted it for myself. Tempers were short that morning on both sides. He pecked at it and grabbed it, and I gave him a whack on the head to make him leave go. And at that he went for me. Lord!

"He gave me this in the face." The man indicated his scar. "Then he kicked me. It was like a cart horse. I got up, and seeing he hadn't finished I started off full tilt with my arms doubled up over my face. But he ran on those gawky legs of his faster than a racehorse, and kept landing out at me with sledgehammer kicks, and bringing his pickaxe down on the back of my head. I made for the lagoon, and went in up to my neck. He stopped at the water, for he hated getting his feet wet, and began to make a shindy, something like a peacock's, only hoarser. He started strutting up and down the beach. I'll admit I felt small to see this blessed fossil lording it there. And my head and face were all bleeding, and—well, my body just one jelly of bruises.

"I decided to swim across the lagoon and leave him alone for a bit, until the affair blew over. I shinned up the tallest palm tree and sat there thinking of it all. I don't suppose I ever felt so hurt by anything before or since. It was the brutal ingratitude of the creature. I'd been more than a brother to him. I'd hatched him. Educated him. A great, gawky, out-of-date bird! And me a human being—heir of the ages and all that.

"I thought after a time he'd begin to see things in that light himself, and feel a little sorry for his behavior. I thought if I was to catch some nice little bits of fish, perhaps, and go to him presently in a casual kind of way, and offer them to him, he might do the sensible thing. It took me some time to learn how unforgiving and cantankerous an extinct bird can be. Malice!

"I won't tell you all the little devices I tried to get that bird round again. I simply can't. It makes my cheek burn with shame even now to think of the snubs and buffets I had from this infernal curiosity. I tried violence. I chucked lumps of coral at him from a safe distance, but he only swallowed them. I shied my open knife at him and almost lost it, though it was too big for him to swallow. I tried starving him out and struck fishing, but he took to picking along the beach at low water after worms, and rubbed along on that. Half my time I spent up to my neck in the lagoon, and the rest up the palm trees. One of them was scarcely high enough, and when he caught me up it he had a regular Bank Holiday with the calves of my legs. It got unbearable. I don't know if you have ever tried sleeping up a palm tree. It gave me the most horrible nightmares. Think of the shame of it too! Here was this extinct animal mooning about my island like a sulky duke, and me not allowed to rest the sole of my foot on the place. I used to cry with weariness and vexation. I told him straight that I didn't mean to be chased about a desert island by any damned anachronisms. I told him to go and peck a navigator of his own age. But he only snapped his beak at me. Great ugly bird—all legs and neck!

"I shouldn't like to say how long that went on altogether. I'd have killed him sooner if I'd known how. However, I hit on a way of settling him at last. It's a South American dodge. I joined all my fishing lines together with stems of seaweed and things, and made a stoutish string, perhaps twelve yards in length or more, and I fastened two lumps of coral rock to the ends of this. It took me some time to do, because every now and then I had to go into the lagoon or up a tree as the fancy took me. This I whirled rapidly round my head and then let it go at him. The first time I missed, but the next time the string caught his legs beautifully and wrapped round them again and again. Over he went. I threw it standing waist-deep in the lagoon, and as soon as he went down I was out of the water and sawing at his neck with my knife——

"I don't like to think of that even now. I felt like a murderer while I did it, though my anger was hot against him. When I stood over him and saw him bleeding on the

100

white sand and his beautiful great legs and neck writhing in his last agony—Pah!

"With that tragedy, loneliness came upon me like a curse. Good Lord! you can't imagine how I missed that bird. I sat by his corpse and sorrowed over him, and shivered as I looked round the desolate, silent reef. I thought of what a jolly little bird he had been when he was hatched, and of a thousand pleasant tricks he had played before he went wrong. I thought if I'd only wounded him I might have nursed him round into a better understanding. If I'd had any means of digging into the coral rock I'd have buried him. I felt exactly as if he was human. As it was I couldn't think of eating him, so I put him in the lagoon and the little fishes picked him clean. Then one day a chap cruising about in a yacht had a fancy to see if my atoll still existed.

"He didn't come a moment too soon, for I was about sick enough of the desolation of it, and only hesitating whether I should walk out into the sea and finish up the business that way, or fall back on the green things.

"I sold the bones to a man named Winslow—a dealer near the British Museum, and he says he sold them to old Havers. It seems Havers didn't understand they were extra large, and it was only after his death they attracted attention. They called 'em Æpyornis—what was it?"

"*Æpyornis vastus*," said I. "It's funny, the very thing was mentioned to me by a friend of mine. When they found an Æpyornis with a thigh a yard long they thought they had reached the top of the scale and called him *Æpyornis maximus*. Then some one turned up another thigh bone four feet six or more, and that they called *Æpyornis Titan*. Then your *vastus* was found after old Havers died, in his collection, and then a *vastissimus* turned up."

"Winslow was telling me as much," said the man with the scar. "If they get any more Æpyornises, he reckons some scientific swell will go and burst a blood vessel. But it was a queer thing to happen to a man! wasn't it—altogether?"

The Terror of Blue John Gap

by A. Conan Doyle

The following narrative was found among the papers of Dr. James Hardcastle, who died of phthisis on February 4, 1908, at 36, Upper Coventry Flats, South Kensington. Those who knew him best, while refusing to express an opinion upon this particular statement, are unanimous in asserting that he was a man of a sober and scientific turn of mind, absolutely devoid of imagination, and most unlikely to invent any abnormal series of events. The paper was contained in an envelope, which was docketed, "A Short Account of the Circumstances which occurred near Miss Allerton's Farm in Northwest Derbyshire in the Spring of Last Year." The envelope was sealed, and on the other side was written in pencil—

DEAR SEATON,

It may interest, and perhaps pain you, to know that the incredulity with which you met my story has prevented me from ever opening my mouth upon the subject again. I leave this record after my death, and perhaps strangers may be found to have more confidence in me than my friend.

Inquiry has failed to elicit who this Seaton may have been. I may add that the visit of the deceased to Allerton's Farm, and the general nature of the alarm there, apart from his particular explanation, have been absolutely established. With this foreword I append his account exactly as he left it. It is in the form of a diary, some entries in which have been expanded, while a few have been erased.

April 17. Already I feel the benefit of this wonderful upland air. The farm of the Allertons lies 1420 feet above sea level, so it may well be a bracing climate. Beyond the usual morning cough I have very little discomfort, and, what with the fresh milk and the home-grown mutton, I have every chance of putting on weight. I think Saunderson will be pleased.

The two Miss Allertons are charmingly quaint and kind, two dear little hard-working old maids, who are ready to lavish all the heart which might have gone out to husband and to children upon an invalid stranger. Truly, the old maid is a most useful person, one of the reserve forces of the community. They talk of superfluous woman, but what would the poor superfluous man do without her kindly presence? By the way, in their simplicity they very quickly let out the reason why Saunderson recommended their farm. The professor rose from the ranks himself, and I believe that in his youth he was not above scaring crows in these very fields.

It is a most lonely spot, and the walks are picturesque in the extreme. The farm consists of grazing land lying at the bottom of an irregular valley. On each side are the fantastic limestone hills, formed of rock so soft that you can break it away with your hands. All this country is hollow. Could you strike it with some gigantic hammer it would boom like a drum, or possibly cave in altogether and expose some huge subterranean sea. A great sea there must surely be, for on all sides the streams run into the mountain itself, never to reappear. There are gaps everywhere amid the rocks, and when you pass through them you find yourself in great caverns, which wind down into the bowels of the earth. I have a small bicycle lamp, and it is a perpetual joy to me to carry it into these weird solitudes, and to see the wonderful silver and black effects when I throw its light upon the stalactites which drape the lofty roofs. Shut off the lamp, and you are in the blackest darkness. Turn it on, and it is a scene from the Arabian Nights.

But there is one of these strange openings in the earth which has a special interest, for it is the handiwork, not of nature, but of man. I had never heard of Blue John when I came to these parts. It is the name given to a peculiar mineral of a beautiful purple shade, which is only found at one or two places in the world. It is so rare that an ordinary vase of Blue John would be valued at a great price. The Romans, with that extraordinary instinct of theirs, discovered that it was to be found in this valley, and sank a horizontal shaft deep into the mountainside. The opening of their mine has been called Blue John Gap, a clean-cut arch in the rock, the mouth all overgrown with bushes. It is a goodly passage which the Roman miners have cut, and it intersects some of the great water-worn caves, so that if you enter Blue John Gap you would do well to mark your steps and to have a good store of candles, or you may never make your way back to the daylight again. I have not yet gone deeply into it, but this very day I stood at the mouth of the arched tunnel, and peering down into the black recesses beyond, I vowed that when my health returned I would devote some holiday to exploring those mysterious depths and finding out for myself how far the Roman had penetrated into the Derbyshire hills.

Strange how superstitious these countrymen are! I should have thought better of young Armitage, for he is a man of some education and character, and a very fine fellow for his station in life. I was standing at the Blue John Gap when he came across the field to me.

"Well, doctor," said he, "you're not afraid, anyhow."

"Afraid!" I answered. "Afraid of what?"

"Of it," said he, with a jerk of his thumb towards the black vault, "of the Terror that lives in the Blue John Cave."

How absurdly easy it is for a legend to arise in a lonely countryside! I examined him as to the reasons for his weird belief. It seems that from time to time sheep have been missing from the fields, carried bodily away, according to Armitage. That they could have wandered away of their own accord and disappeared among the mountains was an explanation to which he would not listen. On one occasion a pool of blood had been found, and some tufts of wool. That also, I pointed out, could be explained in a perfectly natural way. Further, the nights upon which sheep disappeared were invariably very dark, cloudy nights with no moon. This I met with the obvious retort that those were the nights which a commonplace sheep stealer would naturally choose for his work. On one occasion a gap had been made in a wall, and some of the stones scattered for a considerable distance. Human agency again, in my opinion. Finally, Armitage clinched all his arguments by telling me that he had actually heard the Creature—indeed, that anyone could hear it who remained long enough at the Gap. It was a distant roaring of an immense volume. I could not but smile at this, knowing, as I do, the strange reverberations which come out of an underground water system running amid the chasms of a limestone formation. My incredulity annoyed Armitage so that he turned and left me with some abruptness.

And now comes the queer point about the whole business. I was still standing near the mouth of the cave, turning over in my mind the various statements of Armitage, and reflecting how readily they could be explained away, when suddenly, from the depth of the tunnel beside me, there issued a most extraordinary sound. How shall I describe it? First of all, it seemed to be a great distance away, far down in the bowels of the earth. Secondly, in spite of this suggestion of distance, it was very loud. Lastly, it was not a boom, nor a crash, such as one would associate with falling water or tumbling rock, but it was a high whine, tremulous and vibrating, almost like the whinnying of a horse. It was certainly a most remarkable experience, and one which for a moment, I must admit, gave a new significance to Armitage's words. I waited by the Blue John Gap for half an hour or more, but there was no return of the sound, so at last I wandered back to the farmhouse, rather mystified by what had occurred. Decidedly I shall explore that cavern when my strength is restored. Of course, Armitage's explanation is too absurd for discussion, and yet that sound was certainly very strange. It still rings in my ears as I write.

April 20. In the last three days I have made several expeditions to the Blue John Gap, and have even penetrated some short distance, but my bicycle lantern is so small and weak that I dare not trust myself very far. I shall do the thing more systematically. I have heard no sound at all, and could almost believe that I had been the victim of some hallucination suggested, perhaps, by Armitage's conversation. Of course, the whole idea is absurd, and yet I must confess that those bushes at the entrance of the cave do present an appearance as if some heavy creature had forced its way through them. I begin to be keenly interested. I have said nothing to the Miss Allertons, for they are quite superstitious enough already, but I have bought some candles, and mean to investigate for myself.

I observed this morning that among the numerous tufts of sheep's wool which lay among the bushes near the cavern there was one which was smeared with blood. Of course, my reason tells me that if sheep wander into such rocky places they are likely to injure themselves, and yet somehow that splash of crimson gave me a sudden shock, and for a moment I found myself shrinking back in horror from the old Roman arch. A fetid breath seemed to ooze from the black depths into which I peered. Could it indeed be possible that some nameless thing, some dreadful presence, was lurking down yonder? I should have been incapable of such feelings in the days of my strength, but one grows more nervous and fanciful when one's health is shaken.

For the moment I weakened in my resolution, and was ready to leave the secret of the old mine, if one exists,

105

forever unsolved. But tonight my interest has returned and my nerves grown more steady. Tomorrow I trust that I shall have gone more deeply into this matter.

April 22. Let me try and set down as accurately as I can my extraordinary experience of yesterday. I started in the afternoon, and made my way to the Blue John Gap. I confess that my misgivings returned as I gazed into its depths, and I wished that I had brought a companion to share my exploration. Finally, with a return of resolution, I lit my candle, pushed my way through the briars, and descended into the rock shaft.

It went down at an acute angle for some fifty feet, the floor being covered with broken stone. Thence there extended a long, straight passage cut in the solid rock. I am no geologist, but the lining of this corridor was certainly of some harder material than limestone, for there were points where I could actually see the tool-marks which the old miners had left in their excavation, as fresh as if they had been done yesterday. Down this strange, old-world corridor I stumbled, my feeble flame throwing a dim circle of light around me, which made the shadows beyond the more threatening and obscure. Finally, I came to a spot where the Roman tunnel opened into a water-worn cavern—a huge hall, hung with long white icicles of lime deposit. From this central chamber I could dimly perceive that a number of passages worn by the subterranean streams wound away into the depths of the earth. I was standing there wondering whether I had better return, or whether I dare venture farther into this dangerous labyrinth, when my eyes fell upon something at my feet which strongly arrested my attention.

The greater part of the floor of the cavern was covered with boulders of rock or with hard incrustations of lime, but at this particular point there had been a drip from the distant roof, which had left a patch of soft mud. In the very center of this there was a huge mark—an ill-defined blotch, deep, broad and irregular, as if a great boulder had fallen upon it. No loose stone lay near, however, nor was there anything to account for the impression. It was far too large to be caused by any possible animal, and besides, there was only the one, and the patch of mud was of such a size that no reasonable stride could have covered it. As I rose from the examination of that singular mark and then looked round into the black shadows which hemmed me in, I must confess that I felt for a moment a most unpleasant sinking of my heart, and that, do what I could, the candle trembled in my outstretched hand.

I soon recovered my nerve, however, when I reflected how absurd it was to associate so huge and shapeless a mark with the track of any known animal. Even an elephant could not have produced it. I determined, therefore, that I would not be scared by vague senseless fears from carrying out my exploration. Before proceeding, I took good note of a curious rock formation in the wall by which I could recognize the entrance of the Roman tunnel. The precaution was very necessary, for the great cave, so far as I could see it, was intersected by passages. Having made sure of my position, and reassured myself by examining my spare candles and my matches, I advanced slowly over the rocky and uneven surface of the cavern.

And now I come to the point where I met with such sudden and desperate disaster. A stream, some twenty feet broad, ran across my path, and I walked for some little distance along the bank to find a spot where I could cross dry-shod. Finally, I came to a place where a single flat boulder lay near the center, which I could reach in a stride. As it chanced, however, the rock had been cut away and made top-heavy by the rush of the stream, so that it tilted over as I landed on it and shot me into the ice-cold water. My candle went out, and I found myself floundering about in utter and absolute darkness.

I staggered to my feet again, more amused than alarmed by my adventure. The candle had fallen from my hand, and was lost in the stream, but I had two others in my pocket, so that it was of no importance. I got one of them ready, and drew out my box of matches to light it. Only then did I realize my position. The box had been soaked in my fall into the river. It was impossible to strike the matches.

A cold hand seemed to close round my heart as I realized my position. The darkness was opaque and horrible. It was so utter that one put one's hand up to one's face as if to press off something solid. I stood still, and by an effort I steadied myself. I tried to reconstruct in my mind a map of the floor of the cavern as I had last seen it. Alas! the bearings which had impressed themselves upon my mind were high on the wall, and not to be found by touch. Still, I remembered in a general way how the sides were situated, and I hoped that by groping my way along them I should at last come to the opening of the Roman tunnel. Moving very slowly, and continually striking against the rocks, I set out on this desperate quest.

But I very soon realized how impossible it was. In that black, velvety darkness one lost all one's bearings in an instant. Before I had made a dozen paces, I was utterly bewildered as to my whereabouts. The rippling of the stream, which was the one sound audible, showed me where it lay, but the moment that I left its bank I was utterly lost. The idea of finding my way back in absolute darkness through that limestone labyrinth was clearly an impossible one.

I sat down upon a boulder and reflected upon my unfortunate plight. I had not told anyone that I proposed to come to the Blue John mine, and it was unlikely that a search party would come after me. Therefore I must trust to my own resources to get clear of the danger. There was only one hope, and that was that the matches might dry. When I fell into the river, only half of me had got thoroughly wet. My left shoulder had remained above the water. I took the box of matches, therefore, and put it into my left armpit. The moist air of the cavern might possibly be counteracted by the heat of my body, but even so, I knew that I could not hope to get a light for many hours. Meanwhile there was nothing for it but to wait.

By good luck I had slipped several biscuits into my pocket before I left the farmhouse. These I now devoured, and washed them down with a draught from that wretched stream which had been the cause of all my misfortunes. Then I felt about for a comfortable seat among the rocks, and, having discovered a place where I could get a support for my back, I stretched out my legs and settled myself down to wait. I was wretchedly damp and cold, but I tried to cheer myself with the reflection that modern science prescribed open windows and walks in all weather for my disease. Gradually, lulled by the monotonous gurgle of the stream, and by the absolute darkness, I sank into an uneasy slumber.

How long this lasted I cannot say. It may have been for an hour, it may have been for several. Suddenly I sat up on my rock couch, with every nerve thrilling and every sense acutely on the alert. Beyond all doubt I had heard a sound—some sound very distinct from the gurgling of the water. It had passed, but the reverberation of it still lingered in my ear. Was it a search party? They would most certainly have shouted, and vague as this sound was which had awakened me, it was very distinct from the human voice. I sat palpitating and hardly daring to breathe. There it was again! And again! Now it had become continuous. It was a tread—yes, surely it was the tread of some living creature. But what a

108

tread it was! It gave one the impression of enormous weight carried upon spongelike feet, which gave forth a muffled but earsplitting sound. The darkness was as complete as ever, but the tread was regular and decisive. And it was coming beyond all question in my direction.

My skin grew cold, and my hair stood on end as I listened to that steady and ponderous footfall. There was some creature there, and surely by the speed of its advance, it was one which could see in the dark. I crouched low on my rock and tried to blend myself into it. The steps grew nearer still, then stopped, and presently I was aware of a loud lapping and gurgling. The creature was drinking at the stream. Then again there was silence, broken by a succession of long sniffs and snorts of tremendous volume and energy. Had it caught the scent of me? My own nostrils were filled by a low fetid odor, mephitic and abominable. Then I heard the steps again. They were on my side of the stream now. The stones rattled within a few yards of where I lay. Hardly daring to breathe, I crouched upon my rock. Then the steps drew away. I heard the splash as it returned across the river, and the sound died away into the distance in the direction from which it had come.

For a long time I lay upon the rock, too much horrified to move. I thought of the sound which I had heard coming from the depths of the cave, of Armitage's fears, of the strange impression in the mud, and now came this final and absolute proof that there was indeed some inconceivable monster, something utterly unearthly and dreadful, which lurked in the hollow of the mountain. Of its nature or form I could frame no conception, save that it was both light-footed and gigantic. The combat between my reason, which told me that such things could not be, and my senses, which told me that they were, raged within me as I lay. Finally, I was almost ready to persuade myself that this experience had been part of some evil dream, and that my abnormal condition might have conjured up a hallucination. But there remained one final experience which removed the last possibility of doubt from my mind.

I had taken my matches from my armpit and felt them. They seemed perfectly hard and dry. Stooping down into a crevice of the rocks, I tried one of them. To my delight it took fire at once. I lit the candle, and, with a terrified backward glance into the obscure depths of the cavern, I hurried in the direction of the Roman passage. As I did so I passed the patch of mud on which I had seen the huge imprint. Now I stood astonished before it, for there were three similar imprints upon its surface, enormous in size, irregular in outline, of a depth which indicated the ponderous weight which had left them. Then a great terror surged over me. Stooping and shading my candle with my hand, I ran in a frenzy of fear to the rocky archway, hastened up it, and never stopped until, with weary feet and panting lungs, I rushed up the final slope of stones, broke through the tangle of briars, and flung myself exhausted upon the soft grass under the peaceful light of the stars. It was three in the morning when I reached the farmhouse, and today I am all unstrung and quivering after my terrific adventure. As yet I have told no one. I must move warily in the matter. What would the poor lonely women, or the uneducated yokels here think of it if I were to tell them my experience? Let me go to someone who can understand and advise.

April 25. I was laid up in bed for two days after my incredible adventure in the cavern. I use the adjective with a very definite meaning, for I have had an experience since which has shocked me almost as much as the other. I have said that I was looking round for someone who could advise me. There is a Dr. Mark Johnson who practices some few miles away, to whom I had a note of recommendation from Professor Saunderson. To him I drove, when I was strong enough to get about, and I recounted to him my whole strange experience. He listened intently, and then carefully examined me, paying special attention to my reflexes and to the pupils of my eyes. When he had finished, he refused to discuss my adventure, saying that it was entirely beyond him, but he gave me the card of a Mr. Picton at Castleton, with the advice that I should instantly go to him and tell him the story exactly as I had done to himself. He was, according to my adviser, the very man who was preeminently suited to help me. I went on to the station, therefore, and made my way to the little town, which is some ten miles away. Mr. Picton appeared to be a man of importance, as his brass plate was displayed upon the door of a considerable building on the outskirts of the town. I was about to ring his bell, when some misgiving came into my mind, and, crossing to a neighboring shop, I asked the man behind the counter if he could tell me anything of Mr. Picton. "Why," said he, "he is the best mad doctor in Derbyshire, and yonder is his asylum." You can imagine that it was not long before I had shaken the dust of Castleton from my feet and returned to the farm, cursing all unimaginative pedants who cannot conceive that there may be things in creation which have never yet chanced to come across their mole's vision. After all, now that I am cooler, I can afford to admit that I have been no more sympathetic to Armitage than Dr. Johnson has been to me.

April 27. When I was a student I had the reputation of being a man of courage and enterprise. I remember that when there was a ghost hunt at Coltbridge it was I who sat up in the haunted house. Is it advancing years (after all, I am only thirty-five), or is it this physical malady which has caused degeneration? Certainly my heart quails when I think of that horrible cavern in the hill, and the certainty that it has some monstrous occupant. What shall I do? There is not an hour in the day that I do not debate the question. If I say nothing, then the mystery remains unsolved. If I do say anything, then I have the alternative of mad alarm over the whole country-side, or of absolute incredulity which may end in consigning me to an asylum. On the whole, I think that my best course is to wait, and to prepare for some expedition which shall be more deliberate and better thought-out than the last. As a first step I have been to Castleton and obtained a few essentials—a large acetylene lantern for one thing, and a good double-barreled sporting rifle for another. The latter I have hired, but I have bought a dozen heavy game car-tridges, which would bring down a rhinoceros. Now I am ready for my troglodyte friend. Give me better health and a little spate of energy, and I shall try conclusions with him yet. But who and what is he? Ah! there is the question which stands between me and my sleep. How many theories do I form, only to discard each in turn! It is all so utterly unthinkable. And yet the cry, the footmark, the tread in the cavern—no reasoning can get past these. I think of the old-world legends of dragons and of other monsters. Were they, perhaps, not such fairy tales as we thought? Can it be that there is some fact which underlies them, and am I, of all mortals, the one who is chosen to expose it?

May 3. For several days I have been laid up by the vagaries of an English spring, and during those days there have been many developments, the true and sinister meaning of which no one can appreciate save myself. I may say that we have had cloudy and moonless nights of late, which according to my information were the seasons upon which sheep disappeared. Well, sheep *have* disappeared. Two of Miss Allerton's, one of old Pearson's of the Cat Walk, and one of Mrs. Moulton's. Four in all during three nights. No trace is left of them at all, and the countryside is buzzing with rumors of Gypsies and of sheep stealers.

But there is something more serious than that. Young Armitage has disappeared also. He left his moorland cottage early on Wednesday night and has never been heard of since. He was an unattached man, so there is less sensation than would otherwise be the case. The popular explanation is that he owes money, and has found a situation in some other part of the country, whence he will presently write for his belongings. But I have great misgivings. Is it not much more likely that the recent tragedy of the sheep has caused him to take some steps which may have ended in his own destruction? He may, for example, have lain in wait for the creature and been carried off by it into the recesses of the mountains. What an inconceivable fate for a civilized Englishman of the twentieth century! And yet I feel that it is possible and even probable. But in that case, how far am I answerable both for his death and for any other mishap which may occur? Surely with the knowledge I already possess it must be my duty to see that something is done, or if necessary to do it myself. It must be the latter, for this morning I went down to the local police station and told my story. The inspector entered it all in a large book and bowed me out with commendable gravity, but I heard a burst of laughter before I had got down his garden path. No doubt he was recounting my adventure to his family.

June 10. I am writing this, propped up in bed, six weeks after my last entry in this journal. I have gone through a terrible shock both to mind and body, arising from such an experience as has seldom befallen a human being before. But I have attained my end. The danger from the Terror which dwells in the Blue John Gap has passed never to return. Thus much at least I, a broken invalid, have done for the common good. Let me now recount what occurred as clearly as I may.

The night of Friday, May 3, was dark and cloudy—the very night for the monster to walk. About eleven o'clock I went from the farmhouse with my lantern and my rifle, having first left a note upon the table of my bedroom in which I said that, if I were missing, search should be made for me in the direction of the Gap. I made my way to the mouth of the Roman shaft, and, having perched myself among the rocks close to the opening, I shut off my lantern and waited patiently with my loaded rifle ready to my hand.

It was a melancholy vigil. All down the winding valley I

could see the scattered lights of the farmhouses, and the church clock of Chapel-le-Dale tolling the hours came faintly to my ears. These tokens of my fellow men served only to make my own position seem the more lonely, and to call for a greater effort to overcome the terror which tempted me continually to get back to the farm, and abandon forever this dangerous quest. And yet there lies deep in every man a rooted self-respect which makes it hard for him to turn back from that which he has once undertaken. This feeling of personal pride was my salvation now, and it was that alone which held me fast when every instinct of my nature was dragging me away. I am glad now that I had the strength. In spite of all that it has cost me, my manhood is at least above reproach.

Twelve o'clock struck in the distant church, then one, then two. It was the darkest hour of the night. The clouds were drifting low, and there was not a star in the sky. An owl was hooting somewhere among the rocks, but no other sound, save the gentle sough of the wind, came to my ears. And then suddenly I heard it! From far away down the tunnel came those muffled steps, so soft and yet so ponderous. I heard also the rattle of stones as they gave way under that giant tread. They drew nearer. They were close upon me. I heard the crashing of the bushes round the entrance, and then dimly through the darkness I was conscious of the loom of some enormous shape, some monstrous inchoate creature, passing swiftly and very silently out from the tunnel. I was paralyzed with fear and amazement. Long as I had waited, now that it had actually come I was unprepared for the shock. I lay motionless and breathless, whilst the great dark mass whisked by me and was swallowed up in the night.

But now I nerved myself for its return. No sound came from the sleeping countryside to tell of the horror which was loose. In no way could I judge how far off it was, what it was doing, or when it might be back. But not a second time should my nerve fail me, not a second time should it pass unchallenged. I swore it between my clenched teeth as I laid my cocked rifle across the rock.

And yet it nearly happened. There was no warning of approach now as the creature passed over the grass. Suddenly, like a dark, drifting shadow, the huge bulk loomed up once more before me, making for the entrance of the cave. Again came that paralysis of volition which held my crooked forefinger impotent upon the trigger. But with a desperate effort I shook it off. Even as the brushwood rustled, and the

113

monstrous beast blended with the shadow of the Gap, I fired at the retreating form. In the blaze of the gun I caught a glimpse of a great shaggy mass, something with rough and bristling hair of a withered gray color, fading away to white in its lower parts, the huge body supported upon short, thick, curving legs. I had just that glance, and then I heard the rattle of the stones as the creature tore down into its burrow. In an instant, with a triumphant revulsion of feeling, I had cast my fears to the wind, and uncovering my powerful lantern, with my rifle in my hand, I sprang down from my rock and rushed after the monster down the old Roman shaft.

My splendid lamp cast a brilliant flood of vivid light in front of me, very different from the yellow glimmer which had aided me down the same passage only twelve days before. As I ran, I saw the great beast lurching along before me, its huge bulk filling up the whole space from wall to wall. Its hair looked like coarse faded oakum, and hung down in long, dense masses which swayed as it moved. It was like an enormous unclipped sheep in its fleece, but in size it was far larger than the largest elephant, and its breadth seemed to be nearly as great as its height. It fills me with amazement now to think that I should have dared to follow such a horror into the bowels of the earth, but when one's blood is up, and when one's quarry seems to be flying, the old primeval hunting spirit awakes and prudence is cast to the wind. Rifle in hand, I ran at the top of my speed upon the trail of the monster.

I had seen that the creature was swift. Now I was to find out to my cost that it was also very cunning. I had imagined that it was in panic flight, and that I had only to pursue it. The idea that it might turn upon me never entered my excited brain. I have already explained that the passage down which I was racing opened into a great central cave. Into this I rushed, fearful lest I should lose all trace of the beast. But he had turned upon his own traces, and in a moment we were face to face.

That picture, seen in the brilliant white light of the lantern, is etched forever upon my brain. He had reared up on his hind legs as a bear would do, and stood above me, enormous, menacing—such a creature as no nightmare had ever brought to my imagination. I have said that he reared like a bear, and there was something bear-like—if one could conceive a bear which was tenfold the bulk of any bear seen upon earth—in his whole pose and attitude, in his great

114

crooked forelegs with their ivory-white claws, in his rugged skin, and in his red, gaping mouth, fringed with monstrous fangs. Only in one point did he differ from the bear, or from any other creature which walks the earth, and even at that supreme moment a shudder of horror passed over me as I observed that the eyes which glistened in the glow of my lantern were huge, projecting bulbs, white and sightless. For a moment his great paws swung over my head. The next he fell forward upon me, I and my broken lantern crashed to the earth, and I remember no more.

When I came to myself I was back in the farmhouse of the Allertons. Two days had passed since my terrible adventure in the Blue John Gap. It seems that I had lain all night in the cave insensible from concussion of the brain, with my left arm and two ribs badly fractured. In the morning my note had been found, a search party of a dozen farmers assembled, and I had been tracked down and carried back to my bedroom, where I had lain in high delirium ever since. There was, it seems, no sign of the creature, and no bloodstain which would show that my bullet had found him as he passed. Save for my own plight and the marks upon the mud, there was nothing to prove that what I said was true.

Six weeks have now elapsed, and I am able to sit out once more in the sunshine. Just opposite me is the steep hillside, gray with shaly rock, and yonder on its flank is the dark cleft which marks the opening of the Blue John Gap. But it is no longer a source of terror. Never again through that ill-omened tunnel shall any strange shape flit out into the world of men. The educated and the scientific, the Dr. Johnsons and the like, may smile at my narrative, but the poorer folk of the countryside had never a doubt as to its truth. On the day after my recovering consciousness they assembled in their hundreds round the Blue John Gap. As the *Castleton Courier* said:

It was useless for our correspondent, or for any of the adventurous gentlemen who had come from Matlock, Buxton, and other parts, to offer to descend, to explore the cave to the end, and to finally test the extraordinary narrative of Dr. James Hardcastle. The country people had taken the matter into their own hands, and from an early hour of the morning they had worked hard in stopping up the entrance of the tunnel. There is a sharp slope where the shaft begins, the great boulders, rolled along by many willing hands, were thrust down it until the Gap was absolutely sealed. So ends the episode which has caused such excite-

115

ment throughout the country. Local opinion is fiercely divided upon the subject. On the one hand are those who point to Dr. Hardcastle's impaired health, and to the possibility of cerebral lesions of tubercular origin giving rise to strange hallucinations. Some *idée fixe*, according to these gentlemen, caused the doctor to wander down the tunnel, and to fall among the rocks was sufficient to account for his injuries. On the other hand, a legend of a strange creature in the Gap has existed for some months back, and the farmers look upon Dr. Hardcastle's narrative and his personal injuries as a final corroboration. So the matter stands, and so the matter will continue to stand, for no definite solution seems to us to be now possible. It transcends human wit to give any scientific explanation which could cover the alleged facts.

Perhaps before the *Courier* published these words they would have been wise to send their representative to me. I have thought the matter out, as no one else has occasion to do, and it is possible that I might have removed some of the more obvious difficulties of the narrative and brought it one degree nearer to scientific acceptance. Let me then write down the only explanation which seems to me to elucidate what I know to my cost to have been a series of facts. My theory may seem to be wildly improbable, but at least no one can venture to say that it is impossible.

My view is—and it was formed, as is shown by my diary, before my personal adventure—that in this part of England there is a vast subterranean lake or sea, which is fed by the great number of streams which pass down through the limestone. Where there is a large collection of water there must also be some evaporation, mists or rain, and a possibility of vegetation. This in turn suggests that there may be animal life, arising, as the vegetable life would also do, from those seeds and types which had been introduced at an early period of the world's history, when communication with the outer air was more easy. This place had then developed a fauna and flora of its own, including such monsters as the one which I had seen, which may well have been the old cave bear, enormously enlarged and modified by its new environment. For countless aeons the internal and the external creation had kept apart, growing steadily away from each other. Then there had come some rift in the depths of the mountain which had enabled one creature to wander up and, by means of the Roman tunnel, to reach the open air. Like all subterranean life, it had lost the power of sight, but this had no doubt been compensated for by nature in other directions. Certainly it had some means of finding its way

116

about, and of hunting down the sheep upon the hillside. As to its choice of dark nights, it is part of my theory that light was painful to those great white eyeballs, and that it was only a pitch-black world which it could tolerate. Perhaps, indeed, it was the glare of my lantern which saved my life at that awful moment when we were face to face. So I read the riddle. I leave these facts behind me, and if you can explain them, do so; or if you choose to doubt them, do so. Neither your belief nor your incredulity can alter them, nor affect one whose task is nearly over.

So ended the strange narrative of Dr. James Hardcastle.

The Birds

by Daphne du Maurier

On December the third the wind changed overnight and it was winter. Until then the autumn had been mellow, soft. The leaves had lingered on the trees, golden-red, and the hedgerows were still green. The earth was rich where the plough had turned it.

Nat Hocken, because of a wartime disability, had a pension and did not work full-time at the farm. He worked three days a week, and they gave him the lighter jobs: hedging, thatching, repairs to the farm buildings.

Although he was married, with children, his was a solitary disposition; he liked best to work alone. It pleased him when he was given a bank to build up, or a gate to mend at the far end of the peninsula, where the sea surrounded the farmland on either side. Then, at midday, he would pause and eat the pasty that his wife had baked for him, and, sitting on the cliff's edge, would watch the birds. Autumn was best for this, better than spring. In spring the birds flew inland, purposeful, intent; they knew where they were bound, the rhythm and ritual of their life brooked no delay. In autumn those that had not migrated overseas but remained to pass the winter were caught up in the same driving urge, but because migration was denied them followed a pattern of their own. Great flocks of them came to the peninsula, restless, uneasy, spending themselves in motion; now wheeling, circling in the sky, now settling to feed on the rich new-turned soil, but even when they fed it was as though they did so without hunger, without desire. Restlessness drove them to the skies again.

Black and white, jackdaw and gull, mingled in strange partnership, seeking some sort of liberation, never satisfied, never still. Flocks of starlings, rustling like silk, flew to fresh pasture, driven by the same necessity of movement, and the smaller birds, the finches and the larks, scattered from tree to hedge as if compelled.

Nat watched them, and he watched the sea birds too. Down in the bay they waited for the tide. They had more patience. Oyster catchers, redshank, sanderling, and curlew watched by the water's edge; as the slow sea sucked at the shore and then withdrew, leaving the strip of seaweed bare and the shingle churned, the sea birds raced and ran upon the beaches. Then that same impulse to flight seized upon them too. Crying, whistling, calling, they skimmed the placid sea and left the shore. Make haste, make speed, hurry and begone; yet where, and to what purpose? The restless urge of autumn, unsatisfying, sad, had put a spell upon them and they must flock, and wheel, and cry; they must spill themselves of motion before winter came.

"Perhaps," thought Nat, munching his pasty by the cliff's edge, "a message comes to the birds in autumn, like a warning. Winter is coming. Many of them perish. And like people who, apprehensive of death before their time, drive themselves to work or folly, the birds do likewise."

The birds had been more restless than ever this fall of the year, the agitation more marked because the days were still. As the tractor traced its path up and down the western hills, the figure of the farmer silhouetted on the driving seat, the whole machine and the man upon it would be lost momentarily in the great cloud of wheeling, crying birds. There were many more than usual, Nat was sure of this. Always, in autumn, they followed the plough, but not in great flocks like these, not with such clamor.

Nat remarked upon it when hedging was finished for the day. "Yes," said the farmer, "there are more birds about than usual; I've noticed it too. And daring, some of them, taking no notice of the tractor. One or two gulls came so close to my head this afternoon I thought they'd knock my cap off! As it was, I could scarcely see what I was doing, when they were overhead and I had the sun in my eyes. I have a notion the weather will change. It will be a hard winter. That's why the birds are restless."

Nat, tramping home across the fields and down the lane to his cottage, saw the birds still flocking over the western hills, in the last glow of the sun. No wind, and the gray sea calm and full. Campion in bloom yet in the hedges, and the air mild. The farmer was right, though, and it was that night the weather turned. Nat's bedroom faced east. He woke just after two and heard the wind in the chimney. Not the storm and bluster of a sou'westerly gale, bringing the rain, but east wind, cold and dry. It sounded hollow in the chimney, and a loose slate rattled on the roof. Nat listened, and he could hear the sea roaring in the bay. Even the air in the small bedroom had turned chill: a draft came under the skirting of the door, blowing upon the bed. Nat drew the blanket round him, leant closer to the back of his sleeping wife, and stayed wakeful, watchful, aware of misgiving without cause.

Then he heard the tapping on the window. There was no creeper on the cottage walls to break loose and scratch upon the pane. He listened and the tapping continued until, irritated by the sound, Nat got out of bed and went to the window. He opened it, and as he did so something brushed his hand, jabbing at his knuckles, grazing the skin. Then he saw the flutter of the wings and it was gone, over the roof, behind the cottage.

It was a bird; what kind of bird he could not tell. The wind must have driven it to shelter on the sill.

He shut the window and went back to bed, but, feeling his knuckles wet, put his mouth to the scratch. The bird had drawn blood. Frightened, he supposed, and bewildered, the bird, seeking shelter, had stabbed at him in the darkness. Once more he settled himself to sleep.

Presently the tapping came again, this time more forceful, more insistent, and now his wife woke at the sound and turning in the bed, said to him, "See to the window, Nat, it's rattling."

"I've already seen to it," he told her; "there's some bird there trying to get in. Can't you hear the wind? It's blowing from the east, driving the birds to shelter."

"Send them away," she said, "I can't sleep with that noise."

He went to the window for the second time, and now when he opened it there was not one bird upon the sill but half a dozen; they flew straight into his face, attacking him.

He shouted, striking out at them with his arms, scattering

119

them; like the first one, they flew over the roof and disappeared. Quickly he let the window fall and latched it.

"Did you hear that?" he said. "They went for me. Tried to peck my eyes." He stood by the window, peering into the darkness, and could see nothing. His wife, heavy with sleep, murmured from the bed.

"I'm not making it up," he said, angry at her suggestion. "I tell you the birds were on the sill, trying to get into the room."

Suddenly a frightened cry came from the room across the passage where the children slept.

"It's Jill," said his wife, roused at the sound, sitting up in bed. "Go to her, see what's the matter."

Nat lit the candle, but when he opened the bedroom door to cross the passage the draft blew out the flame.

There came a second cry of terror, this time from both children, and stumbling into their room, he felt the beating of wings about him in the darkness. The window was wide open. Through it came the birds, hitting first the ceiling and the walls, then swerving in mid-flight, turning to the children in their beds.

"It's all right, I'm here," shouted Nat, and the children flung themselves, screaming, upon him, while in the darkness the birds rose and dived and came for him again.

"What is it, Nat, what's happened?" his wife called from the further bedroom, and swiftly he pushed the children through the door to the passage and shut it upon them, so that he was alone now in their bedroom with the birds.

He seized a blanket from the nearest bed and, using it as a weapon, flung it to right and left about him in the air. He felt the thud of bodies, heard the fluttering of wings, but they were not yet defeated, for again and again they returned to the assault, jabbing his hands, his head, the little stabbing beaks sharp as pointed forks. The blanket became a weapon of defense; he wound it about his head, and then in greater darkness beat at the birds with his bare hands. He dared not stumble to the door and open it, lest in doing so the birds should follow him.

How long he fought with them in the darkness he could not tell, but at last the beating of the wings about him lessened and then withdrew, and through the density of the blanket he was aware of light. He waited, listened, there was no sound except the fretful crying of one of the children from the bedroom beyond. The fluttering, the whirring of the wings had ceased.

He took the blanket from his head and stared about him. The cold gray morning light exposed the room. Dawn and the open window had called the living birds; the dead lay on the floor. Nat gazed at the little corpses, shocked and horrified. They were all small birds, none of any size; there must have been fifty of them lying there upon the floor. There were robins, finches, sparrows, blue tits, larks, and bramblings, birds that by nature's law kept to their own flock and their own territory, and now, joining one with another in their urge for battle, had destroyed themselves against the bedroom walls, or in the strife had been destroyed by him. Some had lost feathers in the fight; others had blood, his blood, upon their beaks.

Sickened, Nat went to the window and stared out across his patch of garden to the fields.

It was bitter cold, and the ground had all the hard black look of frost. Not white frost, to shine in the morning sun, but the black frost that the east wind brings. The sea, fiercer now with the turning tide, white-capped and steep, broke harshly in the bay. Of the birds there was no sign. Not a sparrow chattered in the hedge beyond the garden gate, no early missel thrush or blackbird pecked on the grass for worms. There was no sound at all but the east wind and the sea.

Nat shut the window and the door of the small bedroom, and went back across the passage to his own. His wife sat up in bed, one child asleep beside her, the smaller in her arms, his face bandaged. The curtains were tightly drawn across the window, the candles lit. Her face looked garish in the yellow light. She shook her head for silence.

"He's sleeping now," she whispered, "but only just. Something must have cut him, there was blood at the corner of his eyes. Jill said it was the birds. She said she woke up, and the birds were in the room."

His wife looked up at Nat, searching his face for confirmation. She looked terrified, bewildered, and he did not want her to know that he was also shaken, dazed almost, by the events of the past few hours.

"There are birds in there," he said, "dead birds, nearly fifty of them. Robins, wrens, all the little birds from hereabouts. It's as though a madness seized them, with the east wind." He sat down on the bed beside his wife, and held her hand. "It's the weather," he said, "it must be that, it's the hard weather. They aren't the birds, maybe, from here around. They've been driven down from upcountry."

"But Nat," whispered his wife, "it's only this night that the weather turned. There's been no snow to drive them. And they can't be hungry yet. There's food for them out there in the fields."

"It's the weather," repeated Nat. "I tell you, it's the weather."

His face, too, was drawn and tired, like hers. They stared at one another for a while without speaking.

"I'll go downstairs and make a cup of tea," he said.

The sight of the kitchen reassured him. The cups and saucers, neatly stacked upon the dresser, the table and chairs, his wife's roll of knitting on her basket chair, the children's toys in a corner cupboard.

He knelt down, raked out the old embers, and relit the fire. The glowing sticks brought normality, the steaming kettle and the brown teapot comfort and security. He drank his tea, carried a cup up to his wife. Then he washed in the scullery, and, putting on his boots, opened the back door.

The sky was hard and leaden, and the brown hills that had gleamed in the sun the day before looked dark and bare. The east wind, like a razor, stripped the trees, and the leaves, crackling and dry, shivered and scattered with the wind's blast. Nat stubbed the earth with his boot. It was frozen hard. He had never known a change so swift and sudden. Black winter had descended in a single night.

The children were awake now. Jill was chattering upstairs and young Johnny crying once again. Nat heard his wife's voice, soothing, comforting. Presently they came down. He had breakfast ready for them, and the routine of the day began.

"Did you drive away the birds?" asked Jill, restored to calm because of the kitchen fire, because of day, because of breakfast.

"Yes, they've all gone now," said Nat. "It was the east wind brought them in. They were frightened and lost, they wanted shelter."

"They tried to peck us," said Jill. "They went for Johnny's eyes."

"Fright made them do that," said Nat. "They didn't know where they were in the dark bedroom."

"I hope they won't come again," said Jill. "Perhaps if we put bread for them outside the window they will eat that and fly away."

She finished her breakfast and then went for her coat and hood, her schoolbooks and her satchel. Nat said nothing, but

122

his wife looked at him across the table. A silent message passed between them.

"I'll walk with her to the bus," he said. "I don't go to the farm today."

And while the child was washing in the scullery he said to his wife, "Keep all the windows closed, and the doors too. Just to be on the safe side. I'll go to the farm. Find out if they heard anything in the night." Then he walked with his small daughter up the lane. She seemed to have forgotten her experience of the night before. She danced ahead of him, chasing the leaves, her face whipped with the cold and rosy under the pixie hood.

"Is it going to snow, Dad?" she said. "It's cold enough."

He glanced up at the bleak sky, felt the wind tear at his shoulders.

"No," he said, "it's not going to snow. This is a black winter, not a white one."

All the while he searched the hedgerows for the birds, glanced over the top of them to the fields beyond, looked to the small wood above the farm where the rooks and jackdaws gathered. He saw none.

The other children waited by the bus stop, muffled, hooded like Jill, their faces white and pinched with cold.

Jill ran to them, waving. "My Dad says it won't snow," she called, "it's going to be a black winter."

She said nothing of the birds. She began to push and struggle with another little girl. The bus came ambling up the hill. Nat saw her onto it, then turned and walked back towards the farm. It was not his day for work, but he wanted to satisfy himself that all was well. Jim, the cowman, was clattering in the yard.

"Boss around?" asked Nat.

"Gone to market," said Jim. "It's Tuesday, isn't it?"

He clumped off round the corner of a shed. He had no time for Nat. Nat was said to be superior. Read books, and the like. Nat had forgotten it was Tuesday. This showed how the events of the preceding night had shaken him. He went to the back door of the farmhouse and heard Mrs. Trigg singing in the kitchen, the wireless making a background to her song.

"Are you there, missus?" called out Nat.

She came to the door, beaming, broad, a good-tempered woman.

"Hullo, Mr. Hocken," she said. "Can you tell me where this cold is coming from? Is it Russia? I've never seen such a change. And it's going on, the wireless says. Something to do with the Arctic Circle."

"We didn't turn on the wireless this morning," said Nat. "Fact is, we had trouble in the night."

"Kiddies poorly?"

"No . . ." He hardly knew how to explain it. Now, in daylight, the battle of the birds would sound absurd.

He tried to tell Mrs. Trigg what had happened, but he could see from her eyes that she thought his story was the result of a nightmare.

"Sure they were real birds," she said, smiling, "with proper feathers and all? Not the funny-shaped kind that the men see after closing hours on a Saturday night?"

"Mrs. Trigg," he said, "there are fifty dead birds, robins, wrens, and such, lying low on the floor of the children's bedroom. They went for me; they tried to go for young Johnny's eyes."

Mrs. Trigg stared at him doubtfully.

"Well there, now," she answered, "I suppose the weather brought them. Once in the bedroom, they wouldn't know where they were to. Foreign birds maybe, from that Arctic Circle."

"No," said Nat, "they were the birds you see about here every day."

"Funny thing," said Mrs. Trigg, "no explaining it, really. You ought to write up and ask the *Guardian*. They'd have some answer for it. Well, I must be getting on."

She nodded, smiled, and went back into the kitchen.

Nat, dissatisfied, turned to the farm gate. Had it not been for those corpses on the bedroom floor, which he must now collect and bury somewhere, he would have considered the tale exaggeration too.

Jim was standing by the gate.

"Had any trouble with the birds?" asked Nat.

"Birds? What birds?"

"We got them up our place last night. Scores of them, came in the children's bedroom. Quite savage they were."

"Oh?" It took time for anything to penetrate Jim's head. "Never heard of birds acting savage," he said at length. "They get tame, like, sometimes. I've seen them come to the windows for crumbs."

"The birds last night weren't tame."

"No? Cold, maybe. Hungry. You put out some crumbs."

Jim was no more interested than Mrs. Trigg had been. It was, Nat thought, like air raids in the war. None down this end of the country knew what the Plymouth folk had seen and suffered. You had to endure something yourself before it touched you. He walked back along the lane and crossed the stile to his cottage. He found his wife in the kitchen with young Johnny.

"See anyone?" she asked.

"Mrs. Trigg and Jim," he answered. "I don't think they believed me. Anyway, nothing wrong up there."

"You might take the birds away," she said. "I daren't go into the room to make the beds until you do. I'm scared."

"Nothing to scare you now," said Nat. "They're dead, aren't they?"

He went up with a sack and dropped the stiff bodies into it, one by one. Yes, there were fifty of them, all told. Just the ordinary common birds of the hedgerow, nothing as large even as a thrush. It must have been fright that made them act the way they did. Blue tits, wrens—it was incredible to think of the power of their small beaks jabbing at his face and hands the night before. He took the sack out into the garden and was faced now with a fresh problem. The ground was too hard to dig. It was frozen solid, yet no snow had fallen, nothing had happened in the past hours but the coming of the east wind. It was unnatural, queer. The weather prophets must be right. The change was something connected with the Arctic Circle.

The wind seemed to cut him to the bone as he stood there uncertainly, holding the sack. He could see the white-capped seas breaking down under in the bay. He decided to take his birds to the shore and bury them.

When he reached the beach below the headland he could scarcely stand, the force of the east wind was so strong. It hurt to draw breath, and his bare hands were blue. Never had he known such cold, not in all the bad winters he could remember. It was low tide. He crunched his way over the shingle to the softer sand and then, his back to the wind, ground a pit in the sand with his heel. He meant to drop the birds into it, but as he opened up the sack the force of the wind carried them, lifted them, as though in flight again, and they were blown away from him along the beach, tossed like feathers, spread and scattered, the bodies of the fifty frozen birds. There was something ugly in the sight. He did not like it. The dead birds were swept away from him by the wind.

"The tide will take them when it turns," he said to himself.

He looked out to sea and watched the crested breakers, combing green. They rose stiffly, curled, and broke again,

125

and because it **was** ebb tide the roar was distant, more remote, lacking the sound and thunder of the flood.

Then he saw them. The gulls. Out the**re**, riding the seas.

What he had thought at first to be the whitecaps of the waves were gulls. Hundreds, thousands, tens of thousands . . . They rose and fell in the trough of the seas, heads to the wind, like a mighty fleet at anchor, waiting on the tide. To eastward, and to the west, the gulls were there. They stretched as far as his eye could reach, in close formation, line upon line. Had the sea been still they would have covered the bay like a white cloud, head to head, body packed to body. Only the east wind, whipping the sea to breakers, hid them from the shore.

Nat turned and, leaving the beach, climbed the steep path home. Someone should know of this. Someone should be told. Something was happening, because of the wind and the weather, that he did not understand. He wondered if he should go to the call box by the bus stop and ring up the police. Yet what could they do? What could anyone do? Tens of thousands of gulls riding the sea there in the bay because of storm, because of hunger. The police would think him mad, or drunk, or take the statement from him with great calm. "Thank you. Yes, the matter has already been reported. The hard weather is driving the birds inland in great numbers." Nat looked about him. Still no sign of any other bird. Perhaps the cold had sent them all from upcountry? As he drew near to the cottage his wife came to meet him at the door. She called to him, excited. "Nat," she said, "it's on the wireless. They've just read out a special news bulletin. I've written it down."

"What's on the wireless?" he said.

"About the birds," she said. "It's not only here, it's everywhere. In London, all over the country. Something has happened to the birds."

Together they went into the kitchen. He read the piece of paper lying on the table.

"Statement from the Home Office at 11 A.M. today. Reports from all over the country are coming in hourly about the vast quantity of birds flocking above towns, villages, and outlying districts, causing obstruction and damage and even attacking individuals. It is thought that the Arctic air stream, at present covering the British Isles, is causing birds to migrate south in immense numbers, and that intense hunger may drive these birds to attack human beings. Householders are warned to see to their windows, doors, and chimneys, and to take reasonable precautions for the safety of their children. A further statement will be issued later."

A kind of excitement seized Nat; he looked at his wife in triumph.

"There you are," he said. "Let's hope they'll hear that at the farm. Mrs. Trigg will know it wasn't any story. It's true. All over the country. I've been telling myself all morning there's something wrong. And just now, down on the beach, I looked out to sea and there are gulls, thousands of them, tens of thousands—you couldn't put a pin between their heads—and they're all out there, riding on the sea, waiting."

"What are they waiting for, Nat?" she asked.

He stared at her, then looked down again at the piece of paper.

"I don't know," he said slowly. "It says here the birds are hungry."

He went over to the drawer where he kept his hammer and tools.

"What are you going to do, Nat?"

"See to the windows and the chimneys too, like they tell you."

"You think they would break in, with the windows shut? Those sparrows and robins and such? Why, how could they?"

He did not answer. He was not thinking of the robins and the sparrows. He was thinking of the gulls. . . .

He went upstairs and worked there the rest of the morning, boarding the windows of the bedrooms, filling up the chimney bases. Good job it was his free day and he was not working at the farm. It reminded him of the old days, at the beginning of the war. He was not married then, and he had made all the blackout boards for his mother's house in Plymouth. Made the shelter too. Not that it had been of any use when the moment came. He wondered if they would take these precautions up at the farm. He doubted it. Too easygoing, Harry Trigg and his missus. Maybe they'd laugh at the whole thing. Go off to a dance or a whist drive.

"Dinner's ready." She called him, from the kitchen.

"All right. Coming down."

He was pleased with his handiwork. The frames fitted nicely over the little panes and at the bases of the chimneys.

When dinner was over and his wife was washing up, Nat switched on the one o'clock news. The same announcement was repeated, the one which she had taken down during the morning, but the news bulletin enlarged upon it. "The flocks of birds have caused dislocation in all areas," read the announcer, "and in London the sky was so dense at ten o'clock this morning that it seemed as if the city was covered by a vast black cloud.

"The birds settled on rooftops, on window ledges, and on chimneys. The species included blackbird, thrush, the common house sparrow, and, as might be expected in the metropolis, a vast quantity of pigeons and starlings, and that frequenter of the London river, the black-headed gull. The sight has been so unusual that traffic came to a standstill in many thoroughfares, work was abandoned in shops and offices, and the streets and pavements were crowded with people standing about to watch the birds."

Various incidents were recounted, the suspected reason of cold and hunger stated again, and warnings to householders repeated. The announcer's voice was smooth and suave. Nat had the impression that this man, in particular, treated the whole business as he would an elaborate joke. There would be others like him, hundreds of them, who did not know what it was to struggle in darkness with a flock of birds. There would be parties tonight in London, like the ones they gave on election nights. People standing about, shouting and laughing, getting drunk. "Come and watch the birds!"

Nat switched off the wireless. He got up and started work on the kitchen windows. His wife watched him, young Johnny at her heels.

"What, boards for down here too?" she said. "Why, I'll have to light up before three o'clock. I see no call for boards down here."

"Better be sure than sorry," answered Nat. "I'm not going to take any chances."

"What they ought to do," she said, "is to call the Army out and shoot the birds. That would soon scare them off."

"Let them try," said Nat. "How'd they set about it?"

"They have the Army to the docks," she answered, "when the dockers strike. The soldiers go down and unload the ships."

"Yes," said Nat, "and the population of London is eight million or more. Think of all the buildings, all the flats and houses. Do you think they've enough soldiers to go round shooting birds from every roof?"

"I don't know. But something should be done. They ought to do something."

Nat thought to himself that "they" were no doubt considering the problem at that very moment, but whatever "they" decided to do in London and the big cities would not help the people here, three hundred miles away. Each householder must look after his own.

"How are we off for food?" he said.

"Now, Nat, whatever next?"

"Never mind. What have you got in the larder?"

"It's shopping day tomorrow, you know that. I don't keep uncooked food hanging about, it goes off. Butcher doesn't call till the day after. But I can bring back something when I go in tomorrow."

Nat did not want to scare her. He thought it possible that she might not go to town tomorrow. He looked in the larder for himself, and in the cupboard where she kept her tins. They would do for a couple of days. Bread was low.

"What about the baker?"

"He comes tomorrow too."

He saw she had flour. If the baker did not call she had enough to bake one loaf.

"We'd be better off in old days," he said, "when the women baked twice a week, and had pilchards salted, and there was food for a family to last a siege, if need be."

"I've tried the children with tinned fish, they don't like it," she said.

Nat went on hammering the boards across the kitchen windows. Candles. They were low in candles too. That must be another thing she meant to buy tomorrow. Well, it could not be helped. They must go early to bed tonight. That was, if . . .

He got up and went out of the back door and stood in the garden, looking down towards the sea. There had been no sun all day, and now, at barely three o'clock, a kind of darkness had already come, the sky sullen, heavy, colorless like salt. He could hear the vicious sea drumming on the rocks. He walked down the path, halfway to the beach. And then he stopped. He could see the tide had turned. The rock that had shown in midmorning was now covered, but it was not the sea that held his eyes. The gulls had risen. They were circling, hundreds of them, thousands of them, lifting their wings against the wind. It was the gulls that made the darkening of the sky. And they were silent. They made not a sound. They just went on soaring and circling, rising, falling, trying their strength against the wind.

Nat turned. He ran up the path, back to the cottage. "I'm going for Jill," he said. "I'll wait for her at the bus stop."

"What's the matter?" asked his wife. "You've gone quite white."

"Keep Johnny inside," he said. "Keep the door shut. Light up now, and draw the curtains."

"It's only just gone three," she said.

"Never mind. Do what I tell you."

He looked inside the tool shed outside the back door. Nothing there of much use. A spade was too heavy, and a fork no good. He took the hoe. It was the only possible tool, and light enough to carry.

He started walking up the lane to the bus stop, and now and again glanced back over his shoulder.

The gulls had risen higher now, their circles were broader, wider, they were spreading out in huge formation across the sky.

He hurried on; although he knew the bus would not come to the top of the hill before four o'clock he had to hurry. He passed no one on his way. He was glad of this. No time to stop and chatter.

At the top of the hill he waited. He was much too soon. There was half an hour still to go. The east wind came whipping across the fields from the higher ground. He stamped his feet and blew upon his hands. In the distance he could see the clay hills, white and clean, against the heavy pallor of the sky. Something black rose from behind them, like a smudge at first, then widening, becoming deeper, and the smudge became a cloud, and the cloud divided again into five other clouds, spreading north, east, south, and west, and they were not clouds at all; they were birds. He watched them travel across the sky, and as one section passed overhead, within two or three hundred feet of him, he knew, from their speed, they were bound inland, upcountry; they had no business with the people here on the peninsula. They were rooks, crows, jackdaws, magpies, jays, all birds that usually preyed upon the smaller species; but this afternoon they were bound on some other mission.

"They've been given the towns," thought Nat; "they know what they have to do. We don't matter so much here. The gulls will serve for us. The others go to the towns."

He went to the call box, stepped inside, and lifted the receiver. The exchange would do. They would pass the message on.

"I'm speaking from Highway," he said, "by the bus stop. I want to report large formations of birds travelling upcountry. The gulls are also forming in the bay."

"All right," answered the voice, laconic, weary.

"You'll be sure and pass this message on to the proper quarter?"

"Yes . . . yes . . ." Impatient now, fed-up. The buzzing note resumed.

"She's another," thought Nat, "she doesn't care. Maybe she's had to answer calls all day. She hopes to go to the pictures tonight. She'll squeeze some fellow's hand, and point up at the sky, and 'Look at all them birds!' She doesn't care."

The bus came lumbering up the hill. Jill climbed out, and three or four other children. The bus went on towards the town.

"What's the hoe for, Dad?"

They crowded around him, laughing, pointing.

"I just brought it along," he said. "Come on now, let's get home. It's cold, no hanging about. Here, you. I'll watch you across the fields, see how fast you can run."

He was speaking to Jill's companions, who came from different families, living in the council houses. A short cut would take them to the cottages.

"We want to play a bit in the lane," said one of them.

"No, you don't. You go off home or I'll tell your Mammy."

They whispered to one another, round-eyed, then scuttled off across the fields. Jill stared at her father, her mouth sullen.

"We always play in the lane," she said.

"Not tonight, you don't," he said. "Come on now, no dawdling."

He could see the gulls now, circling the fields, coming in towards the land. Still silent. Still no sound.

"Look, Dad, look over there, look at all the gulls."

"Yes. Hurry, now."

"Where are they flying to? Where are they going?"

"Upcountry, I dare say. Where it's warmer."

He seized her hand and dragged her after him along the lane.

"Don't go so fast. I can't keep up."

The gulls were copying the rooks and crows. They were spreading out in formation across the sky. They headed, in bands of thousands, to the four compass points.

"Dad, what is it? What are the gulls doing?"

They were not intent upon their flight, as the crows, as the jackdaws had been. They still circled overhead. Nor did they fly so high. It was as though they waited upon some signal.

131

As though some decision had yet to be given. The order was not clear.

"Do you want me to carry you, Jill? Here, come pick-a-back."

This way he might put on speed; but he was wrong. Jill was heavy. She kept slipping. And she was crying too. His sense of urgency, of fear, had communicated itself to the child.

"I wish the gulls would go away. I don't like them. They're coming closer to the lane."

He put her down again. He started running, swinging Jill after him. As they went past the farm turning he saw the farmer backing his car out of the garage. Nat called to him.

"Can you give us a lift?" he said.

"What's that?"

Mr. Trigg turned in the driving seat and stared at them. Then a smile came to his cheerful, rubicund face.

"It looks as though we're in for some fun," he said. "Have you seen the gulls? Jim and I are going to take a crack at them. Everyone's gone bird-crazy, talking of nothing else. I hear you were troubled in the night. Want a gun?"

Nat shook his head.

The small car was packed. There was just room for Jill, if she crouched on top of petrol tins on the back seat.

"I don't want a gun," said Nat, "but I'd be obliged if you'd run Jill home. She's scared of the birds."

He spoke briefly. He did not want to talk in front of Jill.

"Okay," said the farmer. "I'll take her home. Why don't you stop behind and join the shooting match? We'll make the feathers fly."

Jill climbed in, and, turning the car, the driver sped up the lane. Nat followed after. Trigg must be crazy. What use was a gun against a sky of birds?

Now Nat was not responsible for Jill, he had time to look about him. The birds were circling still above the fields. Mostly herring gull, but the black-backed gull amongst them. Usually they kept apart. Now they were united. Some bond had brought them together. It was the black-backed gull that attacked the smaller birds, and even newborn lambs, so he'd heard. He'd never seen it done. He remembered this now, though, looking above him in the sky. They were coming in towards the farm. They were circling lower in the sky, and the black-backed gulls were to the front, the black-backed gulls were leading. The farm, then, was their target. They were making for the farm.

Nat increased his pace towards his own cottage. He saw the farmer's car turn and come back along the lane. It drew up beside him with a jerk.

"The kid has run inside," said the farmer. "Your wife was watching for her. Well, what do you make of it? They're saying in town the Russians have done it. The Russians have poisoned the birds."

"How could they do that?" asked Nat.

"Don't ask me. You know how stories get around. Will you join my shooting match?"

"No, I'll get along home. The wife will be worried else."

"My missus says if you could eat gull there'd be some sense in it," said Trigg. "We'd have roast gull, baked gull, and pickle 'em into the bargain. You wait until I let off a few barrels into the brutes. That'll scare 'em."

"Have you boarded your windows?" asked Nat.

"No. Lot of nonsense. They like to scare you on the wireless. I've had more to do today than to go round boarding up my windows."

"I'd board them now, if I were you."

"Garn. You're windy. Like to come to our place to sleep?"

"No, thanks all the same."

"All right. See you in the morning. Give you a gull breakfast."

The farmer grinned and turned his car to the farm entrance.

Nat hurried on. Past the little wood, past the old barn, and then across the stile to the remaining field.

As he jumped the stile he heard the whir of wings. A black-backed gull dived down at him from the sky, missed, swerved in flight, and rose to dive again. In a moment it was joined by others, six, seven, a dozen, black-backed and herring mixed. Nat dropped his hoe. The hoe was useless. Covering his head with his arms, he ran towards the cottage. They kept coming at him from the air, silent save for the beating wings. The terrible, fluttering wings. He would feel the blood on his hands, his wrists, his neck. Each stab of a swooping beak tore his flesh. If only he could keep them from his eyes. Nothing else mattered. He must keep them from his eyes. They had not learnt yet how to cling to a shoulder, how to rip clothing, how to dive in mass upon the head, upon the body. But with each dive, with each attack, they became bolder. And they had no thought for themselves. When they dived low and missed, they crashed, bruised and broken, on the ground. As Nat ran he stumbled, kicking their spent bodies in front of him.

He found the door; he hammered upon it with his bleeding hands. Because of the boarded windows no light shone. Everything was dark.

"Let me in," he shouted, "it's Nat. Let me in."

He shouted loud to make himself heard above the whir of the gulls' wings.

Then he saw the gannet, poised for the dive, above him in the sky. The gulls circled, retired, soared, one after another, against the wind. Only the gannet remained. One single gannet above him in the sky. The wings folded suddenly to its body. It dropped like a stone. Nat screamed, and the door opened. He stumbled across the threshold, and his wife threw her weight against the door.

They heard the thud of the gannet as it fell.

His wife dressed his wounds. They were not deep. The backs of his hands had suffered most, and his wrists. Had he not worn a cap they would have reached his head. As to the gannet . . . the gannet could have split his skull.

The children were crying, of course. They had seen the blood on their father's hands.

"It's all right now," he told them. "I'm not hurt. Just a few scratches. You play with Johnny, Jill. Mammy will wash these cuts."

He half shut the door to the scullery so that they could not see. His wife was ashen. She began running water from the sink.

"I saw them overhead," she whispered. "They began collecting just as Jill ran in with Mr. Trigg. I shut the door fast, and it jammed. That's why I couldn't open it at once when you came."

"Thank God they waited for me," he said. "Jill would have fallen at once. One bird alone would have done it."

Furtively, so as not to alarm the children, they whispered together as she bandaged his hands and the back of his neck.

"They're flying inland," he said, "thousands of them. Rooks, crows, all the bigger birds. I saw them from the bus stop. They're making for the towns."

"But what can they do, Nat?"

"They'll attack. Go for everyone out in the streets. Then they'll try the windows, the chimneys."

"Why don't the authorities to something? Why don't they get the Army, get machine guns, anything?"

"There's been no time. Nobody's prepared. We'll hear what they have to say on the six o'clock news."

Nat went back into the kitchen, followed by his wife. Johnny was playing quietly on the floor. Only Jill looked anxious.

"I can hear the birds," she said. "Listen, Dad."

Nat listened. Muffled sounds came from the windows, from the door. Wings brushing the surface, sliding, scraping, seeking a way of entry. The sound of many bodies, pressed together, shuffling on the sills. Now and again came a thud, a crash, as some bird dived and fell. "Some of them will kill themselves that way," he thought, "but not enough. Never enough."

"All right," he said aloud, "I've got boards over the windows, Jill. The birds can't get in."

He went and examined all the windows. His work had been thorough. Every gap was closed. He would make extra certain, however. He found wedges, pieces of old tin, strips of wood and metal, and fastened them at the sides to reinforce the boards. His hammering helped to deafen the sound of the birds, the shuffling, the tapping, and more ominous— he did not want his wife or the children to hear it—the splinter of cracked glass.

"Turn on the wireless," he said, "let's have the wireless."

This would drown the sound also. He went upstairs to the bedrooms and reinforced the windows there. Now he could hear the birds on the roof, the scraping of claws, a sliding, jostling sound.

He decided they must sleep in the kitchen, keep up the fire, bring down the mattresses, and lay them out on the floor. He was afraid of the bedroom chimneys. The boards he had placed at the chimney bases might give way. In the kitchen they would be safe because of the fire. He would have to make a joke of it. Pretend to the children they were playing at camp. If the worst happened, and the birds forced an entry down the bedroom chimneys, it would be hours, days perhaps, before they could break down the doors. The birds would be imprisoned in the bedrooms. They could do no harm there. Crowded together, they would stifle and die.

He began to bring the mattresses downstairs. At sight of them his wife's eyes widened in apprehension. She thought the birds had already broken in upstairs.

"All right," he said cheerfully, "we'll all sleep together in the kitchen tonight. More cozy here by the fire. Then we shan't be worried by those silly old birds tapping at the windows."

He made the children help him rearrange the furniture, and he took the precaution of moving the dresser, with his wife's help, across the window. It fitted well. It was an added safeguard. The mattresses could now be lain, one beside the other, against the wall where the dresser had stood.

"We're safe enough now," he thought. "We're snug and tight, like an air-raid shelter. We can hold out. It's just the food that worries me. Food, and coal for the fire. We've enough for two or three days, not more. By that time . . ."

No use thinking ahead as far as that. And they'd be giving directions on the wireless. People would be told what to do. And now, in the midst of many problems, he realized that it was dance music only coming over the air. Not Children's Hour, as it should have been. He glanced at the dial. Yes, they were on the Home Service all right. Dance records. He switched to the Light program. He knew the reason. The usual programs had been abandoned. This only happened at exceptional times. Elections and such. He tried to remember if it had happened in the war, during the heavy raids on London. But of course. The B.B.C. was not stationed in London during the war. The programs were broadcast from other, temporary quarters. "We're better off here," he thought; "we're better off here in the kitchen, with the windows and the doors boarded, than they are up in the towns. Thank God we're not in the towns."

At six o'clock the records ceased. The time signal was given. No matter if it scared the children, he must hear the news. There was a pause after the pips. Then the announcer spoke. His voice was solemn, grave. Quite different from midday.

"This is London," he said. "A National Emergency was proclaimed at four o'clock this afternoon. Measures are being taken to safeguard the lives and property of the population, but it must be understood that these are not easy to effect immediately, owing to the unforeseen and unparalleled nature of the present crisis. Every householder must take precautions to his own building, and where several people live together, as in flats and apartments, they must unite to do the utmost they can to prevent entry. It is absolutely imperative that every individual stay indoors tonight and that no one at all remain on the streets, or roads, or anywhere withoutdoors. The birds, in vast numbers, are attacking any-one on sight, and have already begun an assault upon buildings; but these, with due care, should be impenetrable. The population is asked to remain calm and not to panic. Owing to the exceptional nature of the emergency, there will be no further transmission from any broadcasting station until seven A.M. tomorrow."

They played the National Anthem. Nothing more happened. Nat switched off the set. He looked at his wife. She stared back at him.

"What's it mean?" said Jill. "What did the news say?"

"There won't be any more programs tonight," said Nat. "There's been a breakdown at the B.B.C."

"Is it the birds?" asked Jill. "Have the birds done it?"

"No," said Nat, "it's just that everyone's very busy, and then of course they have to get rid of the birds, messing everything up, in the towns. Well, we can manage without the wireless for one evening."

"I wish we had a gramophone," said Jill. "That would be better than nothing."

She had her face turned to the dresser backed against the windows. Try as they did to ignore it, they were all aware of the shuffling, the stabbing, the persistent beating and sweeping of wings.

"We'll have supper early," suggested Nat, "something for a treat. Ask Mammy. Toasted cheese, eh? Something we all like?"

He winked and nodded at his wife. He wanted the look of dread, of apprehension, to go from Jill's face.

He helped with the supper, whistling, singing, making as much clatter as he could, and it seemed to him that the shuffling and the tapping were not so intense as they had been at first. Presently he went up to the bedrooms and listened, and he no longer heard the jostling for place upon the roof.

"They've got reasoning powers," he thought; "they know it's hard to break in here. They'll try elsewhere. They won't waste their time with us."

Supper passed without incident, and then, when they were clearing away, they heard a new sound, droning, familiar, a sound they all knew and understood.

His wife looked up at him, her face alight. "It's planes," she said; "they're sending out planes after the birds. That's what I said they ought to do all along. That will get them. Isn't that gunfire? Can't you hear guns?"

It might be gunfire out at sea. Nat could not tell. Big naval guns might have an effect upon the gulls out at sea, but the

137

gulls were inland now. The guns couldn't shell the shore because of the population.

"It's good, isn't it," said his wife, "to hear the planes?" And Jill, catching her enthusiasm, jumped up and down with Johnny. "The planes will get the birds. The planes will shoot them."

Just then they heard a crash about two miles distant, followed by a second, then a third. The droning became more distant, passed away out to sea.

"What was that?" asked his wife. "Were they dropping bombs on the birds?"

"I don't know," answered Nat. "I don't think so."

He did not want to tell her that the sound they had heard was the crashing of aircraft. It was, he had no doubt, a venture on the part of the authorities to send out reconnaissance forces, but they might have known the venture was suicidal. What could aircraft do against birds that flung themselves to death against propeller and fuselage, but hurtle to the ground themselves? This was being tried now, he supposed, over the whole country. And at a cost. Someone high up had lost his head.

"Where have the planes gone, Dad?" asked Jill.

"Back to base," he said. "Come on, now, time to truck down for bed."

It kept his wife occupied, undressing the children before the fire, seeing to the bedding, one thing and another, while he went round the cottage again, making sure that nothing had worked loose. There was no further drone of aircraft, and the naval guns had ceased. "Waste of life and effort," Nat said to himself. "We can't destroy enough of them that way. Cost too heavy. There's always gas. Maybe they'll try spraying with gas, mustard gas. We'll be warned first, of course, if they do. There's one thing, the best brains of the country will be on to it tonight."

Somehow the thought reassured him. He had a picture of scientists, naturalists, technicians, and all those chaps they called the back-room boys, summoned to a council; they'd be working on the problem now. This was not a job for the government, for the chiefs of staff—they would merely carry out the orders of the scientists.

"They'll have to be ruthless," he thought. "Where the trouble's worst they'll have to risk more lives, if they use gas. All the livestock, too, and the soil—all contaminated. As long as everyone doesn't panic. That's the trouble. People panick-

138

ing, losing their heads. The B.B.C. was right to warn us of that."

Upstairs in the bedrooms all was quiet. No further scraping and stabbing at the windows. A lull in battle. Forces regrouping. Wasn't that what they called it in the old wartime bulletins? The wind hadn't dropped, though. He could still hear it roaring in the chimneys. And the sea breaking down on the shore. Then he remembered the tide. The tide would be on the turn. Maybe the lull in battle was because of the tide. There was some law the birds obeyed, and it was all to do with the east wind and the tide.

He glanced at his watch. Nearly eight o'clock. It must have gone high water an hour ago. That explained the lull: the birds attacked with the flood tide. It might not work that way inland, upcountry, but it seemed as if it was so this way on the coast. He reckoned the time limit in his head. They had six hours to go without attack. When the tide turned again, around one-twenty in the morning, the birds would come back. . . .

There were two things he could do. The first to rest, with his wife and the children, and all of them snatch what sleep they could, until the small hours. The second to go out, see how they were faring at the farm, see if the telephone was still working there, so that they might get news from the exchange.

He called softly to his wife, who had just settled the children. She came halfway up the stairs and he whispered to her.

"You're not to go," she said at once, "you're not to go and leave me alone with the children. I can't stand it."

Her voice rose hysterically. He hushed her, calmed her.

"All right," he said, "all right. I'll wait till morning. And we'll get the wireless bulletin then too, at seven. But in the morning, when the tide ebbs again, I'll try for the farm, and they may let us have bread and potatoes, and milk too."

His mind was busy again, planning against emergency. They would not have milked, of course, this evening. The cows would be standing by the gate, waiting in the yard, with the household inside, battened behind boards, as they were here at the cottage. That is, if they had time to take precautions. He thought of the farmer, Trigg, smiling at him from the car. There would have been no shooting party, not tonight.

The children were asleep. His wife, still clothed, was sitting on her mattress. She watched him, her eyes nervous.

"What are you going to do?" she whispered.

He shook his head for silence. Softly, stealthily, he opened the back door and looked outside.

It was pitch dark. The wind was blowing harder than ever, coming in steady gusts, icy, from the sea. He kicked at the step outside the door. It was heaped with birds. There were dead birds everywhere. Under the windows, against the walls. These were the suicides, the divers, the ones with broken necks. Wherever he looked he saw dead birds. No trace of the living. The living had flown seaward with the turn of the tide. The gulls would be riding the seas now, as they had done in the forenoon.

In the far distance, on the hill where the tractor had been two days before, something was burning. One of the aircraft that had crashed; the fire, fanned by the wind, had set light to a stack.

He looked at the bodies of the birds, and he had a notion that if he heaped them, one upon the other, on the window sills they would make added protection for the next attack. Not much, perhaps, but something. The bodies would have to be clawed at, pecked, and dragged aside before the living birds could gain purchase on the sills and attack the panes. He set to work in the darkness. It was queer, he hated touching them. The bodies were still warm and bloody. The blood matted their feathers. He felt his stomach turn, but he went on with his work. He noticed grimly that every window-pane was shattered. Only the boards had kept the birds from breaking in. He stuffed the cracked panes with the bleeding bodies of the birds.

When he had finished he went back into the cottage. He barricaded the kitchen door, made it doubly secure. He took off his bandages, sticky with the birds' blood, not with his own cuts, and put on fresh plaster.

His wife had made him cocoa and he drank it thirstily: he was very tired.

"All right," he said, smiling, "don't worry. We'll get through."

He lay down on his mattress and closed his eyes. He slept at once. He dreamt uneasily, because through his dreams there ran a thread of something forgotten. Some piece of work, neglected, that he should have done. Some precaution that he had known well but had not taken, and he could not put a name to it in his dreams. It was connected in some way with the burning aircraft and the stack upon the hill. He went on sleeping, though; he did not awake. It was his wife shaking his shoulder that awoke him finally.

"They've begun," she sobbed, "they've started this last hour. I can't listen to it any longer alone. There's something smelling bad too, something burning."

Then he remembered. He had forgotten to make up the fire. It was smoldering, nearly out. He got up swiftly and lit the lamp. The hammering had started at the windows and the doors, but it was not that he minded now. It was the smell of singed feathers. The smell filled the kitchen. He knew at once what it was. The birds were coming down the chimney, squeezing their way down to the kitchen range.

He got sticks and paper and put them on the embers, then reached for the can of paraffin.

"Stand back," he shouted to his wife. "We've got to risk this."

He threw the paraffin onto the fire. The flame roared up the pipe, and down upon the fire fell the scorched, blackened bodies of the birds.

The children woke, crying. "What is it?" said Jill. "What happened?"

Nat had no time to answer. He was raking the bodies from the chimney, clawing them out onto the floor. The flames still roared, and the danger of the chimney catching fire was one he had to take. The flames would send away the living birds from the chimney top. The lower joint was the difficulty, though. This was choked with the smoldering helpless bodies of the birds caught by the fire. He scarcely heeded the attack on the windows and the door: let them beat their wings, break their beaks, lose their lives, in the attempt to force an entry into his home. They would not break in. He thanked God he had one of the old cottages, with small windows, stout walls. Not like the new council houses. Heaven help them up the lane in the new council houses.

"Stop crying," he called to the children. "There's nothing to be afraid of, stop crying."

He went on raking at the burning, smoldering bodies as they fell into the fire.

"This'll fetch them," he said to himself, "the draft and the flames together. We're all right, as long as the chimney doesn't catch. I ought to be shot for this. It's all my fault. Last thing, I should have made up the fire. I knew there was something."

Amid the scratching and tearing at the window boards came the sudden homely striking of the kitchen clock. Three

A.M. A little more than four hours yet to go. He could not be sure of the exact time of high water. He reckoned it would not turn much before half past seven, twenty to eight.

"Light up the Primus," he said to his wife. "Make us some tea, and the kids some cocoa. No use sitting around doing nothing."

That was the line. Keep her busy, and the children too. Move about, eat, drink; always best to be on the go.

He waited by the range. The flames were dying. But no more blackened bodies fell from the chimney. He thrust his poker up as far as it could go and found nothing. It was clear. The chimney was clear. He wiped the sweat from his forehead.

"Come on now, Jill," he said, "bring me some more sticks. We'll have a good fire going directly." She wouldn't come near him, though. She was staring at the heaped singed bodies of the birds.

"Never mind them," he said, "we'll put those in the passage when I've got the fire steady."

The danger of the chimney was over. It could not happen again, not if the fire was kept burning day and night.

"I'll have to get more fuel from the farm tomorrow," he thought. "This will never last. I'll manage, though. I can do all that with the ebb tide. It can be worked, fetching what we need, when the tide's turned. We've just got to adapt ourselves, that's all."

They drank tea and cocoa and ate slices of bread and Bovril. Only half a loaf left, Nat noticed. Never mind though, they'd get by.

"Stop it," said young Johnny, pointing to the windows with his spoon, "stop it, you old birds."

"That's right," said Nat, smiling, "we don't want the old beggars, do we? Had enough of 'em."

They began to cheer when they heard the thud of the suicide birds.

"There's another, Dad," cried Jill, "he's done for."

"He's had it," said Nat. "There he goes, the blighter."

This was the way to face up to it. This was the spirit. If they could keep this up, hang on like this until seven, when the first news bulletin came through, they would not have done too badly.

"Give us a fag," he said to his wife. "A bit of a smoke will clear away the smell of the scorched feathers."

"There's only two left in the packet," she said. "I was going to buy you some from the Co-op."

"I'll have one," he said, "t'other will keep for a rainy day."

No sense trying to make the children rest. There was no rest to be got while the tapping and the scratching went on at the windows. He sat with one arm round his wife and the other round Jill, with Johnny on his mother's lap and the blankets heaped about them on the mattress.

"You can't help admiring the beggars," he said; "they've got persistence. You'd think they'd tire of the game, but not a bit of it."

Admiration was hard to sustain. The tapping went on and on and a new rasping note struck Nat's ear, as though a sharper beak than any hitherto had come to take over from its fellows. He tried to remember the names of birds; he tried to think which species would go for this particular job. It was not the tap of the woodpecker. That would be light and frequent. This was more serious, because if it continued long the wood would splinter as the glass had done. Then he remembered the hawks. Could the hawks have taken over from the gulls? Were there buzzards now upon the sills, using talons as well as beaks? Hawks, buzzards, kestrels, falcons—he had forgotten the birds of prey. He had forgotten the gripping power of the birds of prey. Three hours to go, and while they waited, the sound of the splintering wood, the talons tearing at the wood.

Nat looked about him, seeing what furniture he could destroy to fortify the door. The windows were safe because of the dresser. He was not certain of the door. He went upstairs, but when he reached the landing he paused and listened. There was a soft patter on the floor of the children's bedroom. The birds had broken through.... He put his ear to the door. No mistake. He could hear the rustle of wings and the light patter as they searched the floor. The other bedroom was still clear. He went into it and began bringing out the furniture, to pile at the head of the stairs should the door of the children's bedroom go. It was a preparation. It might never be needed. He could not stack the furniture against the door, because it opened inward. The only possible thing was to have it at the top of the stairs.

"Come down, Nat, what are you doing?" called his wife.

"I won't be long," he shouted. "Just making everything shipshape up here."

He did not want her to come, he did not want her to hear the pattering of the feet in the children's bedroom, the brushing of those wings against the door.

At five thirty he suggested breakfast, bacon and fried

143

bread, if only to stop the growing look of panic in his wife's eyes and to calm the fretful children. She did not know about the birds upstairs. The bedroom, luckily, was not over the kitchen. Had it been so, she could not have failed to hear the sound of them up there, tapping the boards. And the silly, senseless thud of the suicide birds, the death and glory boys, who flew into the bedroom, smashing their heads against the walls. He knew them of old, the herring gulls. They had no brains. The black-backs were different; they knew what they were doing. So did the buzzards, the hawks . . .

He found himself watching the clock, gazing at the hands that went so slowly round the dial. If his theory was not correct, if the attack did not cease with the turn of the tide, he knew they were beaten. They could not continue through the long day without air, without rest, without more fuel, without . . . His mind raced. He knew there were so many things they needed to withstand siege. They were not fully prepared. They were not ready. It might be that it would be safer in the towns after all. If he could get a message through on the farm telephone to his cousin, only a short journey by train upcountry, they might be able to hire a car. That would be quicker—hire a car between tides . . .

His wife's voice, calling his name, drove away the sudden, desperate desire for sleep.

"What is it? What now?" he said sharply.

"The wireless," said his wife. "I've been watching the clock. It's nearly seven."

"Don't twist the knob," he said, impatient for the first time. "It's on the Home where it is. They'll speak from the Home."

They waited. The kitchen clock struck seven. There was no sound. No chimes, no music. They waited until a quarter past, switching to the Light. The result was the same. No news bulletin came through.

"We've heard wrong," he said. "They won't be broadcasting until eight o'clock."

They left it switched on, and Nat thought of the battery, wondered how much power was left in it. It was generally recharged when his wife went shopping in the town. If the battery failed they would not hear the instructions.

"It's getting light," whispered his wife. "I can't see it, but I can feel it. And the birds aren't hammering so loud."

She was right. The rasping, tearing sound grew fainter every moment. So did the shuffling, the jostling for place upon the step, upon the sills. The tide was on the turn. By eight there was no sound at all. Only the wind. The children, lulled at last by the stillness, fell asleep. At half past eight Nat switched the wireless off.

"What are you doing? We'll miss the news," said his wife.

"There isn't going to be any news," said Nat. "We've got to depend upon ourselves."

He went to the door and slowly pulled away the barricades. He drew the bolts and, kicking the bodies from the step outside the door, breathed the cold air. He had six working hours before him, and he knew he must reserve his strength for the right things, not waste it in any way. Food, and light, and fuel; these were the necessary things. If he could get them in sufficiency, they could endure another night.

He stepped into the garden, and as he did so he saw the living birds. The gulls had gone to ride the sea, as they had done before; they sought sea food, and the buoyancy of the tide, before they returned to the attack. Not so the land birds. They waited and watched. Nat saw them, on the hedgerows, on the soil, crowded in the trees, outside in the field, line upon line of birds, all still, doing nothing.

He went to the end of his small garden. The birds did not move. They went on watching him.

"I've got to get food," said Nat to himself. "I've got to go to the farm to find food."

He went back to the cottage. He saw to the windows and the doors. He went upstairs and opened the children's bedroom. It was empty, except for the dead birds on the floor. The living were out there, in the garden, in the fields. He went downstairs.

"I'm going to the farm," he said.

His wife clung to him. She had seen the living birds from the open door.

"Take us with you," she begged. "We can't stay here alone. I'd rather die than stay here alone."

He considered the matter. He nodded.

"Come on, then," he said. "Bring baskets, and Johnny's pram. We can load up the pram."

They dressed against the biting wind, wore gloves and scarves. His wife put Johnny in the pram. Nat took Jill's hand.

"The birds," she whimpered, "they're all out there in the fields."

"They won't hurt us," he said, "not in the light."

They started walking across the field towards the stile, and

145

the birds did not move. They waited, their heads turned to the wind.

When they reached the turning to the farm, Nat stopped and told his wife to wait in the shelter of the hedge with the two children.

"But I want to see Mrs. Trigg," she protested. "There are lots of things we can borrow if they went to market yesterday; not only bread, and ..."

"Wait here," Nat interrupted. "I'll be back in a moment."

The cows were lowing, moving restlessly in the yard, and he could see a gap in the fence where the sheep had knocked their way through, to roam unchecked in the front garden before the farmhouse. No smoke came from the chimneys. He was filled with misgiving. He did not want his wife or the children to go down to the farm.

"Don't gib now," said Nat, harshly, "do what I say."

She withdrew with the pram into the hedge, screening herself and the children from the wind.

He went down alone to the farm. He pushed his way through the herd of bellowing cows, which turned this way and that, distressed, their udders full. He saw the car standing by the gate, not put away in the garage. The windows of the farmhouse were smashed. There were many dead gulls lying in the yard and around the house. The living birds perched on the group of trees behind the farm and on the roof of the house. They were quite still. They watched him.

Jim's body lay in the yard ... what was left of it. When the birds had finished, the cows had trampled him. His gun was beside him. The door of the house was shut and bolted, but as the windows were smashed it was easy to lift them and climb through. Trigg's body was close to the telephone. He must have been trying to get through to the exchange when the birds came for him. The receiver was hanging loose, the instrument torn from the wall. No sign of Mrs. Trigg. She would be upstairs. Was it any use going up? Sickened, Nat knew what he would find.

"Thank God," he said to himself, "there were no children."

He forced himself to climb the stairs, but halfway he turned and descended again. He could see her legs protruding from the open bedroom door. Beside her were the bodies of the black-backed gulls, and an umbrella, broken.

"It's no use," thought Nat, "doing anything. I've only got

146

five hours, less than that. The Triggs would understand. I must load up with what I can find."

He tramped back to his wife and children.

"I'm going to fill up the car with stuff," he said. "I'll put coal in it, and paraffin for the Primus. We'll take it home and return for a fresh load."

"What about the Triggs?" asked his wife.

"They must have gone to friends," he said.

"Shall I come and help you, then?"

"No; there's a mess down there. Cows and sheep all over the place. Wait, I'll get the car. You can sit in it."

Clumsily he backed the car out of the yard and into the lane. His wife and the children could not see Jim's body from there.

"Stay here," he said, "never mind the pram. The pram can be fetched later. I'm going to load the car."

Her eyes watched his all the time. He believed she understood, otherwise she would have suggested helping him to find the bread and groceries.

They made three journeys altogether, backwards and forwards between their cottage and the farm, before he was satisfied they had everything they needed. It was surprising, once he started thinking, how many things were necessary. Almost the most important of all was planking for the windows. He had to go round searching for timber. He wanted to renew the boards on all the windows at the cottage. Candles, paraffin, nails, tinned stuff; the list was endless. Besides all that, he milked three of the cows. The rest, poor brutes, would have to go on bellowing.

On the final journey he drove the car to the bus stop, got out, and went to the telephone box. He waited a few minutes, jangling the receiver. No good, though. The line was dead. He climbed onto a bank and looked over the countryside, but there was no sign of life at all, nothing in the fields but the waiting, watching birds. Some of them slept—he could see the beaks tucked into the feathers.

"You'd think they'd be feeding," he said to himself, "not just standing in that way."

Then he remembered. They were gorged with food. They had eaten their fill during the night. That was why they did not move this morning. . . .

No smoke came from the chimneys of the council house. He thought of the children who had run across the fields the night before.

"I should have known," he thought; "I ought to have taken them home with me."

He lifted his face to the sky. It was colorless and gray. The bare trees on the landscape looked bent and blackened by the east wind. The cold did not affect the living birds waiting out there in the fields.

"This is the time they ought to get them," said Nat; "they're a sitting target now. They must be doing this all over the country. Why don't our aircraft take off now and spray them with mustard gas? What are all our chaps doing? They must know, they must see for themselves."

He went back to the car and got into the driver's seat.

"Go quickly past that second gate," whispered his wife. "The postman's lying there. I don't want Jill to see."

He accelerated. The little Morris bumped and rattled along the lane. The children shrieked with laughter.

"Up-a-down, up-a-down," shouted young Johnny.

It was a quarter to one by the time they reached the cottage. Only an hour to go.

"Better have cold dinner," said Nat. "Hot up something for yourself and the children, some of that soup. I've no time to eat now. I've got to unload all this stuff."

He got everything inside the cottage. It could be sorted later. Give them all something to do during the long hours ahead. First he must see to the windows and the doors.

He went round the cottage methodically, testing every window, every door. He climbed onto the roof also, and fixed boards across every chimney, except the kitchen. The cold was so intense he could hardly bear it, but the job had to be done. Now and again he would look up, searching the sky for aircraft. None came. As he worked he cursed the inefficiency of the authorities.

"It's always the same," he muttered, "they always let us down. Muddle, muddle, from the start. No plan, no real organization. And we don't matter down here. That's what it is. The people upcountry have priority. They're using gas up there, no doubt, and all the aircraft. We've got to wait and take what comes."

He paused, his work on the bedroom chimney finished, and looked out to sea. Something was moving out there. Something gray and white amongst the breakers.

"Good old Navy," he said, "they never let us down. They're coming down-channel, they're turning in the bay."

He waited, straining his eyes, watering in the wind, towards the sea. He was wrong, though. It was not ships. The

Navy was not there. The gulls were rising from the sea. The massed flocks in the fields, with ruffled feathers, rose in formation from the ground and, wing to wing, soared upwards to the sky.

The tide had turned again.

Nat climbed down the ladder and went inside the kitchen. The family were at dinner. It was a little after two. He bolted the door, put up the barricade, and lit the lamp.

"It's nighttime," said young Johnny.

His wife had switched on the wireless once again, but no sound came from it.

"I've been all round the dial," she said, "foreign stations, and that lot. I can't get anything."

"Maybe they have the same trouble," he said, "maybe it's the same right through Europe."

She poured out a plateful of the Triggs' soup, cut him a large slice of the Triggs' bread, and spread their dripping upon it.

They ate in silence. A piece of the dripping ran down young Johnny's chin and fell onto the table.

"Manners, Johnny," said Jill, "you should learn to wipe your mouth."

The tapping began at the windows, at the door. The rustling, the jostling, the pushing for position on the sills. The first thud of the suicide gulls upon the step.

"Won't America do something?" said his wife. "They've always been our allies, haven't they? Surely America will do something?"

Nat did not answer. The boards were strong against the windows, and on the chimneys too. The cottage was filled with stores, with fuel, with all they needed for the next few days. When he had finished dinner he would put the stuff away, stack it neatly, get everything shipshape, handy-like. His wife could help him, and the children too. They'd tire themselves out, between now and a quarter to nine, when the tide would ebb; then he'd tuck them down on their mattresses, see that they slept good and sound until three in the morning.

He had a new scheme for the windows, which was to fix barbed wire in front of the boards. He had brought a great roll of it from the farm. The nuisance was, he'd have to work at this in the dark, when the lull came between nine and three. Pity he had not thought of it before. Still, as long as the wife slept, and the kids, that was the main thing.

The smaller birds were at the window now. He recognized

the light tap-tapping of their beaks and the soft brush of their wings. The hawks ignored the windows. They concentrated their attack upon the door. Nat listened to the tearing sound of splintering wood, and wondered how many million years of memory were stored in those little brains, behind the stabbing beaks, the piercing eyes, now giving them this instinct to destroy mankind with all the deft precision of machines.

"I'll smoke that last fag," he said to his wife. "Stupid of me, it was the one thing I forgot to bring back from the farm."

He reached for it, switched on the silent wireless. He threw the empty packet on the fire, and watched it burn.

The Judge's House

by Bram Stoker

When the time for his examination drew near. Malcolm Malcolmson made up his mind to go somewhere to read by himself. He feared the attractions of the seaside, and also he feared completely rural isolation, for of old he knew its charms, and so he determined to find some unpretentious little town where there would be nothing to distract him. He refrained from asking suggestions from any of his friends, for he argued that each would recommend some place of which he had knowledge, and where he had already acquaintances. As Malcolmson wished to avoid friends he had no wish to encumber himself with the attention of friends' friends, and so he determined to look out for a place for himself. He packed a portmanteau with some clothes and all the books he required, and then took a ticket for the first name on the local timetable which he did not know.

When at the end of three hours' journey he alighted at Benchurch, he felt satisfied that he had so far obliterated his tracks as to be sure of having a peaceful opportunity of pursuing his studies. He went straight to the one inn which the sleepy little place contained, and put up for the night. Benchurch was a market town, and once in three weeks was crowded to excess, but for the remainder of the twenty-one days it was as attractive as a desert. Malcolmson looked around the day after his arrival to try to find quarters more isolated than even so quiet an inn as The Good Traveller afforded. There was only one place which took his fancy, and it certainly satisfied his wildest ideas regarding quiet; in fact, quiet was not the proper word to apply to it—desolation was the only term conveying any suitable idea of its isolation. It was an old rambling, heavy-built house of the Jacobean style, with heavy gables and windows, unusually small, and set higher than was customary in such houses, and was surrounded with a high brick wall massively built. Indeed, on examination, it looked more like a fortified house than an ordinary dwelling. But all these things pleased Malcolmson. "Here," he thought, "is the very spot I have been looking for, and if I can only get opportunity of using it I shall be happy." His joy was increased when he realized beyond doubt that it was not at present inhabited.

From the post office he got the name of the agent, who was really surprised at the application to rent a part of the old house. Mr. Carnford, the local lawyer and agent, was a genial old gentleman, and frankly confessed his delight at anyone being willing to live in the house.

"To tell you the truth," said he, "I should be only too happy, on behalf of the owners, to let anyone have the house rent free for a term of years if only to accustom the people to see it inhabited. It has been so long empty that some kind of absurd prejudice has grown up about it, and this can be best put down by its occupation—if only," he added with a sly glance at Malcolmson, "by a scholar like yourself, who wants it quiet for a time."

Malcolmson thought it needless to ask the agent about the "absurd prejudice"; he knew he would get more information, if he should require it, on that subject from other quarters. He paid his three months' rent, got a receipt, and the name of an old woman who would probably undertake to "do" for him, and came away with the keys in his pocket. He then went to the landlady of the inn, who was a cheerful and most kindly person, and asked her advice as to such stores and provision as he would be likely to require. She threw up her hands in amazement when he told her where he was going to settle himself.

"Not in the Judge's House!" she said, and grew pale as she spoke. He explained the locality of the house, saying that he did not know its name. When he had finished she answered:

"Aye, sure enough—sure enough the very place! It is the

151

Judge's House sure enough." He asked her to tell him about the place, why so called, and what there was against it. She told him that it was so called locally because it had been many years before—how long she could not say, as she was herself from another part of the country, but she thought it must have been a hundred years or more—the abode of a judge who was held in great terror on account of his harsh sentences and his hostility to prisoners at Assizes. As to what there was against the house itself she could not tell. She had often asked, but no one could inform her; but there was a general feeling that there was *something,* and for her own part she would not take all the money in Drinkwater's Bank and stay in the house an hour by herself. Then she apologized to Malcolmson for her disturbing talk.

"It is too bad of me, sir, and you—and a young gentleman, too—if you will pardon me saying it, going to live there all alone. If you were my boy—and you'll excuse me for saying it—you wouldn't sleep there a night, not if I had to go there myself and pull the big alarm bell that's on the roof!" The good creature was so manifestly in earnest, and was so kindly in her intentions, that Malcolmson, although amused, was touched. He told her kindly how much he appreciated her interest in him, and added:

"But, my dear Mrs. Witham, indeed you need not be concerned about me! A man who is reading for the Mathematical Tripos has too much to think of to be disturbed by any of these mysterious 'somethings,' and his work is of too exact and prosaic a kind to allow of his having any corner in his mind for mysteries of any kind. Harmonical progression, permutations and combinations, and elliptic functions have sufficient mysteries for me!" Mrs. Witham kindly undertook to see after his commissions, and he went himself to look for the old woman who had been recommended to him. When he returned to the Judge's House with her, after an interval of a couple of hours, he found Mrs. Witham herself waiting with several men and boys carrying parcels, and an upholsterer's man with a bed in a cart, for she said, though tables and chairs might be all very well, a bed that hadn't been aired for mayhap fifty years was not proper for young bones to lie on. She was evidently curious to see the inside of the house; and though manifestly so afraid of the "somethings" that at the slightest sound she clutched on to Malcolmson, whom she never left for a moment, went over the whole place.

After his examination of the house, Malcolmson decided to take up his abode in the great dining room, which was big enough to serve for all his requirements; and Mrs. Witham, with the aid of the charwoman, Mrs. Dempster, proceeded to arrange matters. When the hampers were brought in and unpacked, Malcolmson saw that with much kind forethought she had sent from her own kitchen sufficient provisions to last for a few days. Before going she expressed all sorts of kind wishes; and at the door turned and said:

"And perhaps, sir, as the room is big and drafty it might be well to have one of those big screens put round your bed at night—though, truth to tell, I would die myself if I were to be so shut in with all kinds of—of 'things,' that put their heads round the sides, or over the top, and look on me!" The image which she had called up was too much for her nerves, and she fled incontinently.

Mrs. Dempster sniffed in a superior manner as the landlady disappeared, and remarked that for her own part she wasn't afraid of all the bogies in the kingdom.

"I'll tell you what it is, sir," she said; "bogies is all kinds and sorts of things—except bogies! Rats and mice, and beetles; and creaky doors, and loose slates, and broken panes, and stiff drawer handles, that stay out when you pull them and then fall down in the middle of the night. Look at the wainscot of the room! It is old—hundreds of years old! Do you think there's no rats and beetles there! And do you imagine, sir, that you won't see none of them? Rats is bogies, I tell you, and bogies is rats; and don't you get to think anything else!"

"Mrs. Dempster," said Malcolmson gravely, making her a polite bow, "you know more than a Senior Wrangler! And let me say, that, as a mark of esteem for your indubitable soundness of head and heart, I shall, when I go, give you possession of this house, and let you stay here by yourself for the last two months of my tenancy, for four weeks will serve my purpose."

"Thank you kindly, sir!" she answered, "but I couldn't sleep away from home a night. I am in Greenhow's Charity, and if I slept a night away from my rooms I should lose all I have got to live on. The rules is very strict; and there's too many watching for a vacancy for me to run any risks in the matter. Only for that, sir, I'd gladly come here and attend on you altogether during your stay."

"My good woman," said Malcolmson hastily, "I have come here on purpose to obtain solitude; and believe me that I am grateful to the late Greenhow for having so organized his admirable charity—whatever it is—that I am perforce denied the opportunity of suffering from such a form of temptation! Saint Anthony himself could not be more rigid on the point!"

The old woman laughed harshly. "Ah, you young gentlemen," she said, "you don't fear for naught; and belike you'll get all the solitude you want here." She set to work with her cleaning; and by nightfall, when Malcolmson returned from his walk—he always had one of his books to study as he walked—he found the room swept and tidied, a fire burning in the old hearth, the lamp lit, and the table spread for supper with Mrs. Witham's excellent fare. "This is comfort, indeed," he said, as he rubbed his hands.

When he had finished his supper, and lifted the tray to the other end of the great oak dining table, he got out his books again, put fresh wood on the fire, trimmed his lamp, and set himself down to a spell of real hard work. He went on without pause till about eleven o'clock, when he knocked off for a bit to fix his fire and lamp, and to make himself a cup of tea. He had always been a tea drinker, and during his college life had sat late at work and had taken tea late. The rest was a great luxury to him, and he enjoyed it with a sense of delicious, voluptuous ease. The renewed fire leaped and sparkled and threw quaint shadows through the great old room; and as he sipped his hot tea he revelled in the sense of isolation from his kind. Then it was that he began to notice for the first time what a noise the rats were making.

"Surely," he thought, "they cannot have been at it all the time I was reading. Had they been, I must have noticed it!" Presently, when the noise increased, he satisfied himself that it was really new. It was evident that at first the rats had been frightened at the presence of a stranger, and the light of fire and lamp; but that as the time went on they had grown bolder and were now disporting themselves as was their wont.

How busy they were! and hark to the strange noises! Up and down behind the old wainscot, over the ceiling and under the floor they raced, and gnawed, and scratched! Malcolmson smiled to himself as he recalled to mind the saying of Mrs. Dempster, "Bogies is rats, and rats is bogies!" The tea began to have its effect of intellectual and nervous stimulus, he saw with joy another long spell of work to be done before the night was past, and in the sense of security which it gave him, he allowed himself the luxury of a good look round the room. He took his lamp in one hand, and went all around, wondering that so quaint and beautiful an old house had been so long neglected. The carving of the oak on the panels of the wainscot was fine, and on and round the doors and windows it was beautiful and of rare merit. There were some old pictures on the walls, but they were coated so thick with dust and dirt that he could not distinguish any detail of them, though he held his lamp as high as he could over his head. Here and there as he went round he saw some crack or hole blocked for a moment by the face of a rat with its bright eyes glittering in the light, but in an instant it was gone, and a squeak and a scamper followed. The thing that most struck him, however, was the rope of the great alarm bell on the roof, which hung down in a corner of the room on the right-hand side of the fireplace. He pulled up close to the hearth a great high-backed carved oak chair, and sat down to his last cup of tea. When this was done he made up the fire, and went back to his work, sitting at the corner of the table, having the fire to his left. For a little while the rats disturbed him somewhat with their perpetual scampering, but he got accustomed to the noise as one does to the ticking of a clock or to the roar of moving water; and he became so immersed in his work that everything in the world, except the problem which he was trying to solve, passed away from him.

He suddenly looked up, his problem was still unsolved, and there was in the air that sense of the hour before the dawn, which is so dread to doubtful life. The noise of the rats had ceased. Indeed it seemed to him that it must have ceased but lately and that it was the sudden cessation which had disturbed him. The fire had fallen low, but still it threw out a deep red glow. As he looked he started in spite of his *sang froid*.

There on the great high-backed carved oak chair by the right side of the fireplace sat an enormous rat, steadily glaring at him with baleful eyes. He made a motion to it as though to hunt it away, but it did not stir. Then he made the motion of throwing something. Still it did not stir, but showed its great white teeth angrily, and its cruel eyes shone in the lamplight with an added vindictiveness.

Malcolmson felt amazed, and seizing the poker from the hearth ran at it to kill it. Before, however, he could strike it, the rat, with a squeak that sounded like the concentration of hate, jumped upon the floor, and, running up the rope of the alarm bell, disappeared in the darkness beyond the range of the green-shaded lamp. Instantly, strange to say, the noisy scampering of the rats in the wainscot began again.

By this time Malcolmson's mind was quite off the problem;

and as a shrill cock crow outside told him of the approach of morning, he went to bed and to sleep.

He slept so soundly that he was not even wakened by Mrs. Dempster coming in to make up his room. It was only when she had tidied up the place and got his breakfast ready and tapped on the screen which closed in his bed that he woke. He was a little tired still after his night's hard work, but a strong cup of tea soon freshened him up, and, taking his book, he went out for his morning walk, bringing with him a few sandwiches lest he should not care to return till dinner time. He found a quiet walk between high elms some way outside the town, and here he spent the greater part of the day studying his Laplace. On his return he looked in to see Mrs. Witham and to thank her for her kindness. When she saw him coming through the diamond-paned bay window of her sanctum she came out to meet him and asked him in. She looked at him searchingly and shook her head as she said:

"You must not overdo it, sir. You are paler this morning than you should be. Too late hours and too hard work on the brain isn't good for any man! But tell me, sir, how did you pass the night? Well, I hope? But, my heart! sir, I was glad when Mrs. Dempster told me this morning that you were all right and sleeping sound when she went in."

"Oh, I was all right," he answered, smiling. "The 'some-things' didn't worry me, as yet. Only the rats; and they had a circus, I tell you, all over the place. There was one wicked-looking old devil that sat up on my own chair by the fire, and wouldn't go till I took the poker to him, and then he ran up the rope of the alarm bell and got to somewhere up the wall or the ceiling—I couldn't see where, it was so dark."

"Mercy on us," said Mrs. Witham, "an old devil, and sitting on a chair by the fireside! Take care, sir! take care! There's many a true word spoken in jest."

"How do you mean? 'Pon my word I don't understand."

"An old devil! The old devil, perhaps. There! sir, you needn't laugh," for Malcolmson had broken into a hearty peal. "You young folks thinks it easy to laugh at things that makes older ones shudder. Never mind, sir! never mind! Please God, you'll laugh all the time. It's what I wish you myself!" And the good lady beamed all over in sympathy with his enjoyment, her fears gone for a moment.

"Oh, forgive me!" said Malcolmson presently. "Don't think me rude; but the idea was too much for me—that the old devil himself was on the chair last night!" And at the thought he laughed again. Then he went home to dinner.

This evening the scampering of the rats began earlier; indeed it had been going on before his arrival, and only ceased while his presence by its freshness disturbed them. After dinner he sat by the fire for a while and had a smoke; and then, having cleared his table, began to work as before. Tonight the rats disturbed him more than they had done on the previous night. How they scampered up and down and under and over! How they squeaked, and scratched, and gnawed! How they, getting bolder by degrees, came to the mouths of their holes and to the chinks and cracks and crannies in the wainscoting till their eyes shone like tiny lamps as the firelight rose and fell. But to him, now doubtless accustomed to them, their eyes were not wicked; only their playfulness touched him. Sometimes the boldest of them made sallies out on the floor or along the moldings of the wainscot. Now and again as they disturbed him Malcolmson made a sound to frighten them, smiting the table with his hand or giving a fierce "Hsh, hssh," so that they fled straightway to their holes.

And so the early part of the night wore on; and despite the noise Malcolmson got more and more immersed in his work.

All at once he stopped, as on the previous night, being overcome by a sudden sense of silence. There was not the faintest sound of gnaw, or scratch, or squeak. The silence was as of the grave. He remembered the odd occurrence of the previous night, and instinctively he looked at the chair standing close by the fireside. And then a very odd sensation thrilled through him.

There, on the great old high-backed carved oak chair beside the fireplace sat the same enormous rat, steadily glaring at him with baleful eyes.

Instinctively he took the nearest thing to his hand, a book of logarithms, and flung it at it. The book was badly aimed and the rat did not stir, so again the poker performance of the previous night was repeated; and again the rat, being closely pursued, fled up the rope of the alarm bell. Strangely too, the departure of this rat was instantly followed by the renewal of the noise made by the general rat community. On this occasion, as on the previous one, Malcolmson could not see at what part of the room the rat disappeared, for the green shade of his lamp left the upper part of the room in darkness, and the fire had burned low.

On looking at his watch he found it was close on midnight; and, not sorry for the *divertissement,* he made up his fire and made himself his nightly pot of tea. He had got through a good spell of work, and thought himself entitled to a cigarette; and so he sat on the great carved oak chair before the fire and enjoyed it. While smoking he began to think that he would like to know where the rat disappeared to, for he had certain ideas for the morrow not entirely disconnected with a rat trap. Accordingly he lit another lamp and placed it so that it would shine well into the right-hand corner of the wall by the fireplace. Then he got all the books he had with him, and placed them handy to throw at the vermin. Finally he lifted the rope of the alarm bell and placed the end of it on the table, fixing the extreme end under the lamp. As he handled it he could not help noticing how pliable it was, especially for so strong a rope, and one not in use. "You could hang a man with it," he thought to himself. When his preparations were made he looked around, and said complacently:

"There now, my friend, I think we shall learn something of you this time!" He began his work again, and though as before somewhat disturbed at first by the noise of the rats, soon lost himself in his propositions and problems.

Again he was called to his immediate surroundings suddenly. This time it might not have been the sudden silence only which took his attention; there was a slight movement of the rope, and the lamp moved. Without stirring, he looked to see if his pile of books was within range, and then cast his eye along the rope. As he looked he saw the great rat drop from the rope on the oak armchair and sit there glaring at him. He raised a book in his right hand, and taking careful aim, flung it at the rat. The latter, with a quick movement, sprang aside and dodged the missile. He then took another book, and a third, and flung them one after another at the rat, but each time unsuccessfully. At last, as he stood with a book poised in his hand to throw, the rat squeaked and seemed afraid. This made Malcolmson more than ever eager to strike, and the book flew and struck the rat a resounding blow. It gave a terrified squeak, and turning on his pursuer a look of terrible malevolence, ran up the chair back and made a great jump to the rope of the alarm bell and ran up it like lightning. The lamp rocked under the sudden strain, but it was a heavy one and did not topple over. Malcolmson kept his eyes on the rat, and saw it by the light of the second lamp leap to a molding of the wainscot and disappear through a hole in one of the great pictures which hung on the wall, obscured and invisible through its coating of dirt and dust.

"I shall look up my friend's habitation in the morning,"

said the student, as he went over to collect his books. The third picture from the fireplace; I shall not forget." He picked up the books one by one, commenting on them as he lifted them. *"Conic Sections* he does not mind, nor *Cycloidal Oscillations,* nor the *Principia,* nor *Quaternions,* nor *Thermodynamics.* Now for the book that fetched him!" Malcolmson took it up and looked at it. As he did so he started, and a sudden pallor overspread his face. He looked round uneasily and shivered slightly, as he murmured to himself:

"The Bible my mother gave me! What an odd coincidence." He sat down to work again, and the rats in the wainscot renewed their gambols. They did not disturb him, however; somehow their presence gave him a sense of companionship. But he could not attend to his work, and after striving to master the subject on which he was engaged gave it up in despair, and went to bed as the first streak of dawn stole in through the eastern window.

He slept heavily but uneasily, and dreamed much; and when Mrs. Dempster woke him late in the morning he seemed ill at ease, and for a few minutes did not seem to realize exactly where he was. His first request rather surprised the servant.

"Mrs. Dempster, when I am out today I wish you would get the steps and dust or wash those pictures—especially that one the third from the fireplace—I want to see what they are."

Late in the afternoon Malcolmson worked at his books in the shaded walk, and the cheerfulness of the previous day came back to him as the day wore on, and he found that his reading was progressing well. He had worked out to a satisfactory conclusion all the problems which had as yet baffled him, and it was in a state of jubilation that he paid a visit to Mrs. Witham at The Good Traveller. He found a stranger in the cozy sitting room with the landlady who was introduced to him as Dr. Thornhill. She was not quite at ease, and this, combined with the doctor's plunging at once into a series of questions, made Malcolmson come to the conclusion that his presence was not an accident, so without preliminary he said:

"Dr. Thornhill, I shall with pleasure answer you any question you may choose to ask me if you will answer me one question first."

The doctor seemed surprised, but he smiled and answered at once, "Done! What is it?"

"Did Mrs. Witham ask you to come here and see me and advise me?"

Dr. Thornhill for a moment was taken aback, and Mrs. Witham got fiery red and turned away; but the doctor was a frank and ready man, and he answered at once and openly:

"She did: but she didn't intend you to know it. I suppose it was my clumsy haste that made you suspect. She told me that she did not like the idea of your being in that house all by yourself and that she thought you took too much strong tea. In fact, she wants me to advise you if possible to give up the tea and the very late hours. I was a keen student in my time, so I suppose I may take the liberty of a college man and, without offense, advise you not quite as a stranger."

Malcolmson with a bright smile held out his hand. "Shake! as they say in America," he said. "I must thank you for your kindness and Mrs. Witham too, and your kindness deserves a return on my part. I promise to take no more strong tea—no tea at all till you let me—and I shall go to bed tonight at one o'clock at latest. Will that do?"

"Capital," said the doctor. "Now tell us all that you noticed in the old house," and so Malcolmson then and there told in minute detail all that had happened in the last two nights. He was interrupted every now and then by some exclamation from Mrs. Witham, till finally when he told of the episode of the Bible the landlady's pent-up emotions found vent in a shriek; and it was not till a stiff glass of brandy and water had been administered that she grew composed again. Dr. Thornhill listened with a face of growing gravity, and when the narrative was complete and Mrs. Witham had been restored he asked:

"The rat always went up the rope of the alarm bell?"

"Always."

"I suppose you know," said the doctor after a pause, "what the rope is?"

"No!"

"It is," said the doctor slowly, "the very rope which the hangman used for all the victims of the Judge's judicial rancor!" Here he was interrupted by another scream from Mrs. Witham, and steps had to be taken for her recovery. Malcolmson having looked at his watch, and found that it was close to his dinner hour, had gone home before her complete recovery.

When Mrs. Witham was herself again she almost assailed the doctor with angry questions as to what he meant by putting such horrible ideas into the poor young man's mind. "He has quite enough there already to upset him," she added. Dr. Thornhill replied:

"My dear madam, I had a distinct purpose in it! I wanted to draw his attention to the bell rope, and to fix it there. It may be that he is in a highly overwrought state, and has been studying too much, although I am bound to say that he seems as sound and healthy a young man, mentally and bodily, as ever I saw—but then the rats—and that suggestion of the devil." The doctor shook his head and went on. "I would have offered to go and stay the first night with him but that I felt sure it would have been a cause of offense. He may get in the night some strange fright or hallucination; and if he does I want him to pull that rope. All alone as he is it will give us warning, and we may reach him in time to be of service. I shall be sitting up pretty late tonight and shall keep my ears open. Do not be alarmed if Benchurch gets a surprise before morning."

"Oh, Doctor, what do you mean? What do you mean?"

"I mean this; that possibly—nay, more probably—we shall hear the great alarm bell from the Judge's House tonight," and the doctor made about as effective an exit as could be thought of.

When Malcolmson arrived home he found that it was a little after his usual time, and Mrs. Dempster had gone away—the rules of Greenhow's Charity were not to be neglected. He was glad to see that the place was bright and tidy with a cheerful fire and a well-trimmed lamp. The evening was colder than might have been expected in April, and a heavy wind was blowing with such rapidly increasing strength that there was every promise of a storm during the night. For a few minutes after his entrance the noise of the rats ceased; but so soon as they became accustomed to his presence they began again. He was glad to hear them, for he felt once more the feeling of companionship in their noise, and his mind ran back to the strange fact that they only ceased to manifest themselves when that other—the great rat with the baleful eyes—came upon the scene. The reading lamp only was lit and its green shade kept the ceiling and the upper part of the room in darkness, so that the cheerful light from the hearth spreading over the floor and shining on the white cloth laid over the end of the table was warm and cheery. Malcolmson sat down to his dinner with a good appetite and a buoyant spirit. After his dinner and a cigarette he sat steadily down to work, determined not to let anything disturb him, for he remembered his promise to the doctor, and made up his mind to make the best of the time at his disposal.

For an hour or so he worked all right, and then his thoughts began to wander from his books. The actual circumstances around him, the calls on his physical attention, and his nervous susceptibility were not to be denied. By this time the wind had become a gale, and the gale a storm. The old house, solid though it was, seemed to shake to its foundations, and the storm roared and raged through its many chimneys and its queer old gables, producing strange, unearthly sounds in the empty rooms and corridors. Even the great alarm bell on the roof must have felt the force of the wind, for the rope rose and fell slightly, as though the bell were moved a little from time to time, and the limber rope fell on the oak floor with a hard and hollow sound.

As Malcolmson listened to it he bethought himself of the doctor's words, "It is the rope which the hangman used for the victims of the Judge's judicial rancor," and he went over to the corner of the fireplace and took it in his hand to look at it. There seemed a sort of deadly interest in it, and as he stood there he lost himself for a moment in speculation as to who these victims were, and the grim wish of the Judge to have such a ghastly relic ever under his eyes. As he stood there the swaying of the bell on the roof still lifted the rope now and again; but presently there came a new sensation—a sort of tremor in the rope, as though something was moving along it.

Looking up instinctively Malcolmson saw the great rat coming slowly down towards him, glaring at him steadily. He dropped the rope and started back with a muttered curse, and the rat turning ran up the rope again and disappeared, and at the same instant Malcolmson became conscious that the noise of the rats, which had ceased for a while, began again.

All this set him thinking, and it occurred to him that he had not investigated the lair of the rat or looked at the pictures, as he had intended. He lit the other lamp without the shade, and, holding it up, went and stood opposite the third picture from the fireplace on the right-hand side where he had seen the rat disappear on the previous night.

At the first glance he started back so suddenly that he almost dropped the lamp, and a deadly pallor overspread his face. His knees shook, and heavy drops of sweat came on his forehead, and he trembled like an aspen. But he was young and plucky, and pulled himself together, and after the pause of a few seconds stepped forward again, raised the lamp, and examined the picture which had been dusted and washed, and now stood out clearly.

It was of a judge dressed in his robes of scarlet and ermine. His face was strong and merciless, evil, crafty, and vindictive, with a sensual mouth, hooked nose of ruddy color, and shaped like the beak of a bird of prey. The rest of the face was of a cadaverous color. The eyes were of peculiar brilliance and with a terribly malignant expression. As he looked at them, Malcolmson grew cold, for he saw there the very counterpart of the eyes of the great rat. The lamp almost fell from his hand, he saw the rat with its baleful eyes peering out through the hole in the corner of the picture, and noted the sudden cessation of the noise of the other rats. However, he pulled himself together, and went on with his examination of the picture.

The Judge was seated in a great high-backed carved oak chair, on the right-hand side of a great stone fireplace where, in the corner, a rope hung down from the ceiling, its end lying coiled on the floor. With a feeling of something like horror, Malcolmson recognized the scene of the room as it stood, and gazed around him in an awestruck manner as though he expected to find some strange presence behind him. Then he looked over to the corner of the fireplace—and with a loud cry he let the lamp fall from his hand.

There, in the judge's armchair, with the rope hanging behind, sat the rat with the Judge's baleful eyes, now intensified and with a fiendish leer. Save for the howling of the storm without there was silence.

The fallen lamp recalled Malcolmson to himself. Fortunately it was of metal, and so the oil was not spilt. However, the practical need of attending to it settled at once his nervous apprehensions. When he had turned it out, he wiped his brow and thought for a moment.

"This will not do," he said to himself. "If I go on like this I shall become a crazy fool. This must stop! I promised the doctor I would not take tea. Faith, he was pretty right! My nerves must have been getting into a queer state. Funny I did not notice it. I never felt better in my life. However, it is all right now, and I shall not be such a fool again."

Then he mixed himself a good stiff glass of brandy and water and resolutely sat down to his work.

It was nearly an hour when he looked up from his book, disturbed by the sudden stillness. Without, the wind howled and roared louder than ever, and the rain drove in sheets against the windows, beating like hail on the glass; but within

163

there was no sound whatever save the echo of the wind as it roared in the great chimney, and now and then a hiss as a few raindrops found their way down the chimney in a lull of the storm. The fire had fallen low and had ceased to flame, though it threw out a red glow. Malcolmson listened attentively, and presently heard a thin, squeaking noise, very faint. It came from the corner of the room where the rope hung down, and he thought it was the creaking of the rope on the floor as the swaying of the bell raised and lowered it. Looking up, however, he saw in the dim light the great rat clinging to the rope and gnawing it. The rope was already nearly gnawed through—he could see the lighter color where the strands were laid bare. As he looked the job was completed, and the severed end of the rope fell clattering on the oaken floor, while for an instant the great rat remained like a knob or tassel at the end of the rope, which now began to sway to and fro. Malcolmson felt for a moment another pang of terror as he thought that now the possibility of calling the outer world to his assistance was cut off, but an intense anger took its place, and seizing the book he was reading he hurled it at the rat. The blow was well aimed, but before the missile could reach him the rat dropped off and struck the floor with a soft thud. Malcolmson instantly rushed over towards him, but it darted away and disappeared in the darkness of the shadows of the room. Malcolmson felt that his work was over for the night, and determined then and there to vary the monotony of the proceedings by a hunt for the rat, and took off the green shade of the lamp so as to insure a wider spreading light. As he did so the gloom of the upper part of the room was relieved, and in the new flood of light, great by comparison with the previous darkness, the pictures on the wall stood out boldly. From where he stood, Malcolmson saw right opposite to him the third picture on the wall from the right of the fireplace. He rubbed his eyes in surprise, and then a great fear began to come upon him.

In the center of the picture was a great irregular patch of brown canvas, as fresh as when it was stretched on the frame. The background was as before, with chair and chimney corner and rope, but the figure of the Judge had disappeared.

Malcolmson, almost in a chill of horror, turned slowly round, and then he began to shake and tremble like a man in a palsy. His strength seemed to have left him, and he was incapable of action or movement, hardly even of thought. He could only see and hear.

There, on the great high-backed carved oak chair sat the Judge in his robes of scarlet and ermine, with his baleful eyes glaring vindictively, and a smile of triumph on the resolute, cruel mouth, as he lifted with his hands a *black cap*. Malcolmson felt as if the blood was running from his heart, as one does in moments of prolonged suspense. There was a singing in his ears. Without, he could hear the roar and howl of the tempest, and through it, swept on the storm, came the striking of midnight by the great chimes in the market place. He stood for a space of time that seemed to him endless, still as a statue, and with wide-open, horror-struck eyes, breathless. As the clock struck, so the smile of triumph on the Judge's face intensified, and at the last stroke of midnight he placed the black cap on his head.

Slowly and deliberately the Judge rose from his chair and picked up the piece of the rope of the alarm bell which lay on the floor, drew it through his hands as if he enjoyed its touch, and then deliberately began to knot one end of it, fashioning it into a noose. This he tightened and tested with his foot, pulling hard at it till he was satisfied and then making a running noose of it, which he held in his hand. Then he began to move along the table on the opposite side to Malcolmson, keeping his eyes on him until he had passed him, when with a quick movement he stood in front of the door. Malcolmson then began to feel that he was trapped, and tried to think of what he should do. There was some fascination in the Judge's eyes, which he never took off him, and he had perforce to look. He saw the Judge approach— still keeping between him and the door—and raise the noose and throw it towards him as if to entangle him. With a great effort he made a quick movement to one side, and saw the rope fall beside him, and heard it strike the oaken floor. Again the Judge raised the noose and tried to ensnare him, ever keeping his baleful eyes fixed on him, and each time by a mighty effort the student just managed to evade it. So this went on for many times, the Judge seeming never discouraged nor discomposed at failure, but playing as a cat does with a mouse. At last in despair, which had reached its climax, Malcolmson cast a quick glance round him. The lamp seemed to have blazed up, and there was a fairly good light in the room. At the many rat holes and in the chinks and crannies of the wainscot he saw the rats' eyes; and this aspect, that was purely physical, gave him a gleam of comfort. He looked around and saw that the rope of the great alarm bell was laden with rats. Every inch of it was covered with them, and more and more were pouring through the small circular hole in the ceiling whence it emerged, so that with their weight the bell was beginning to sway.

Hark! it had swayed till the clapper had touched the bell. The sound was but a tiny one, but the bell was only beginning to sway, and it would increase.

At the sound the Judge, who had been keeping his eyes fixed on Malcolmson, looked up, and a scowl of diabolical anger overspread his face. His eyes fairly glowed like hot coals, and he stamped his foot with a sound that seemed to make the house shake. A dreadful peal of thunder broke overhead as he raised the rope again, while the rats kept running up and down the rope as though working against time. This time, instead of throwing it, he drew close to his victim, and held open the noose as he approached. As he came closer there seemed something paralyzing in his very presence, and Malcolmson stood rigid as a corpse. He felt the Judge's icy fingers touch his throat as he adjusted the rope. The noose tightened—tightened. Then the Judge, taking the rigid form of the student in his arms, carried him over and placed him standing in the oak chair, and stepping up beside him, put his hand up and caught the end of the swaying rope of the alarm bell. As he raised his hand the rats fled squeaking, and disappeared through the hole in the ceiling. Taking the end of the noose which was round Malcolmson's neck he tied it to the hanging-bell rope, and then descending pulled away the chair.

When the alarm bell of the Judge's House began to sound a crowd soon assembled. Lights and torches of various kinds appeared, and soon a silent crowd was hurrying to the spot. They knocked loudly at the door, but there was no reply. Then they burst in the door, and poured into the great dining room, the doctor at the head.

There at the end of the rope of the great alarm bell hung the body of the student, and on the face of the Judge in the picture was a malignant smile.

The Kill

by Peter Fleming

In the cold waiting room of a small railway station in the west of England two men were sitting. They had sat there for an hour, and were likely to sit there longer. There was a thick fog outside. Their train was indefinitely delayed.

The waiting room was a barren and unfriendly place. A naked electric bulb lit it with wan, disdainful efficiency. A notice, NO SMOKING, stood on the mantelpiece; when you turned it round, it said NO SMOKING on the other side, too. Printed regulations relating to an outbreak of swine fever in 1924 were pinned neatly to one wall, almost, but maddeningly not quite, in the center of it. The stove gave out a hot, thick smell, powerful already but increasing. A pale leprous flush on the black and beaded window showed that a light was burning on the platform outside, in the fog. Somewhere water dripped with infinite reluctance onto corrugated iron.

The two men sat facing each other over the stove on chairs of an unswerving woodenness. Their acquaintance was no older than their vigil. From such talk as they had had, it seemed likely that they were to remain strangers.

The younger of the two resented the lack of contact in their relationship more than the lack of comfort in their surroundings. His attitude towards his fellow beings had but recently undergone a transition from the subjective to the objective. As with many of his class and age, the routine, unrecognized as such, of an expensive education, with the triennial alternative of those delights normal to wealth and gentility, had atrophied many of his curiosities. For the first twenty-odd years of his life he had read humanity in terms of relevance rather than reality, looking on people who held no ordained place in his own existence much as a buck in a park watches visitors walking up the drive: mildly, rather resentfully inquiring—not inquisitive. Now, hot in reaction from this unconscious provincialism, he treated mankind as a museum, gaping conscientiously at each fresh exhibit, hunting for the noncumulative evidence of man's complexity with

167

indiscriminate zeal. To each magic circle of individuality he saw himself as a kind of free-lance tangent. He aspired to be a connoisseur of men.

There was undoubtedly something arresting about the specimen before him. Of less than medium height, the stranger had yet that sort of ranging leanness that lends vicarious inches. He wore a long black overcoat, very shabby, and his shoes were covered with mud. His face had no color in it, though the impression it produced was not one of pallor; the skin was of a dark sallow, tinged with gray. The nose was pointed, the jaw sharp and narrow. Deep vertical wrinkles, running down towards it from the high cheekbones, sketched the permanent groundwork of a broader smile than the deep-set honey-colored eyes seemed likely to authorize. The most striking thing about the face was the incongruity of its frame. On the back of his head the stranger wore a bowler hat with a very narrow brim. No word of such casual implications as a tilt did justice to its angle. It was clamped, by something at least as holy as custom, to the back of his skull, and that thin, questing face confronted the world fiercely from under a black halo of nonchalance. The man's whole appearance suggested *difference* rather than aloofness. The unnatural way he wore his hat had the significance of indirect comment, like the antics of a performing animal. It was as if he was part of some older thing, of which *Homo sapiens* in a bowler hat was an expurgated edition. He sat with his shoulders hunched and his hands thrust into his overcoat pockets. The hint of discomfort in his attitude seemed due not so much to the fact that his chair was hard as to the fact that it was a chair.

The young man had found him uncommunicative. The most mobile sympathy, launching consecutive attacks on different fronts, had failed to draw him out. The reserved adequacy of his replies conveyed a rebuff more effectively than sheer surliness. Except to answer him, he did not look at the young man. When he did, his eyes were full of an abstracted amusement. Sometimes he smiled, but for no immediate cause.

Looking back down their hour together, the young man saw a field of endeavor on which frustrated banalities lay thick, like the discards of a routed army. But resolution, curiosity, and the need to kill time all clamored against an admission of defeat.

"If he will not talk," thought the young man, "then I will. The sound of my own voice is infinitely preferable to the sound of none. I will tell him what has just happened to me. It is really a most extraordinary story. I will tell it as well as I can, and I shall be very much surprised if its impact on his mind does not shock this man into some form of self-revelation. He is unaccountable without being *outré*, and I am inordinately curious about him."

Aloud he said, in a brisk and engaging manner: "I think you said you were a hunting man?"

The other raised his quick, honey-colored eyes. They gleamed with inaccessible amusement. Without answering, he lowered them again to contemplate the little beads of light thrown through the ironwork of the stove onto the skirts of his overcoat. Then he spoke. He had a husky voice.

"I came here to hunt," he agreed.

"In that case," said the young man, "you will have heard of Lord Fleer's private pack. Their kennels are not far from here."

"I know them," replied the other.

"I have just been staying there," the young man continued. "Lord Fleer is my uncle."

The other looked up, smiled, and nodded, with the bland inconsequence of a foreigner who does not understand what is being said to him. The young man swallowed his impatience.

"Would you," he continued, using a slightly more peremptory tone than heretofore, "would you care to hear a new and rather remarkable story about my uncle? Its dénouement is not two days old. It is quite short."

From the vastness of some hidden joke, those light eyes mocked the necessity of a definite answer. At length: "Yes," said the stranger, "I would." The impersonality in his voice might have passed for a parade of sophistication, a reluctance to betray interest. But the eyes hinted that interest was alive elsewhere.

"Very well," said the young man.

Drawing his chair a little closer to the stove, he began:

As perhaps you know, my uncle, Lord Fleer, leads a retired, though by no means an inactive life. For the last two or three hundred years, the currents of contemporary thought have passed mainly through the hands of men whose gregarious instincts have been constantly awakened and almost invariably indulged. By the standards of the eighteenth century, when Englishmen first became self-conscious about solitude, my uncle would have been considered unsociable. In the early nineteenth century, those not personally acquainted with him would have thought him romantic. Today, his attitude towards the sound and fury of modern life is too negative to excite comment as an oddity; yet even now, were he to be involved in any occurrence which could be called disastrous or interpreted as discreditable, the press would pillory him as a "Titled Recluse."

The truth of the matter is, my uncle has discovered the elixer, or, if you prefer it, the opiate, of self-sufficiency. A man of extremely simple tastes, not cursed with overmuch imagination, he sees no reason to cross frontiers of habit which the years have hallowed into rigidity. He lives in his castle (it may be described as commodious rather than comfortable), runs his estate at a slight profit, shoots a little, rides a great deal, and hunts as often as he can. He never sees his neighbors except by accident, thereby leading them to suppose, with sublime but unconscious arrogance, that he must be slightly mad. If he is, he can at least claim to have padded his own cell.

My uncle has never married. As the only son of his only brother, I was brought up in the expectation of being his heir. During the war, however, an unforeseen development occurred.

In this national crisis my uncle, who was of course too old for active service, showed a lack of public spirit which earned him locally a good deal of unpopularity. Briefly, he declined to recognize the war, or, if he did recognize it, gave no sign of having done so. He continued to lead his own vigorous but (in the circumstances) rather irrelevant life. Though he found himself at last obliged to recruit his hunt servants from men of advanced age and uncertain mettle in any crisis of the chase, he contrived to mount them well, and twice a week during the season himself rode two horses to a standstill after the hill foxes which, as no doubt you know, provide the best sport the Fleer country has to offer.

When the local gentry came and made representations to him, saying that it was time he did something for his country besides destroying its vermin by the most unreliable and expensive method ever devised, my uncle was very sensible. He now saw, he said, that he had been standing too aloof from a struggle of whose progress (since he never read the paper) he had been only indirectly aware. The next day he wrote to London and ordered *The Times* and a Belgian refugee. It was the least he could do, he said. I think he was right.

The Belgian refugee turned out to be a female, and dumb. Whether one or both of these characteristics had been stipulated for by my uncle, nobody knew. At any rate, she took up her quarters at Fleer: a heavy, unattractive girl of twenty-five, with a shiny face and small black hairs on the backs of her hands. Her life appeared to be modeled on that of the larger ruminants, except, of course, that the greater part of it took place indoors. She ate a great deal, slept with a will, and had a bath every Sunday, remitting this salubrious custom only when the housekeeper, who enforced it, was away on her holiday. Much of her time she spent sitting on a sofa, on the landing outside her bedroom, with Prescott's *Conquest of Mexico* open on her lap. She read either exceptionally slowly or not at all, for to my knowledge she carried the first volume about with her for eleven years. Hers, I think, was the contemplative type of mind.

The curious, and from my point of view the unfortunate, aspect of my uncle's patriotic gesture was the gradually increasing affection with which he came to regard this unlovable creature. Although, or more probably because, he saw her only at meals, when her features were rather more animated than at other times, his attitude towards her passed from the detached to the courteous, and from the courteous to the paternal. At the end of the war there was no question of her return to Belgium, and one day in 1919 I heard with pardonable mortification that my uncle had legally adopted her, and was altering his will in her favor.

Time, however, reconciled me to being disinherited by a being who, between meals, could scarcely be described as sentient. I continued to pay an annual visit to Fleer, and to ride with my uncle after his big-boned Welsh hounds over the sullen, dark-gray hill country in which—since its possession was no longer assured to me—I now began to see a powerful, though elusive, beauty.

I came down here three days ago, intending to stay for a week. I found my uncle, who is a tall, fine-looking man with a beard, in his usual unassailable good health. The Belgian, as always, gave me the impression of being impervious to disease, to emotion, or indeed to anything short of an act of God. She had been putting on weight since she came to live with my uncle, and was now a very considerable figure of a woman, though not, as yet, unwieldy.

It was at dinner, on the evening of my arrival, that I first noticed a certain *malaise* behind my uncle's brusque, laconic manner. There was evidently something on his mind. After dinner he asked me to come into his study. I detected, in the delivery of the invitation, the first hint of embarrassment I had known him to betray.

The walls of the study were hung with maps and the extremities of foxes. The room was littered with bills, catalogues, old gloves, fossils, rat-traps, cartridges, and feathers which had been used to clean his pipe—a stale diversity of jetsam which somehow managed to produce an impression of relevance and continuity, like the debris in an animal's lair. I had never been in the study before.

"Paul," said my uncle as soon as I had shut the door, "I am very much disturbed."

I assumed an air of sympathetic inquiry.

"Yesterday," my uncle went on, "one of my tenants came to see me. He is a decent man, who farms a strip of land outside the park wall to the northward. He said that he had lost two sheep in a manner for which he was wholly unable to account. He said he thought they had been killed by some wild animal."

My uncle paused. The gravity of his manner was really portentous.

"Dogs?" I suggested, with the slightly patronizing diffidence of one who has probability on his side.

My uncle shook his head judiciously. "This man had often seen sheep which had been killed by dogs. He said that they were always badly torn—nipped about the legs, driven into a corner, worried to death; it was never a clean piece of work. These two sheep had not been killed like that. I went down to see them for myself. Their throats had been torn out. They were not bitten or nuzzled. They had both died in the open, not in a corner. Whatever did it was an animal more powerful and more cunning than a dog."

I said, "It couldn't have been something that had escaped from a traveling menagerie, I suppose?"

"They don't come into this part of the country," replied my uncle; "there are no fairs."

We were both silent for a moment. It was hard not to show more curiosity than sympathy as I waited on some further revelation to stake out my uncle's claim on the latter emotion. I could put no interpretation on those two dead sheep wild enough to account for his evident distress.

He spoke again, but with obvious reluctance.

"Another was killed early this morning," he said in a low voice, "on the Home Farm. In the same way."

For lack of any better comment, I suggested beating the nearby coverts. There might be some——

"We've scoured the woods," interrupted my uncle brusquely.

"And found nothing?"

"Nothing . . . . Except some tracks."

"What sort of tracks?"

My uncle's eyes were suddenly evasive. He turned his head away.

"They were a man's tracks," he said slowly. A log fell over in the fireplace.

Again a silence. The interview appeared to be causing him pain rather than relief. I decided that the situation could lose nothing through the frank expression of my curiosity. Plucking up courage, I asked him roundly what cause he had to be upset? Three sheep, the property of his tenants, had died deaths which, though certainly unusual, were unlikely to remain for long mysterious. Their destroyer, whatever it was, would inevitably be caught, killed, or driven away in the course of the next few days. The loss of another sheep or two was the worst he had to fear.

When I had finished, my uncle gave me an anxious, almost a guilty look. I was suddenly aware that he had a confession to make.

"Sit down," he said. "I wish to tell you something."

This is what he told me:

A quarter of a century ago, my uncle had had occasion to engage a new housekeeper. With the blend of fatalism and sloth which is the foundation of the bachelor's attitude to the servant problem, he took on the first applicant. She was a tall, black, slant-eyed woman from the Welsh border, aged about thirty. My uncle said nothing about her character, but described her as having "powers." When she had been at Fleer some months, my uncle began to notice her, instead of taking her for granted. She was not averse to being noticed.

One day she came and told my uncle that she was with child by him. He took it calmly enough till he found that she expected him to marry her, or pretended to expect it. Then he flew into a rage, called her a whore, and told her she must leave the house as soon as the child was born. Instead of breaking down or continuing the scene, she began to croon to herself in Welsh, looking at him sideways with a certain amusement. This frightened him. He forbade her to come near him again, had her things moved into an unused wing of the castle, and engaged another housekeeper.

173

A child was born, and they came and told my uncle that the woman was going to die; she asked for him continually, they said. As much frightened as distressed, he went through passages long unfamiliar to her room. When the woman saw him, she began to gabble in a preoccupied kind of way, looking at him all the time, as if she were repeating a lesson. Then she stopped, and asked that he should be shown the child.

It was a boy. The midwife, my uncle noticed, handled it with a reluctance almost amounting to disgust.

"That is your heir," said the dying woman in a harsh, unstable voice. "I have told him what he is to do. He will be a good son to me, and jealous of his birthright." And she went off, my uncle said, into a wild yet cogent rigmarole about a curse, embodied in the child, which would fall on any whom he made his heir over the bastard's head. At last her voice trailed away, and she fell back, exhausted and staring.

As my uncle turned to go, the midwife whispered to him to look at the child's hands. Gently unclasping the podgy, futile little fists, she showed him that on each hand the third finger was longer than the second. . . .

Here I interrupted. The story had a certain queer force behind it, perhaps from its obvious effect on the teller. My uncle feared and hated the things he was saying.

"What did that mean," I asked; "the third finger longer than the second?"

"It took me a long time to discover," replied my uncle. "My own servants, when they saw I did not know, would not tell me. But at last I found out through the doctor, who had it from an old woman in the village. People born with their third finger longer than their second become werewolves. At least"—he made a perfunctory effort at amused indulgence—"that is what the common people here think."

"And what does that—what is that supposed to mean?" I, too, found myself throwing rather hasty sops to skepticism. I was growing strangely credulous.

"A werewolf," said my uncle, dabbling in improbability without self-consciousness, "is a human being who becomes, at intervals, to all intents and purposes a wolf. The transformation—or the supposed transformation—takes place at night. The werewolf kills men and animals, and is supposed to drink their blood. Its preference is for men. All through the Middle Ages, down to the seventeenth century, there were innumerable cases (especially in France) of men and women being legally tried for offenses which they had committed as animals. Like the witches, they were rarely acquitted, but, unlike the witches, they seem seldom to have been unjustly condemned." My uncle paused. "I have been reading the old books," he explained. "I wrote to a man in London who is interested in these things when I heard what was believed about the child."

"What became of the child?" I asked.

"The wife of one of my keepers took it in," said my uncle. "She was a stolid woman from the North who, I think, welcomed the opportunity to show what little store she set by the local superstitions. The boy lived with them till he was ten. Then he ran away. I had not heard of him since then till"—my uncle glanced at me almost apologetically—"till yesterday."

We sat for a moment in silence, looking at the fire. My imagination had betrayed my reason in its full surrender to the story. I had not got it in me to dispel his fears with a parade of sanity. I was a little frightened myself.

"You think it is your son, the werewolf, who is killing the sheep?" I said at length.

"Yes. For a boast: or for a warning: or perhaps out of spite, at a night's hunting wasted."

"Wasted?"

My uncle looked at me with troubled eyes.

"His business is not with sheep," he said uneasily.

For the first time I realized the implications of the Welshwoman's curse. The hunt was up. The quarry was the heir to Fleer. I was glad to have been disinherited.

"I have told Germaine not to go out after dusk," said my uncle, coming in pat on my train of thought.

The Belgian was called Germaine; her other name was Vom.

I confess I spent no very tranquil night. My uncle's story had not wholly worked in me that "suspension of disbelief" which someone speaks of as being the prime requisite of good drama. But I have a powerful imagination. Neither fatigue nor common sense could quite banish the vision of that metamorphosed malignancy ranging, with design, the black and silver silences outside my window. I found myself listening for the sound of loping footfalls on a frost-baked crust of beech leaves. . . .

Whether it was in my dream that I heard, once, the sound of howling, I do not know. But the next morning I saw, as I dressed, a man walking quickly up the drive. He looked like a shepherd. There was a dog at his heels, trotting with a noticeable lack of assurance. At breakfast my uncle told me that another sheep had been killed, almost under the noses of the watchers. His voice shook a little. Solicitude sat oddly on his features as he looked at Germaine. She was eating porridge, as if for a wager.

After breakfast we decided on a campaign. I will not weary you with the details of its launching and its failure. All day we quartered the woods with thirty men, mounted and on foot. Near the scene of the kill our dogs picked up a scent which they followed for two miles and more, only to lose it on the railway line. But the ground was too hard for tracks, and the men said it could only have been a fox or a polecat, so surely and readily did the dogs follow it.

The exercise and the occupation were good for our nerves. But late in the afternoon my uncle grew anxious; twilight was closing in swiftly under a sky heavy with clouds, and we were some distance from Fleer. He gave final instructions for the penning of the sheep by night, and we turned our horses' heads for home.

We approached the castle by the back drive, which was little used: a dank, unholy alley, running the gauntlet of a belt of firs and laurels. Beneath our horses' hooves flints chinked remotely under a thick carpet of moss. Each consecutive cloud from their nostrils hung with an air of permanency, as if bequeathed to the unmoving air.

We were perhaps three hundred yards from the tall gates leading to the stableyard when both horses stopped dead, simultaneously. Their heads were turned towards the trees on our right, beyond which, I knew, the sweep of the main drive converged on ours.

My uncle gave a short, inarticulate cry in which premonition stood aghast at the foreseen. At the same moment something howled on the other side of the trees. There was relish, and a kind of sobbing laughter, in that hateful sound. It rose and fell luxuriously, and rose and fell again, fouling the night. Then it died away, fawning on society in a throaty whimper.

The forces of silence fell unavailingly on its rear; its filthy echoes still went reeling through our heads. We were aware that feet went loping lightly down the iron-hard drive . . . two feet.

My uncle flung himself off his horse and dashed through the trees. I followed. We scrambled down a bank and out into the open. The only figure in sight was motionless.

Germaine Vom lay doubled up in the drive, a solid, black mark against the shifting values of the dusk. We ran forward. . . .

To me she had always been an improbable cipher rather than a real person. I could not help reflecting that she died, as she had lived, in the livestock tradition. Her throat had been torn out.

The young man leant back in his chair, a little dizzy from talking and from the heat of the stove. The inconvenient realities of the waiting room, forgotten in his narrative, closed in on him again. He sighed, and smiled rather apologetically at the stranger.

"It is a wild and improbable story," he said. "I do not expect you to believe the whole of it. For me, perhaps, the reality of its implications has obscured its almost ludicrous lack of verisimilitude. You see, by the death of the Belgian I am heir to Fleer."

The stranger smiled: a slow, but no longer an abstracted smile. His honey-colored eyes were bright. Under his long black overcoat his body seemed to be stretching itself in sensual anticipation. He rose silently to his feet.

The other found a sharp, cold fear drilling into his vitals. Something behind those shining eyes threatened him with appalling immediacy, like a sword at his heart. He was sweating. He dared not move.

The stranger's smile was now a grin, a ravening convulsion of the face. His eyes blazed with a hard and purposeful delight. A thread of saliva dangled from the corner of his mouth.

Very slowly he lifted one hand and removed his bowler hat. Of the fingers crooked about its brim, the young man saw that the third was longer than the second.

Mrs. Amworth

by E. F. Benson

The village of Maxley, where, last summer and autumn, these strange events took place, lies on a heathery and pine-clad upland of Sussex. In all England you could not find a sweeter and saner situation. Should the wind blow from the south, it comes laden with the spices of the sea; to the east high downs protect it from the inclemencies of March; and from the west and north the breezes which reach it travel over miles of aromatic forest and heather. The village itself is insignificant enough in point of population, but rich in amenities and beauty. Halfway down the single street, with its broad road and spacious areas of grass on each side, stands the little Norman church and the antique graveyard long disused: for the rest there are a dozen small, sedate Georgian houses, red-bricked and long-windowed, each with a square of flower garden in front, and an ampler strip behind; a score of shops, and a couple of score of thatched cottages belonging to laborers on neighboring estates, complete the entire cluster of its peaceful habitations. The general peace, however, is sadly broken on Saturdays and Sundays, for we lie on one of the main roads between London and Brighton and our quiet street becomes a racecourse for flying motorcars and bicycles. A notice just outside the village begging them to go slowly only seems to encourage them to accelerate their speed, for the road lies open and straight, and there is really no reason why they should do otherwise. By way of protest, therefore, the ladies of Maxley cover their noses and mouths with their handkerchiefs as they see a motorcar approaching, though, as the street is asphalted, they need not really take these precautions against dust. But late on Sunday night the horde of scorchers has passed, and we settle down again to five days of cheerful and leisurely seclusion. Railway strikes which agitate the country so much leave us undisturbed because most of the inhabitants of Maxley never leave it at all.

I am the fortunate possessor of one of these small Georgian houses, and consider myself no less fortunate in having so interesting and stimulating a neighbor as Francis Urcombe, who, the most confirmed of Maxleyites, has not slept away from his house, which stands just opposite to mine in the village street, for nearly two years, at which date, though still in middle life, he resigned his Physiological Professorship at Cambridge University, and devoted himself to the study of those occult and curious phenomena which seem equally to concern the physical and the psychical sides of human nature. Indeed his retirement was not unconnected with his passion for the strange uncharted places that lie on the confines and borders of science, the existence of which is so stoutly denied by the more materialistic minds, for he advocated that all medical students should be obliged to pass some sort of examination in mesmerism, and that one of the tripos papers should be designed to test their knowledge in such subject as appearances at time of death, haunted houses, vampirism, automatic writing, and possession.

"Of course they wouldn't listen to me," ran his account of the matter, "for there is nothing that these seats of learning are so frightened of as knowledge, and the road to knowledge lies in the study of things like these. The functions of the human frame are, broadly speaking, known. They are a country, anyhow, that has been charted and mapped out. But outside that lie huge tracts of undiscovered country, which certainly exist, and the real pioneers of knowledge are those who, at the cost of being derided as credulous and superstitious, want to push on into those misty and probably perilous places. I felt that I could be of more use by setting out without compass or knapsack into the mists than by sitting in a cage like a canary and chirping about what was known. Besides, teaching is very very bad for a man who knows himself only to be a learner: you only need to be a self-conceited ass to teach."

Here, then, in Francis Urcombe, was a delightful neighbor to one who, like myself, has an uneasy and burning curiosity about what he called the "misty and perilous places"; and this last spring we had a further and most welcome addition to our pleasant little community, in the person of Mrs. Amworth, widow of an Indian civil servant. Her husband had been a judge in the northwest provinces, and after his death at Peshawar she came back to England, and after a year in London found herself starving for the ampler air and sunshine of the country to take the place of the fogs and griminess of town. She had, too, a special reason for settling in Maxley, since her ancestors up till a hundred years ago had long been native to the place, and in the old churchyard, now disused, are many gravestones bearing her maiden name of Chaston. Big and energetic, her vigorous and genial personality speedily woke Maxley up to a higher degree of sociality than it had ever known. Most of us were bachelors or spinsters or elderly folk not much inclined to exert ourselves in the expense and effort of hospitality, and hitherto the gaiety of a small tea party, with bridge afterwards and galoshes (when it was wet) to trip home in again for a solitary dinner, was about the climax of our festivities. But Mrs. Amworth showed us a more gregarious way, and set an example of luncheon parties and little dinners, which we began to follow. On other nights when no such hospitality was on foot, a lone man like myself found it pleasant to know that a call on the telephone to Mrs. Amworth's house not a hundred yards off, and an enquiry as to whether I might come over after dinner for a game of piquet before bedtime, would probably evoke a response of welcome. There she would be, with a comrade-like eagerness for companionship, and there was a glass of port and a cup of coffee and a cigarette and a game of piquet. She played the piano, too, in a free and exuberant manner, and had a charming voice and sang to her own accompaniment; and as the days grew long and the light lingered late, we played our game in her garden, which in the course of a few months she had turned from being a nursery for slugs and snails into a glowing patch of luxuriant blossomings. She was always cheery and jolly; she was interested in everything; and in music, in gardening, in games of all sorts was a competent performer. Everybody (with one exception) liked her, everybody felt her to bring with her the tonic of a sunny day. That one exception was Francis Urcombe; he, though he confessed he did not like her, acknowledged that he was vastly interested in her. This always seemed strange to me, for pleasant and jovial as she was, I could see nothing in her that could call forth conjecture or intrigued surmise, so healthy and unmysterious a figure did she present. But of the genuineness of Urcombe's interest there could be no doubt; one could see him watching and scrutinizing her. In matter of age, she frankly volunteered the information that she was forty-five; but her briskness, her activity, her unravaged skin, her coal-black hair, made it difficult to believe that she was not adopting an unusual device, and adding ten years on to her age instead of subtracting them.

Often, also, as our quite unsentimental friendship ripened, Mrs. Amworth would ring me up and propose her advent. If I was busy writing, I was to give her, so we definitely bargained, a frank negative, and in answer I could hear her jolly laugh and her wishes for a successful evening of work. Sometimes, before her proposal arrived, Urcombe would already have stepped across from his house opposite for a smoke and a chat, and he, hearing who my intended visitor was, always urged me to beg her to come. She and I should play our piquet, said he, and he would look on, if we did not object, and learn something of the game. But I doubt whether he paid much attention to it, for nothing could be clearer than that, under that penthouse of forehead and thick eyebrows, his attention was fixed not on the cards, but on one of the players. But he seemed to enjoy an hour spent thus, and often, until one particular evening in July, he would watch her with the air of a man who has some deep problem in front of him. She, enthusiastically keen about our game, seemed not to notice his scrutiny. Then came that evening when, as I see in the light of subsequent events, began the first twitching of the veil that hid the secret horror from my eyes. I did not know it then, though I noticed that thereafter, if she rang up to propose coming round, she always asked not only if I was at leisure, but whether Mr. Urcombe was with me. If so, she said, she would not spoil the chat of two old bachelors, and laughingly wished me good night. Urcombe, on this occasion, had been with me for some half hour before Mrs. Amworth's appearance, and had been talking to me about the medieval beliefs concerning vampirism, one of those borderland subjects which he declared had not been sufficiently studied before it had been consigned by the medical profession to the dustheap of exploded superstitions. There he sat, grim and eager, tracing with that pellucid clearness which had made him in his Cambridge days so admirable a lecturer, the history of those mysterious visitations. In them all there were the same general features: one of those ghoulish spirits took up its abode in a living man or woman, conferring supernatural powers of batlike flight and glutting itself with nocturnal blood-feasts. When its host died it continued to dwell in the corpse, which remained undecayed. By day it rested, by night it left the grave and went on its awful errands. No European country in the Middle Ages seemed to have escaped them; earlier yet, parallels were to be found in Roman and Greek and in Jewish history.

"It's a large order to set all that evidence aside as being moonshine," he said. "Hundreds of totally independent witnesses in many ages have testified to the occurrence of these phenomena, and there's no explanation known to me which covers all the facts. And if you feel inclined to say 'Why, then, if these are facts, do we not come across them now?' there are two answers I can make you. One is that there were diseases known in the Middle Ages, such as the black death, which were certainly existent then and which have become extinct since, but for that reason we do not assert that such diseases never existed. Just as the black death visited England and decimated the population of Norfolk, so here in this very district about three hundred years ago there was certainly an outbreak of vampirism, and Maxley was the center of it. My second answer is even more convincing, for I tell you that vampirism is by no means extinct now. An outbreak of it certainly occurred in India a year or two ago."

At that moment I heard my knocker plied in the cheerful and peremptory manner in which Mrs. Amworth is accustomed to announce her arrival, and I went to the door to open it.

"Come in at once," I said, "and save me from having my blood curdled. Mr. Urcombe has been trying to alarm me."

Instantly her vital, voluminous presence seemed to fill the room.

"Ah, but how lovely!" she said. "I delight in having my blood curdled. Go on with your ghost story, Mr. Urcombe. I adore ghost stories."

I saw that, as his habit was, he was intently observing her.

"It wasn't a ghost story exactly," said he. "I was only telling our host how vampirism was not extinct yet. I was saying that there was an outbreak of it in India only a few years ago."

There was a more than perceptible pause, and I saw that, if Urcombe was observing her, she on her side was observing him with fixed eye and parted mouth. Then her jolly laugh invaded that rather tense silence.

"Oh, what a shame!" she said. "You're not going to curdle my blood at all. Where did you pick up such a tale, Mr. Urcombe? I have lived for years in India and never heard a rumor of such a thing. Some storyteller in the bazaars must have invented it: they are famous at that."

I could see that Urcombe was on the point of saying something further, but checked himself.

"Ah! very likely that was it," he said.

But something had disturbed our usual peaceful sociability that night, and something had damped Mrs. Amworth's usual high spirits. She had no gusto for her piquet, and left after a couple of games. Urcombe had been silent too, indeed he hardly spoke again till she departed.

"That was unfortunate," he said, "for the outbreak of—of a very mysterious disease, let us call it, took place at Peshawar where she and her husband were. And——"

"Well?" I asked.

"He was one of the victims of it," said he. "Naturally I had quite forgotten that when I spoke."

The summer was unreasonably hot and rainless, and Maxley suffered much from drought, and also from a plague of big black night-flying gnats, the bite of which was very irritating and virulent. They came sailing in of an evening, settling on one's skin so quietly that one perceived nothing till the sharp stab announced that one had been bitten. They did not bite the hands or face, but chose always the neck and throat for their feeding-ground, and most of us, as the poison spread, assumed a temporary goiter. Then about the middle of August appeared the first of those mysterious cases of illness which our local doctor attributed to the long-continued heat coupled with the bite of these venomous insects. The patient was a boy of sixteen or seventeen, the son of Mrs. Amworth's gardener, and the symptoms were an anemic pallor and a languid prostration, accompanied by great drowsiness and an abnormal appetite. He had, too, on his throat two small punctures where, so Dr. Ross conjectured, one of these great gnats had bitten him. But the odd thing was that there was no swelling or inflammation round the place where he had been bitten. The heat at this time had begun to abate, but the cooler weather failed to restore him, and the boy, in spite of the quantity of food which he so ravenously swallowed, wasted away to a skin-clad skeleton.

I met Dr. Ross in the street one afternoon about this time, and in answer to my enquiries about his patient he said that he was afraid the boy was dying. The case, he confessed, completely puzzled him: some obscure form of pernicious anemia was all he could suggest. But he wondered whether Mr. Urcombe would consent to see the boy, on the chance of his being able to throw some new light on the case, and since Urcombe was dining with me that night, I proposed to Dr. Ross to join us. He could not do this, but said he would look in later. When he came, Urcombe at once consented to put his skill at the other's disposal, and together they went off at once. Being thus shorn of my sociable evening, I telephoned to Mrs. Amworth to know if I might inflict myself on her for an hour. Her answer was a welcoming affirmative, and between piquet and music the hour lengthened itself into two. She spoke of the boy who was lying so desperately and mysteriously ill, and told me that she had often been to see him, taking him nourishing and delicate food. But today— and her kind eyes moistened as she spoke—she was afraid she had paid her last visit. Knowing the antipathy between her and Urcombe, I did not tell her that he had been called into consultation; and when I returned home she accompanied me to my door, for the sake of a breath of night air, and in order to borrow a magazine which contained an article on gardening which she wished to read.

"Ah, this delicious night air," she said, luxuriously sniffing in the coolness. "Night air and gardening are the great tonics. There is nothing so stimulating as bare contact with rich mother earth. You are never so fresh as when you have been grubbing in the soil—black hands, black nails, and boots covered with mud." She gave her great jovial laugh.

"I'm a glutton for air and earth," she said. "Positively I look forward to death, for then I shall be buried and have the kind earth all round me. No leaden caskets for me—I have given explicit directions. But what shall I do about air? Well, I suppose one can't have everything. The magazine? A thousand thanks, I will faithfully return it. Good night: garden and keep your windows open, and you won't have anemia."

"I always sleep with my windows open," said I.

I went straight up to my bedroom, of which one of the windows looks out over the street, and as I undressed I thought I heard voices talking outside not far away. But I paid no particular attention, put out my lights, and falling asleep plunged into the depths of a most horrible dream, distortedly suggested, no doubt, by my last words with Mrs. Amworth. I dreamed that I woke, and found that both my bedroom windows were shut. Half suffocating, I dreamed that I sprang out of bed, and went across to open them. The blind over the first one was drawn down, and pulling it up I saw, with the indescribable horror of incipient nightmare, Mrs. Amworth's face suspended close to the pane in the darkness outside, nodding and smiling at me. Pulling down the blind again to keep that terror out, I rushed to the second window on the other side of the room, and there again was Mrs. Amworth's face. Then the panic came upon me in full blast; here was I suffocating in the airless room, and whichever window I opened Mrs. Amworth's face would float in, like those noiseless black gnats that bit before one was aware. The nightmare rose to screaming point, and with strangled yells I awoke to find my room cool and quiet with both windows open and blinds up and a half moon high in its course, casting an oblong of tranquil light on the floor. But even when I was awake the horror persisted, and I lay tossing and turning. I must have slept long before the nightmare seized me, for now it was nearly day, and soon in the east the drowsy eyelids of morning began to lift.

I was scarcely downstairs next morning—for after the

184

dawn I slept late—when Urcombe rang up to know if he might see me immediately. He came in, grim and preoccupied, and I noticed that he was pulling on a pipe that was not even filled.

"I want your help," he said, "and so I must tell you first of all what happened last night. I went round with the little doctor to see his patient, and found him just alive, but scarcely more. I instantly diagnosed in my own mind what this anemia, unaccountable by any other explanation, meant. The boy is the prey of a vampire."

He put his empty pipe on the breakfast table, by which I had just sat down, and folded his arms, looking at me steadily from under his overhanging brows.

"Now about last night," he said. "I insisted that he should be moved from his father's cottage into my house. As we were carrying him on a stretcher, whom should we meet but Mrs. Amworth? She expressed shocked surprise that we were moving him. Now why do you think she did that?"

With a start of horror, as I remembered my dream that night before, I felt an idea come into my mind so preposterous and unthinkable that I instantly turned it out again.

"I haven't the smallest idea," I said.

"Then listen, while I tell you about what happened later. I put out all light in the room where the boy lay, and watched. One window was a little open, for I had forgotten to close it, and about midnight I heard something outside, trying apparently to push it farther open. I guessed who it was—yes, it was full twenty feet from the ground—and I peeped round the corner of the blind. Just outside was the face of Mrs. Amworth and her hand was on the frame of the window. Very softly I crept close, and then banged the window down, and I think I just caught the tip of one of her fingers."

"But it's impossible," I cried. "How could she be floating in the air like that? And what had she come for? Don't tell me such——"

Once more, with closer grip, the remembrance of my nightmare seized me.

"I am telling you what I saw," said he. "And all night long, until it was nearly day, she was fluttering outside, like some terrible bat, trying to gain admittance. Now put together various things I have told you."

He began checking them off on his fingers.

"Number one," he said, "there was an outbreak of disease similar to that which this boy is suffering from at Peshawar, and her husband died of it. Number two: Mrs. Amworth protested against my moving the boy to my house. Number three: she, or the demon that inhabits her body, a creature powerful and deadly, tries to gain admittance. And add this, too: in medieval times there was an epidemic of vampirism here at Maxley. The vampire, so the accounts run, was found to be Elizabeth Chaston . . . I see you remember Mrs. Amworth's maiden name. Finally, the boy is stronger this morning. He would certainly not have been alive if he had been visited again. And what do you make of it?"

There was a long silence, during which I found this incredible horror assuming the hues of reality.

"I have something to add," I said, "which may or may not bear on it. You say that the—the specter went away shortly before dawn."

"Yes."

I told him of my dream, and he smiled grimly.

"Yes, you did well to awake," he said. "That warning came from your subconscious self, which never wholly slumbers, and cried out to you of deadly danger. For two reasons, then, you must help me: one to save others, the second to save yourself."

"What do you want me to do?" I asked.

"I want you first of all to help me in watching this boy, and ensuring that she does not come near him. Eventually I want you to help me in tracking the thing down, in exposing and destroying it. It is not human: it is an incarnate fiend. What steps we shall have to take I don't yet know."

It was now eleven of the forenoon, and presently I went across to his house for a twelve-hour vigil while he slept, to come on duty again that night, so that for the next twenty-four hours either Urcombe or myself was always in the room where the boy, now getting stronger every hour, was lying. The day following was Saturday and a morning of brilliant, pellucid weather, and already when I went across to his house to resume my duty the stream of motors down to Brighton had begun. Simultaneously I saw Urcombe with a cheerful face, which boded good news of his patient, coming out of his house, and Mrs. Amworth, with a gesture of salutation to me and a basket in her hand, walking up the broad strip of grass which bordered the road. There we all three met. I noticed (and saw that Urcombe noticed it too) that one finger of her left hand was bandaged.

"Good morning to you both," said she. "And I hear your patient is doing well, Mr. Urcombe. I have come to bring him a bowl of jelly, and to sit with him for an hour. He and I are great friends. I am overjoyed at his recovery."

Urcombe paused a moment, as if making up his mind, and then shot out a pointing finger at her.

"I forbid that," he said. "You shall not sit with him or see him. And you know the reason as well as I do."

I have never seen so horrible a change pass over a human face as that which now blanched hers to the color of a gray mist. She put up her hand as if to shield herself from that pointing finger, which drew the sign of the cross in the air, and shrank back cowering onto the road. There was a wild hoot from a horn, a grinding of brakes, a shout—too late—from a passing car, and one long scream suddenly cut short. Her body rebounded from the roadway after the first wheel had gone over it, and the second followed it. It lay there, quivering and twitching, and was still.

She was buried three days afterwards in the cemetery outside Maxley, in accordance with the wishes she had told me that she had devised about her interment, and the shock which her sudden and awful death had caused to the little community began by degrees to pass off. To two people only, Urcombe and myself, the horror of it was mitigated from the first by the nature of the relief that her death brought; but, naturally enough, we kept our own counsel, and no hint of what greater horror had been thus averted was ever let slip. But, oddly enough, so it seemed to me, he was still not satisfied about something in connection with her, and would give no answer to my questions on the subject. Then as the days of a tranquil mellow September and the October that followed began to drop away like the leaves of the yellowing trees, his uneasiness relaxed. But before the entry of November the seeming tranquility broke into hurricane.

I had been dining one night at the far end of the village, and about eleven o'clock was walking home again. The moon was of an unusual brilliance, rendering all that it shone on as distinct as in some etching. I had just come opposite the house which Mrs. Amworth had occupied, where there was a board up telling that it was to let, when I heard the click of her front gate, and next moment I saw, with a sudden chill and quaking of my very spirit, that she stood there. Her profile, vividly illuminated, was turned to me, and I could not be mistaken in my identification of her. She appeared not to see me (indeed the shadow of the yew hedge in front of her garden enveloped me in its blackness) and she went swiftly across the road, and entered the gate of the house directly opposite. There I lost sight of her completely.

My breath was coming in short pants as if I had been running—and now indeed I ran, with fearful backward glances, along the hundred yards that separated me from my house and Urcombe's. It was to his that my flying steps took me, and next minute I was within.

"What have you come to tell me?" he asked. "Or shall I guess?"

"You can't guess," said I.

"No; it's no guess. She has come back and you have seen her. Tell me about it."

I gave him my story.

"That's Major Pearsall's house," he said. "Come back with me there at once."

"But what can we do?" I asked.

"I've no idea. That's what we have got to find out."

A minute later, we were opposite the house. When I had passed it before, it was all dark; now lights gleamed from a couple of windows upstairs. Even as we faced it, the front door opened, and next moment Major Pearsall emerged from the gate. He saw us and stopped.

"I'm on my way to Dr. Ross," he said quickly. "My wife has been taken suddenly ill. She had been in bed an hour when I came upstairs, and I found her white as a ghost and utterly exhausted. She had been to sleep, it seemed—— But you will excuse me."

"One moment, Major," said Urcombe. "Was there any mark on her throat?"

"How did you guess that?" said he. "There was: one of those beastly gnats must have bitten her twice there. She was streaming with blood."

"And there's someone with her?" asked Urcombe.

"Yes, I roused her maid."

He went off, and Urcombe turned to me. "I know now what we have to do," he said. "Change your clothes, and I'll join you at your house."

"What is it?" I asked.

"I'll tell you on our way. We're going to the cemetery."

He carried a pick, a shovel, and a screwdriver when he rejoined me, and wore round his shoulders a long coil of rope. As we walked, he gave me the outlines of the ghastly hour that lay before us.

"What I have to tell you," he said, "will seem to you now

too fantastic for credence, but before dawn we shall see whether it outstrips reality. By a most fortunate happening, you saw the specter, the astral body, whatever you choose to call it, of Mrs. Amworth, going on its grisly business, and therefore, beyond doubt, the vampire spirit which abode in her during life animates her again in death. That is not exceptional—indeed, all these weeks since her death I have been expecting it. If I am right, we shall find her body undecayed and untouched by corruption."

"But she has been dead nearly two months," said I.

"If she had been dead two years it would still be so, if the vampire has possession of her. So remember: whatever you see done, it will be done not to her, who in the natural course would now be feeding the grasses above her grave, but to a spirit of untold evil and malignancy, which gives a phantom life to her body."

"But what shall I see done?" said I.

"I will tell you. We know that now, at this moment, the vampire clad in her mortal semblance is out; dining out. But it must get back before dawn, and it will pass into the material form that lies in her grave. We must wait for that, and then with your help I shall dig up her body. If I am right, you will look on her as she was in life, with the full vigor of the dreadful nutriment she has received pulsing in her veins. And then, when dawn has come, and the vampire cannot leave the lair of her body, I shall strike her with this"—and he pointed to his pick—"through the heart, and she, who comes to life again only with the animation the fiend gives her, she and her hellish partner will be dead indeed. Then we must bury her again, delivered at last."

We had come to the cemetery, and in the brightness of the moonshine there was no difficulty in identifying her grave. It lay some twenty yards from the small chapel, in the porch of which, obscured by shadow, we concealed ourselves. From there we had a clear and open sight of the grave, and now we must wait till its infernal visitor returned home. The night was warm and windless, yet even if a freezing wind had been raging I think I should have felt nothing of it, so intense was my preoccupation as to what the night and dawn would bring. There was a bell in the turret of the chapel that struck the quarters of the hour, and it amazed me to find how swiftly the chimes succeeded one another.

The moon had long set, but a twilight of stars shone in a clear sky, when five o'clock of the morning sounded from the turret. A few minutes more passed, and then I felt Urcombe's hand softly nudging me; and looking out in the direction of his pointing finger, I saw that the form of a woman, tall and large in build, was approaching from the right. Noiselessly, with a motion more of gliding and floating than walking, she moved across the cemetery to the grave which was the center of our observation. She moved round it as if to be certain of its identity, and for a moment stood directly facing us. In the grayness to which now my eyes had grown accustomed, I could easily see her face, and recognize its features.

She drew her hand across her mouth as if wiping it, and broke into a chuckle of such laughter as made my hair stir on my head. Then she leaped onto the grave, holding her hands high above her head, and inch by inch disappeared into the earth. Urcombe's hand was laid on my arm, in an injunction to keep still, but now he removed it.

"Come," he said.

With pick and shovel and rope we went to the grave. The earth was light and sandy, and soon after six struck we had delved down to the coffin lid. With his pick he loosened the earth round it, and, adjusting the rope through the handles by which it had been lowered, we tried to raise it. This was a long and laborious business, and the light had begun to herald day in the east before we had it out and lying by the side of the grave. With his screwdriver he loosed the fastenings of the lid, and slid it aside, and standing there we looked on the face of Mrs. Amworth. The eyes, once closed in death, were open, the cheeks were flushed with color, the red, full-lipped mouth seemed to smile.

"One blow and it is all over," he said. "You need not look."

Even as he spoke he took up the pick again, and, laying the point of it on her left breast, measured his distance. And though I knew what was coming I could not look away. . . .

He grasped the pick in both hands, raised it an inch or two for the taking of his aim, and then with full force brought it down on her breast. A fountain of blood, though she had been dead so long, spouted high in the air, falling with the thud of a heavy splash over the shroud, and simultaneously from those red lips came one long, appalling cry, swelling up like some hooting siren, and dying away again. With that, instantaneous as a lightning flash, came the touch of corruption on her face, the color of it faded to ash, the plump cheeks fell in, the mouth dropped.

"Thank God, that's over," said he, and without pause slipped the coffin lid back into its place.

Day was coming fast now, and, working like men possessed, we lowered the coffin into its place again, and shoveled the earth over it.... The birds were busy with their earliest pipings as we went back to Maxley.

Skeleton

by Ray Bradbury

It was past time for him to see the doctor again. Mr. Harris turned palely in at the stairwell, and on his way up the flight saw Dr. Burleigh's name gilded over a pointing arrow. Would Dr. Burleigh sigh when he walked in? After all, this would make the tenth trip so far this year. But Burleigh shouldn't complain; he was paid for the examinations!

The nurse looked Mr. Harris over and smiled, a bit amusedly, as she tiptoed to the glazed glass door, opened it, and put her head in. Harris thought he heard her say, "Guess who's here, Doctor." And didn't the doctor's voice reply, faintly, "Oh, my God, *again?*" Harris swallowed uneasily.

When Harris walked in, Dr. Burleigh snorted. "Aches in your bones again! Ah!!" He scowled and adjusted his glasses. "My dear Harris, you've been curried with the finest-toothed combs and bacteria-brushes known to science. You're just nervous. Let's see your fingers. Too many cigarettes. Let's smell your breath. Too much protein. Let's see your eyes. Not enough sleep. My response? Go to bed, stop the protein, no smoking. Ten dollars, please."

Harris stood sulking.

The doctor glanced up from his papers. "*You* still here? You're a hypochondriac! That's *eleven* dollars, now."

"But why should my bones ache?" asked Harris.

Dr. Burleigh spoke as to a child. "You ever had a sore muscle, and kept irritating it, fussing with it, rubbing it? It gets worse, the more you bother it. Then you leave it alone and the pain vanishes. You realize you caused most of the soreness yourself. Well, son, that's what's with you. Leave yourself alone. Take a dose of salts. Get out of here and take that trip to Phoenix you've stewed about for months. Do you good to travel!"

191

Five minutes later, Mr. Harris riffled through a classified phone directory at the corner druggist's. A fine lot of sympathy one got from blind fools like Burleigh! He passed his finger down a list of BONE SPECIALISTS, found one named M. Munigant. Munigant lacked an M.D. or any other academic lettering behind his name, but his office was conveniently near. Three blocks down, one block over. . . .

M. Munigant, like his office, was small and dark. Like his office, he smelled of iodoform, iodine, and other odd things. He was a good listener, though, and listened with eager shiny moves of his eyes, and when he talked to Harris, his accent was such that he softly whistled each word; undoubtedly because of imperfect dentures.

Harris told all.

M. Munigant nodded. He had seen cases like this before. The bones of the body. Man was not aware of his bones. Ah, yes, the bones. The skeleton. Most difficult. Something concerning an imbalance, an unsympathetic coordination between soul, flesh, and skeleton. Very complicated, softly whistled M. Munigant. Harris listened, fascinated. Now, *here* was a doctor who understood his illness! Psychological, said M. Munigant. He moved swiftly, delicately to a dingy wall and slashed down half a dozen X-rays to haunt the room with their look of things found floating in an ancient tide. Here, here! The skeleton surprised! Here luminous portraits of the long, the short, the large, the small bones. Mr. Harris must be aware of his position, his problem! M. Munigant's hand tapped, rattled, whispered, scratched at faint nebulae of flesh in which hung ghosts of cranium, spinal cord, pelvis, lime, calcium, marrow, here, there, this, that, these, those, and others! Look!

Harris shuddered. The X-rays and the paintings blew in a green and phosphorescent wind from a land peopled by the monsters of Dali and Fuseli.

M. Munigant whistled quietly. Did Mr. Harris wish his bones—treated?

"That depends," said Harris.

Well, M. Munigant could not help Harris unless Harris was in the proper mood. Psychologically, one had to *need* help, or the doctor was useless. But (shrugging) M. Munigant would "try."

Harris lay on a table with his mouth open. The lights were switched off, the shades drawn. M. Munigant approached his patient.

Something touched Harris's tongue.

He felt his jawbones forced out. They creaked and made faint cracking noises. One of those skeleton charts on the dim wall seemed to quiver and jump. A violent shudder seized Harris. Involuntarily, his mouth snapped shut.

M. Munigant shouted. His nose had almost been bitten off! No use, no use! Now was not the time! M. Munigant whispered the shades up, dreadfully disappointed. When Mr. Harris felt he could cooperate psychologically, when Mr. Harris really *needed* help and trusted M. Munigant to help him, then maybe something could be done. M. Munigant held out his little hand. In the meantime, the fee was only two dollars. Mr. Harris must begin to think. Here was a sketch for Mr. Harris to take home and study. It would acquaint him with his body. He must be tremblingly aware of himself. He must be on guard. Skeletons were strange, unwieldy things. M. Munigant's eyes glittered. Good day to Mr. Harris. Oh, and would he care for a breadstick? M. Munigant proffered a jar of long hard salty breadsticks to Harris, taking one himself, saying that chewing breadsticks kept him in—ah—practice. Good day, good day, to Mr. Harris! Mr. Harris went home.

The next day, Sunday, Mr. Harris discovered innumerable fresh aches and pains in his body. He spent the morning, his eyes fixed, staring with new interest at the small, anatomically perfect painting of a skeleton M. Munigant had given him.

His wife, Clarisse, startled him at dinner when she cracked her exquisitely thin knuckles, one by one, until he clapped his hands to his ears and cried, "Stop!"

The rest of the afternoon he quarantined himself in his room. Clarisse played bridge in the parlor laughing and chatting with three other ladies while Harris, hidden away, fingered and weighed the limbs of his body with growing curiosity. After an hour he suddenly rose and called:

"Clarisse!"

She had a way of dancing into any room, her body doing all sorts of soft, agreeable things to keep her feet from ever quite touching the nap of a rug. She excused herself from her friends and came to see him now, brightly. She found him re-seated in a far corner and she saw that he was staring at the anatomical sketch. "Are you still brooding, sweet?" she asked. "Please don't." She sat upon his knees.

Her beauty could not distract him now in his absorption. He juggled her lightness, he touched her kneecap, suspiciously. It seemed to move under her pale, glowing skin. "Is it supposed to do that?" he asked, sucking in his breath.

193

"Is what supposed to do what?" she laughed. "You mean my kneecap?"

"Is it supposed to run around on top of your knee that way?"

She experimented. "So it *does*," she marveled.

"I'm glad yours slithers, too," he sighed. "I was beginning to worry."

"About what?"

He patted his ribs. "My ribs don't go all the way down, they stop *here*. And I found some confounded ones that dangle in midair!"

Beneath the curve of her small breasts, Clarisse clasped her hands.

"Of course, silly, everybody's ribs stop at a given point. And those funny short ones are floating ribs."

"I hope they don't float around too much." The joke was most uneasy. Now, above all, he wished to be alone. Further discoveries, newer and stranger archaeological diggings, lay within reach of his trembling hands, and he did not wish to be laughed at.

"Thanks for coming in, dear," he said.

"Any time." She rubbed her small nose softly against his.

"Wait! Here, now . . ." He put his finger to touch his nose and hers. "Did you realize? The nose-bone grows down only *this* far. From there on a lot of gristly tissue fills out the rest!"

She wrinkled hers. "Of course, darling!" And she danced from the room.

Now, sitting alone, he felt the perspiration rise from the pools and hollows of his face, to flow in a thin tide down his cheeks. He licked his lips and shut his eyes. No. . . . now . . . next on the agenda, what . . . ? The spinal cord, yes. Here. Slowly, he examined it, in the same way he operated the many push buttons in his office, thrusting them to summon secretaries, messengers. But now, in these pushings of his spinal column, fears and terrors answered, rushed from a million doors in his mind to confront and shake him! His spine felt horribly—unfamiliar. Like the brittle shards of a fish, freshly eaten, its bones left strewn on a cold china platter. He seized the little rounded knobbins. "Lord! Lord!"

His teeth began to chatter. God Almighty! he thought, why haven't I realized it all these years? All these years I've gone around with a—SKELETON—inside me! How is it we take ourselves for granted? How is it we never question our bodies and our being?

A skeleton. One of those jointed, snowy, hard things, one of those foul, dry, brittle, gouge-eyed, skull-faced, shake-fingered, rattling things that sway from neck-chains in abandoned webbed closets, one of those things found on the desert all long and scattered like dice!

He stood upright, because he could not bear to remain seated. Inside me now—he grasped his stomach, his head—inside my head is a—skull. One of those curved carapaces which holds my brain like an electrical jelly, one of those cracked shells with the holes in front like two holes shot through it by a double-barreled shotgun! With its grottoes and caverns of bone, its revetments and placements for my flesh, my smelling, my seeing, my hearing, my thinking! A skull, encompassing my brain, allowing it exit through its brittle windows to see the outside world!

He wanted to dash into the bridge party, upset it, a fox in a chickenyard, the cards fluttering all around like chicken feathers burst upward in clouds! He stopped himself only with a violent, trembling effort. Now, now, man, control yourself. This is a revelation, take it for what it's worth, understand it, savor it. BUT A SKELETON! screamed his subconscious. I won't stand for it. It's vulgar, it's terrible, it's frightening. Skeletons are horrors; they clink and tinkle and rattle in old castles, hung from oaken beams, making long, indolently rustling pendulums on the wind. . . .

"Darling, will you come meet the ladies?" His wife's clear, sweet voice called from far away.

Mr. Harris stood. His SKELETON held him up! This thing inside, this invader, this horror, was supporting his arms, legs, and head! It was like feeling someone just behind you who shouldn't be there. With every step, he realized how dependent he was on this other Thing.

"Darling, I'll be with you in a moment," he called weakly. To himself he said, Come on, brace up! You've got to go back to work tomorrow. Friday you must make that trip to Phoenix. It's a long drive. Hundreds of miles. Must be in shape for that trip or you won't get Mr. Creldon to invest in your ceramics business. Chin up, now!

A moment later he stood among the ladies, being introduced to Mrs. Withers, Mrs. Abblematt, and Miss Kirthy, all of whom had skeletons inside them, but took it very calmly, because nature had carefully clothed the bare nudity of clavicle, tibia, and femur with breasts, thighs, calves, with coiffure and eyebrow satanic, with bee-stung lips and—LORD! shouted Mr. Harris inwardly—when they talk or eat,

195

part of their skeleton shows—their *teeth!* I never thought of that. "Excuse me," he gasped, and ran from the room only in time to drop his lunch among the petunias over the garden balustrade.

That night, seated on the bed as his wife undressed, he pared his toenails and fingernails scrupulously. These parts, too, were where his skeleton was shoving, indignantly growing out. He must have muttered part of this theory, because next thing he knew his wife, in negligee, was on the bed, her arms about his neck, yawning, "Oh, my darling, fingernails are *not* bone, they're only hardened epidermis!"

He threw the scissors down. "Are you certain? I hope so. I'd feel better." He looked at the curve of her body, marveling. "I hope all people are made the same way."

"If you aren't the darndest hypochondriac!" She held him at arm's length. "Come on. What's wrong? Tell Mama."

"Something inside me," he said. "Something—I ate."

The next morning and all afternoon at his downtown office, Mr. Harris sorted out the sizes, shapes, and constructions of various bones in his body with displeasure. At ten A.M. he asked to feel Mr. Smith's elbow one moment. Mr. Smith obliged, but scowled suspiciously. And after lunch Mr. Harris asked to touch Miss Laurel's shoulder blade and she immediately pushed herself back against him, purring like a kitten and shutting her eyes.

"Miss Laurel!" he snapped. "Stop that!"

Alone, he pondered his neuroses. The war was just over, the pressure of his work, the uncertainty of the future probably had much to do with his mental outlook. He wanted to leave the office, get into business for himself. He had more than a little talent for ceramics and sculpture. As soon as possible he'd head for Arizona, borrow that money from Mr. Creldon, build a kiln and set up shop. It was a worry. What a case he was. But luckily he had contacted M. Munigant, who seemed eager to understand and help him. He would fight it out with himself, not go back to either Munigant or Dr. Burleigh unless he was forced to. The alien feeling would pass. He sat staring into space.

The alien feeling did not pass. It grew.

On Tuesday and Wednesday it bothered him terrifically that his epidermis, hair and other appendages were of a high disorder, while this integumented skeleton within was a slick

196

clean structure of efficient organization. Sometimes, in certain lights with his lips drawn morosely down, weighted with melancholy, he imagined he saw his skull grinning at him behind the flesh.

Let go! he cried. Let go of me! My lungs! Stop!

He gasped convulsively, as if his ribs were crushing the breath from him.

My brain—stop squeezing it!

And terrifying headaches burnt his brain to a blind cinder.

My insides, let them be, for God's sake! Stay away from my heart!

His heart cringed from the fanning motion of ribs like pale spiders crouched and fiddling with their prey.

Drenched with sweat, he lay upon the bed one night while Clarisse was out attending a Red Cross meeting. He tried to gather his wits but only grew more aware of the conflict between his dirty exterior and this beautiful cool clean calciumed thing inside.

His complexion: wasn't it oily and lined with worry?

Observe the flawless, snow-white perfection of the skull.

His nose: wasn't it too large?

Then observe the tiny bones of the skull's nose before that monstrous nasal cartilage begins forming the lopsided proboscis.

His body: wasn't it plump?

Well, consider the skeleton; slender, svelte, economical of line and contour. Exquisitely carved oriental ivory! Perfect, thin as a white praying mantis!

His eyes: weren't they protuberant, ordinary, numb-looking?

Be so kind as to note the eye-sockets of the skull; so deep and rounded, somber, quiet pools, all-knowing, eternal. Gaze deep and you never touch the bottom of their dark understanding. All irony, all life, all everything is there in the cupped darkness.

Compare. Compare. Compare.

He raged for hours. And the skeleton, ever the frail and solemn philosopher, hung quietly inside, saying not a word, suspended like a delicate insect within a chrysalis, waiting and waiting.

Harris sat slowly up.

"Wait a minute. Hold on!" he exclaimed. "You're helpless, too. I've got you, too. I can make you do anything I want! You can't prevent it! I say move your carpales, metacarpals, and phalanges and—sswtt—up they go, as I wave to someone!" He laughed. "I order the fibula and femur to locomote and *Hunn* two three four, *Hunn* two three four—we walk around the block. There!"

Harris grinned.

"It's a fifty-fifty fight. Even-Stephen. And we'll fight it out, we two! After all, I'm the part that *thinks!* Yes, by God! yes. Even if I didn't have you, I could still think!"

Instantly, a tiger's jaw snapped shut, chewing his brain in half. Harris screamed. The bones of his skull grabbed hold and gave him nightmares. Then slowly, while he shrieked, nuzzled and ate the nightmares one by one, until the last one was gone and the light went out. . . .

At the end of the week he postponed the Phoenix trip because of his health. Weighing himself on a penny scale he saw the slow gliding red arrow point to: 165.

He groaned. Why, I've weighed 175 for years. I can't have lost ten pounds! He examined his cheeks in the fly-dotted mirror. Cold, primitive fear rushed over him in odd little shivers. You, you! I know what you're about, *you!*

He shook his fist at his bony face, particularly addressing his remarks to his superior maxillary, his inferior maxillary, to his cranium and to his cervical vertebrae.

"You damn thing, you! Think you can starve me, make me lose weight, eh? Peel the flesh off, leave nothing but skin on bone. Trying to ditch me, so you can be supreme, ah? No, no!"

He fled into a cafeteria.

Turkey, dressing, creamed potatoes, four vegetables, three desserts, he could eat none of it, he was sick to his stomach. He forced himself. His teeth began to ache. Bad teeth, is it! he thought angrily. I'll eat in spite of every tooth clanging and banging and rattling so they fall in my gravy.

His head blazed, his breath jerked in and out of a constricted chest, his teeth raged with pain, but he knew one small victory. He was about to drink milk when he stopped and poured it into a vase of nasturtiums. No calcium for you, my boy, no calcium for you. Never again shall I eat foods with calcium or other bone-fortifying minerals. I'll eat for one of us, not both, my lad.

"One hundred and fifty pounds," he said the following week to his wife. "Do you *see* how I've changed?"

"For the better," said Clarisse. "You were always a little plump for your height, darling." She stroked his chin. "I like

198

your face. It's so much nicer; the lines of it are so firm and strong now."

"They're not *my* lines, they're his, damn him! You mean to say you like him better than you like me?"

"Him? Who's *'him'?*"

In the parlor mirror, beyond Clarisse, his skull smiled back at him behind his fleshy grimace of hatred and despair.

Fuming, he popped malt tablets into his mouth. This was one way of gaining weight when you couldn't keep other foods down. Clarisse noticed the malt pellets.

"But, darling, really, you don't have to regain the weight for me," she said.

Oh, shut up! he felt like saying.

She made him lie with his head in her lap. "Darling," she said, "I've watched you lately. You're so—badly off. You don't say anything, but you look—hunted. You toss in bed at night. Maybe you should go to a psychiatrist. But I think I can tell you everything he would say. I've put it all together from hints you've let escape you. I can tell you that you and your skeleton are one and the same, 'one nation, indivisible, with liberty and justice for all.' United you stand, divided you fall. If you two fellows can't get along like an old married couple in the future, go back and see Dr. Burleigh. But, first, relax. You're in a vicious circle; the more you worry, the more your bones stick out, the more you worry. After all, who picked this fight—you or that anonymous entity you claim is lurking around behind your alimentary canal?"

He closed his eyes. "I did. I guess I did. Go on, Clarisse, keep talking."

"You rest now," she said softly. "Rest and forget."

Mr. Harris felt buoyed up for half a day, then he began to sag. It was all very well to blame his imagination, but this particular skeleton, by God, was fighting back.

Harris set out for M. Munigant's office late in the day. Walking for half an hour until he found the address, he caught sight of the name "M. Munigant" initialed in ancient, flaking gold on a glass plate outside the building. Then, his bones seemed to explode from their moorings, blasted and erupted with pain. Blinded, he staggered away. When he opened his eyes again he had rounded a corner. M. Munigant's office was out of sight.

The pains ceased.

M. Munigant was the man to help him. If the sight of his

199

name could cause so titanic a reaction of course M. Munigant *must* be just the man.

But, not today. Each time he tried to return to that office, the terrible pains took hold. Perspiring, he had to give up and swayed into a cocktail bar.

Moving across the dim lounge, he wondered briefly if a lot of blame couldn't be put on M. Munigant's shoulders. After all, it was Munigant who'd first drawn specific attention to his skeleton, and let the psychological impact of it slam home! Could M. Munigant be using him for some nefarious purpose? But what purpose? Silly to suspect him. Just a little doctor. Trying to be helpful. Munigant and his jar of breadsticks. Ridiculous. M. Munigant was okay, okay . . .

There was a sight within the cocktail lounge to give him hope. A large, fat man, round as a butterball, stood drinking consecutive beers at the bar. Now *there* was a successful man. Harris repressed a desire to go up, clap the fat man's shoulder, and inquire as to how he'd gone about impounding his bones. Yes, the fat man's skeleton was luxuriously closeted. There were pillows of fat here, resilient bulges of it there, with several round chandeliers of fat under his chin. The poor skeleton was lost; it could never fight clear of that blubber. It might have tried once—but not now. Overwhelmed, not a bony echo of the fat man's supporter remained.

Not without envy, Harris approached the fat man as one might cut across the bow of an ocean liner. Harris ordered a drink, drank it, and then dared to address the fat man:

"Glands?"

"You talking to me?" asked the fat man.

"Or is there a special diet?" wondered Harris. "I beg your pardon, but, as you see, I'm down. Can't seem to put on any weight. I'd like a stomach like that one of yours. Did you grow it because you were afraid of something?"

"You," announced the fat man, "are drunk. But—I like drunkards." He ordered more drinks. "Listen close, I'll tell you. Layer by layer," said the fat man, "twenty years, man and boy, I built this." He held his vast stomach like a globe of the world, teaching his audience its gastronomical geography. "It was no overnight circus. The tent was not raised before dawn on the wonders installed within. I have cultivated my inner organs as if they were thoroughbred dogs, cats, and other animals. My stomach is a fat pink Persian tom slumbering, rousing at intervals to purr, mew, growl, and cry for chocolate tidbits. I feed it well, it will 'most sit up for me. And, my dear fellow, my intestines are the rarest pure-bred Indian anacondas you ever viewed in the sleekest, coiled, fine and ruddy health. Keep 'em in prime, I do, all my pets. For fear of something? Perhaps."

This called for another drink for everyone.

"Gain weight?" The fat man savored the words on his tongue. "Here's what you do: get yourself a quarreling bird of a wife, a baker's dozen of relatives who can flush a covey of troubles out from behind the veriest molehill. Add to these a sprinkling of business associates whose prime motivation is snatching your last lonely quid, and you are well on your way to getting fat. How so? In no time you'll begin subconsciously building fat betwixt yourself and them. A buffer epidermal state, a cellular wall. You'll soon find that eating is the only fun on earth. But one needs to be bothered by outside sources. Too many people in this world haven't enough to worry about, then they begin picking on themselves, and they lose weight. Meet all of the vile, terrible people you can possibly meet, and pretty soon you'll be adding the good old fat!"

And with that advice, the fat man launched himself out into the dark tide of night, swaying mightily and wheezing.

"That's exactly what Dr. Burleigh told me, slightly changed," said Harris thoughtfully. "Perhaps that trip to Phoenix, now, at this time——"

The trip from Los Angeles to Phoenix was a sweltering one, crossing, as it did, the Mojave desert on a broiling yellow day. Traffic was thin and inconstant, and for long stretches there would not be a car on the road for miles ahead or behind. Harris twitched his fingers on the steering wheel. Whether or not Creldon, in Phoenix, lent him the money he needed to start his business, it was still a good thing to get away, to put distance behind.

The car moved in the hot sluice of desert wind. The one Mr. H. sat inside the other Mr. H. Perhaps both perspired. Perhaps both were miserable.

On a curve, the inside Mr. H. suddenly constricted the outer flesh, causing him to jerk forward on the hot steering wheel.

The car plunged off the road into boiling sand and turned half over.

Night came, a wind rose, the roof was lonely and silent. The few cars that passed went swiftly on their way, their

201

view obstructed. Mr. Harris lay unconscious, until very late he heard a wind rising out of the desert, felt the sting of little sand needles on his cheeks, and opened his eyes.

Morning found him gritty-eyed and wandering in thoughtless senseless circles, having, in his delirium, got away from the road. At noon he sprawled in the poor shade of a bush. The sun struck him with a keen sword edge, cutting through to his—bones. A vulture circled.

Harris's parched lips cracked open. "So that's it?" he whispered, red-eyed, bristle-cheeked. "One or another you'll walk me, starve me, thirst me, kill me." He swallowed dry burrs of dust. "Sun cook off my flesh so you can peek out. Vultures lunch off me, and there you'll lie, grinning. Grinning with victory. Like a bleached xylophone strewn and played by vultures with an ear for odd music. You'd like that. Freedom."

He walked on through a landscape that shivered and bubbled in the direct pour of sunlight; stumbling, falling flat, lying to feed himself little mouths of fire. The air was blue alcohol flame, and vultures roasted and steamed and glittered as they flew in glides and circles. Phoenix. The road. Car. Water. Safety.

"Hey!"

Someone called from way off in the blue alcohol flame.

Mr. Harris propped himself up.

"Hey!"

The call was repeated. A crunching of footsteps, quick.

With a cry of unbelievable relief, Harris rose, only to collapse again into the arms of someone in a uniform with a badge.

The car tediously hauled, repaired, Phoenix reached, Harris found himself in such an unholy state of mind that the business transaction was a numb pantomime. Even when he got the loan and held the money in his hand, it meant nothing. This Thing within him like a hard white sword in a scabbard tainted his business, his eating, colored his love for Clarisse, made it unsafe to trust an automobile; all in all this Thing had to be put in its place. The desert incident had brushed too close. Too near the bone, one might say with an ironic twist of one's mouth. Harris heard himself thanking Mr. Creldon, dimly, for the money. Then he turned his car and motored back across the long miles, this time cutting across to San Diego, so he would miss that desert stretch between El Centro and Beaumont. He drove north along the coast. He didn't trust that desert. But—careful! Salt waves boomed, hissing on the beach outside Laguna. Sand, fish and crustacea would cleanse his bones as swiftly as vultures. Slow down on the curves over the surf.

Damn, he was sick!

Where to turn? Clarisse? Burleigh? Munigant? Bone specialist. Munigant. Well?

"Darling!" Clarisse kissed him. He winced at the solidness of the teeth and jaw behind the passionate exchange.

"Darling," he said, slowly, wiping his lips with his wrist, trembling.

"You look thinner; oh, darling, the business deal——?"

"It went through. I guess. Yes, it did."

She kissed him again. They ate a slow, falsely cheerful dinner, with Clarisse laughing and encouraging him. He studied the phone; several times he picked it up indecisively, then laid it down.

His wife walked in, putting on her coat and hat. "Well, sorry, but I have to leave." She pinched him on the cheek. "Come on now, cheer up! I'll be back from Red Cross in three hours. You lie around and snooze. I simply *have* to go."

When Clarisse was gone, Harris dialed the phone, nervously.

"M. Munigant?"

The explosions and the sickness in his body after he set the phone down were unbelievable. His bones were racked with every kind of pain, cold and hot, he had ever thought of or experienced in wildest nightmare. He swallowed all the aspirin he could find, in an effort to stave off the assault; but when the doorbell finally rang an hour later, he could not move; he lay weak and exhausted, panting, tears streaming down his cheeks.

"Come in! Come in, for God's sake!"

M. Munigant came in. Thank God the door was unlocked.

Oh, but Mr. Harris looked terrible. M. Munigant stood in the center of the living room, small and dark. Harris nodded. The pains rushed through him, hitting him with large iron hammers and hooks. M. Munigant's eyes glittered as he saw Harris's protuberant bones. Ah, he saw that Mr. Harris was now psychologically prepared for aid. Was it not so? Harris nodded again, feebly, sobbing. M. Munigant still whistled when he talked; something about his tongue and the whistling. No matter. Through his shimmering eyes Harris seemed to see M. Munigant shrink, get smaller. Imagination, of course. Harris sobbed out his story of the Phoenix trip. M. Munigant sympathized. This skeleton was a—a traitor! They would fix him for once and for all!

"M. Munigant," sighed Harris, faintly, "I—I never noticed before. Your tongue. Round, tube-like. Hollow? My eyes. Delirious. What do I do?"

M. Munigant whistled softly, appreciatively, coming closer. If Mr. Harris would relax in his chair, and open his mouth? The lights were switched off. M. Munigant peered into Harris's dropped jaw. Wider, please? It had been so hard, that first visit, to help Harris, with both body and bone in revolt. Now, he had cooperation from the flesh of the man, anyway, even if the skeleton protested. In the darkness, M. Munigant's voice got small, small, tiny, tiny. The whistling became high and shrill. Now. Relax, Mr. Harris. NOW!

Harris felt his jaw pressed violently in all directions, his tongue depressed as with a spoon, his throat clogged. He gasped for breath. Whistle. He couldn't breathe! Something squirmed, corkscrewed his cheeks out, bursting his jaws. Like a hot-water douche, something squirted into his sinuses, his ears clanged! "Ahhhh!" shrieked Harris, gagging. His head, its carapaces riven, shattered, hung loose. Agony shot fire through his lungs.

Harris could breathe again, momentarily. His watery eyes sprang wide. He shouted. His ribs, like sticks, picked up and bundled, were loosened in him. Pain! He fell to the floor, wheezing out his hot breath.

Lights flickered in his senseless eyeballs, he felt his limbs swiftly cast loose and free. Through streaming eyes he saw the parlor.

The room was empty.

"M. Munigant? In God's name, where are you, M. Munigant? Come help me!"

M. Munigant was gone.

"Help!"

Then he heard it.

Deep down in the subterranean fissures of his body, the minute, unbelievable noises; little smackings and twistings and little dry chippings and grindings and nuzzling sounds—like a tiny hungry mouse down in the red-blooded dimness, gnawing ever so earnestly and expertly at what might have been, but was not, a submerged timber . . . !

Clarisse, walking along the sidewalk, held her head high

and marched straight toward her house on Saint James Place. She was thinking of the Red Cross as she turned the corner and almost ran into this little dark man who smelled of iodine.

Clarisse would have ignored him if it were not for the fact that as she passed, he took something long, white and oddly familiar from his coat and proceeded to chew on it, as on a peppermint stick. Its end devoured, his extraordinary tongue darted within the white confection, sucking out the filling, making contented noises. He was still crunching his goody as she proceeded up the sidewalk to her house, turned the doorknob and walked in.

"Darling?" she called, smiling around. "Darling, where are you?" She shut the door, walked down the hall and into the living room. "Darling . . ."

She stared at the floor for twenty seconds, trying to understand.

She screamed.

Outside in the sycamore darkness, the little man pierced a long white stick with intermittent holes; then, softly, sighing, his lips puckered, played a little sad tune upon the improvised instrument to accompany the shrill and awful singing of Clarisse's voice as she stood in the living room.

Many times as a little girl Clarisse had run on the beach sands, stepped on a jellyfish and screamed. It was not so bad, finding an intact, gelatin-skinned jellyfish in one's living room. One could step back from it.

It was when the jellyfish *called you by name . . .*

The Elephant Man

by Sir Frederick Treves

In the Mile End Road, opposite to the London Hospital, there was (and possibly still is) a line of small shops. Among them was a vacant greengrocer's which was to let. The whole of the front of the shop, with the exception of the door, was hidden by a hanging sheet of canvas on which was the announcement that the Elephant Man was to be seen within and that the price of admission was twopence. Painted on the canvas in primitive colors was a life-size portrait of the Elephant Man. This very crude production depicted a frightful creature that could only have been possible in a nightmare. It was the figure of a man with the characteristics of an elephant. The transfiguration was not far advanced. There was still more of the man than of the beast. This fact—that it was still human—was the most repellent attribute of the creature. There was nothing about it of the pitiableness of the misshapen or the deformed, nothing of the grotesqueness of the freak, but merely the loathsome insinuation of a man being changed into an animal. Some palm trees in the background of the picture suggested a jungle and might have led the imaginative to assume that it was in this wild that the perverted object had roamed.

When I first became aware of this phenomenon the exhibition was closed, but a well-informed boy sought the proprietor in a public house and I was granted a private view on payment of a shilling. The shop was empty and gray with dust. Some old tins and a few shriveled potatoes occupied a shelf and some vague vegetable refuse the window. The light in the place was dim, being obscured by the painted placard outside. The far end of the shop—where I expect the late proprietor sat at a desk—was cut off by a curtain or rather by a red tablecloth suspended from a cord by a few rings. The room was cold and dank, for it was the month of November. The year, I might say, was 1884.

The showman pulled back the curtain and revealed a bent figure crouching on a stool and covered by a brown blanket. In front of it, on a tripod, was a large brick heated by a Bunsen burner. Over this the creature was huddled to warm itself. It never moved when the curtain was drawn back. Locked up in an empty shop and lit by the faint blue light of the gas jet, this hunched-up figure was the embodiment of loneliness. It might have been a captive in a cavern or a wizard watching for unholy manifestations in the ghostly flame. Outside the sun was shining and one could hear the footsteps of the passers-by, a tune whistled by a boy, and the companionable hum of traffic in the road.

The showman—speaking as if to a dog—called out harshly: "Stand up!" The thing arose slowly and let the blanket that covered its head and back fall to the ground. There stood revealed the most disgusting specimen of humanity that I have ever seen. In the course of my profession I had come upon lamentable deformities of the face due to injury or disease, as well as mutilations and contortions of the body depending upon like causes; but at no time had I met with such a degraded or perverted version of a human being as this lone figure displayed. He was naked to the waist, his feet were bare, he wore a pair of threadbare trousers that had once belonged to some fat gentleman's dress suit.

From the intensified painting in the street I had imagined the Elephant Man to be of gigantic size. This, however, was a little man below the average height and made to look shorter by the bowing of his back. The most striking feature about him was his enormous and misshapen head. From the brow there projected a huge bony mass like a loaf, while from the back of the head hung a bag of spongy, fungous-looking skin, the surface of which was comparable to brown cauliflower. On the top of the skull were a few long lank hairs. The osseous growth on the forehead almost occluded one eye. The circumference of the head was no less than that of the man's waist. From the upper jaw there projected another mass of bone. It protruded from the mouth like a pink stump, turning the upper lip inside out and making of the mouth a mere slobbering aperture. This growth from the jaw had been so exaggerated in the painting as to appear to be a rudimentary trunk or tusk. The nose was merely a lump of flesh, only recognizable as a nose from its position. The face was no more capable of expression than a block of gnarled wood. The back was horrible, because from it hung, as far down as the middle of the thigh, huge, sack-like masses of flesh covered by the same loathsome cauliflower skin.

The right arm was of enormous size, and shapeless: It suggested the limb of the subject of elephantiasis. It was overgrown also with pendent masses of the same cauliflower-like skin. The hand was large and clumsy—a fin or paddle rather than a hand. There was no distinction between the palm and the back. The thumb had the appearance of a radish, while the fingers might have been thick, tuberous roots. As a limb it was almost useless. The other arm was remarkable by contrast. It was not only normal but was, moreover, a delicately shaped limb covered with fine skin and provided with a beautiful hand which any woman might have envied. From the chest hung a bag of the same repulsive flesh. It was like a dewlap suspended from the neck of a lizard. The lower limbs had the characters of the deformed arm. They were unwieldy, dropsical looking, and grossly misshapen.

To add a further burden to his trouble the wretched man, when a boy, developed hip disease, which had left him permanently lame, so that he could only walk with a stick. He was thus denied all means of escape from his tormentors. As he told me later, he could never run away. One other feature must be mentioned to emphasize his isolation from his kind. Although he was already repellent enough, there arose from the fungous skin-growth with which he was almost covered a very sickening stench which was hard to tolerate. From the showman I learnt nothing about the Elephant Man, except that he was English, that his name was John Merrick, and that he was twenty-one years of age.

As at the time of my discovery of the Elephant Man I was the Lecturer on Anatomy at the Medical College opposite, I was anxious to examine him in detail and to prepare an account of his abnormalities. I therefore arranged with the showman that I should interview his strange exhibit in my room at the college. I became at once conscious of a difficulty. The Elephant Man could not show himself in the streets. He would have been mobbed by the crowd and seized by the police. He was, in fact, as secluded from the world as the Man with the Iron Mask. He had, however, a disguise, although it was almost as startling as he was himself. It consisted of a long black cloak which reached to the ground. Whence the cloak had been obtained I cannot imagine. I had only seen such a garment on the stage wrapped about the figure of a Venetian bravo. The recluse was provided with a pair of bag-like slippers in which to hide his deformed feet. On his head was a cap of a kind that never before was seen. It was black like the cloak, had a wide peak, and the general outline of a yachting cap. As the circumference of Merrick's head was that of a man's waist, the size of this headgear may be imagined. From the attachment of the peak, a gray flannel curtain hung in front of the face. In this mask was cut a wide horizontal slit through which the wearer could look out. This costume, worn by a bent man hobbling along with a stick, is probably the most remarkable and the most uncanny that has as yet been designed. I arranged that Merrick should cross the road in a cab, and to ensure his immediate admission to the college I gave him my card. This card was destined to play a critical part in Merrick's life.

I made a careful examination of my visitor, the result of which I embodied in a paper.* I made little of the man himself. He was shy, confused, not a little frightened, and evidently much cowed. Moreover, his speech was almost unintelligible. The great bony mass that projected from his mouth blurred his utterance and made the articulation of certain words impossible. He returned in a cab to the place of exhibition, and I assumed that I had seen the last of him, especially as I found next day that the show had been forbidden by the police and that the shop was empty.

I supposed that Merrick was imbecile and had been imbecile from birth. The fact that his face was incapable of expression, that his speech was a mere spluttering, and his attitude that of one whose mind was void of all emotions and concerns, gave grounds for this belief. The conviction was no doubt encouraged by the hope that his intellect was the blank I imagined it to be. That he could appreciate his position was unthinkable. Here was a man in the heyday of youth who was so vilely deformed that everyone he met confronted him with a look of horror and disgust. He was taken about the country to be exhibited as a monstrosity and an object of loathing. He was shunned like a leper, housed like a wild beast, and got his only view of the world from a peephole in a showman's cart. He was, moreover, lame, had but one available arm, and could hardly make his utterances understood. It was not until I came to know that Merrick was highly intelligent, that he possessed an acute sensibility and—worse than all—a romantic imagination, that I realized the overwhelming tragedy of his life.

The episode of the Elephant Man was, I imagined, closed; but I was fated to meet him again—two years later—under more dramatic conditions. In England the showman and Merrick had been moved on from place to place by the police, who considered the exhibition degrading and among the things that could not be allowed. It was hoped that in the uncritical retreats of Mile End a more abiding peace would be found. But it was not to be. The official mind there, as elsewhere, very properly decreed that the public exposure of

* *British Medical Journal,* December 1866, and April 1890.

Merrick and his deformities transgressed the limits of decency. The show must close.

The showman, in despair, fled with his charge to the Continent. Whither he roamed at first I do not know; but he came finally to Brussels. His reception was discouraging. Brussels was firm; the exhibition was banned; it was brutal, indecent, and immoral, and could not be permitted within the confines of Belgium. Merrick was thus no longer of value. He was no longer a source of profitable entertainment. He was a burden. He must be got rid of. The elimination of Merrick was a simple matter. He could offer no resistance. He was as docile as a sick sheep. The impresario, having robbed Merrick of his paltry savings, gave him a ticket to London, saw him into the train and no doubt in parting condemned him to perdition.

His destination was Liverpool Street. The journey may be imagined. Merrick was in his alarming outdoor garb. He would be harried by an eager mob as he hobbled along the quay. They would run ahead to get a look at him. They would lift the hem of his cloak to peep at his body. He would try to hide in the train or in some dark corner of the boat, but never could he be free from that ring of curious eyes or from those whispers of fright and aversion. He had but a few shillings in his pocket and nothing either to eat or drink on the way. A panic-dazed dog with a label on his collar would have received some sympathy and possibly some kindness. Merrick received none.

What was he to do when he reached London? He had not a friend in the world. He knew no more of London than he knew of Peking. How could he find a lodging, or what lodginghouse keeper would dream of taking him in? All he wanted was to hide. What most he dreaded were the open street and the gaze of his fellowmen. If even he crept into a cellar the horrid eyes and the still more dreaded whispers would follow him to its depths. Was there ever such a homecoming!

At Liverpool Street he was rescued from the crowd by the police and taken into the third-class waiting room. Here he sank on the floor in the darkest corner. The police were at a loss what to do with him. They had dealt with strange and moldy tramps, but never with such an object as this. He could not explain himself. His speech was so maimed that he might as well have spoken in Arabic. He had, however, something with him which he produced with a ray of hope. It was my card.

The card simplified matters. It made it evident that this curious creature had an acquaintance and that the individual must be sent for. A messenger was dispatched to the London Hospital, which is comparatively near at hand. Fortunately I was in the building and returned at once with the messenger to the station. In the waiting room I had some difficulty in making a way through the crowd, but there, on the floor in the corner, was Merrick. He looked a mere heap. It seemed as if he had been thrown there like a bundle. He was so huddled up and so helpless looking that he might have had both his arms and his legs broken. He seemed pleased to see me, but he was nearly done. The journey and want of food had reduced him to the last stage of exhaustion. The police kindly helped him into a cab, and I drove him at once to the hospital. He appeared to be content, for he fell asleep almost as soon as he was seated and slept to the journey's end. He never said a word, but seemed to be satisfied that all was well.

In the attics of the hospital was an isolation ward with a single bed. It was used for emergency purposes—for a case of delirium tremens, for a man who had become suddenly insane, or for a patient with an undetermined fever. Here the Elephant Man was deposited on a bed, was made comfortable, and was supplied with food. I had been guilty of an irregularity in admitting such a case, for the hospital was neither a refuge nor a home for incurables. Chronic cases were not accepted, but only those requiring active treatment, and Merrick was not in need of such treatment. I applied to the sympathetic chairman of the committee, Mr. Carr Gomm, who not only was good enough to approve my action, but who agreed with me that Merrick must not again be turned out into the world.

Mr. Carr Gomm wrote a letter to *The Times* detailing the circumstances of the refugee and asking for money for his support. So generous is the English public that in a few days—I think in a week—enough money was forthcoming to maintain Merrick for life without any charge upon the hospital funds. There chanced to be two empty rooms at the back of the hospital which were little used. They were on the ground floor, were out of the way, and opened upon a large courtyard called Bedstead Square, because here the iron beds were marshaled for cleaning and painting. The front room

211

was converted into a bed-sitting room and the smaller chamber into a bathroom. The condition of Merrick's skin rendered a bath at least once a day a necessity, and I might here mention that with the use of the bath the unpleasant odor to which I have referred ceased to be noticeable. Merrick took up his abode in the hospital in December 1886.

Merrick had now something he had never dreamed of, never supposed to be possible—a home of his own for life. I at once began to make myself acquainted with him and to endeavor to understand his mentality. It was a study of much interest. I very soon learnt his speech so that I could talk freely with him. This afforded him great satisfaction, for, curiously enough, he had a passion for conversation, yet all his life had had no one to talk to. I—having then much leisure—saw him almost every day, and made a point of spending some two hours with him every Sunday morning when he would chatter almost without ceasing. It was unreasonable to expect one nurse to attend him continuously, but there was no lack of temporary volunteers. As they did not all acquire his speech it came about that I had occasionally to act as an interpreter.

I found Merrick, as I have said, remarkably intelligent. He had learnt to read and had become a most voracious reader. I think he had been taught when he was in the hospital with his diseased hip. His range of books was limited. The Bible and Prayer Book he knew intimately, but he had subsisted for the most part upon newspapers, or rather upon such fragments of old journals as he had chanced to pick up. He had read a few stories and some elementary lesson books, but the delight of his life was a romance, especially a love romance. These tales were very real to him, as real as any narrative in the Bible, so that he would tell them to me as incidents in the lives of people who had lived. In his outlook upon the world he was a child, yet a child with some of the tempestuous feelings of a man. He was an elemental being, so primitive that he might have spent the twenty-three years of his life immured in a cave.

Of his early days I could learn but little. He was very loath to talk about the past. It was a nightmare, the shudder of which was still upon him. He was born, he believed, in or about Leicester. Of his father he knew absolutely nothing. Of his mother he had some memory. It was very faint and had, I think, been elaborated in his mind into something definite. Mothers figured in the tales he had read, and he wanted his

212

mother to be one of those comfortable lullaby-singing persons who are so lovable. In his subconscious mind there was apparently a germ of recollection in which someone figured who had been kind to him. He clung to this conception and made it more real by invention, for since the day when he could toddle no one had been kind to him. As an infant he must have been repellent, although his deformities did not become gross until he had attained his full stature.

It was a favorite belief of his that his mother was beautiful. The fiction was, I am aware, one of his own making, but it was a great joy to him. His mother, lovely as she may have been, basely deserted him when he was very small, so small that his earliest clear memories were of the workhouse to which he had been taken. Worthless and inhuman as this mother was, he spoke of her with pride and even with reverence. Once, when referring to his own appearance, he said: "It *is* very strange, for, you see, Mother was so beautiful."

The rest of Merrick's life up to the time that I met him at Liverpool Street Station was one dull record of degradation and squalor. He was dragged from town to town and from fair to fair as if he were a strange beast in a cage. A dozen times a day he would have to expose his nakedness and his piteous deformities before a gaping crowd who greeted him with such mutterings as "Oh! what a horror! What a beast!" He had had no childhood. He had had no boyhood. He had never experienced pleasure. He knew nothing of the joy of living nor of the fun of things. His sole idea of happiness was to creep into the dark and hide. Shut up alone in a booth, awaiting the next exhibition, how mocking must have sounded the laughter and merriment of the boys and girls outside who were enjoying the "fun of the fair!" He had no past to look back upon and no future to look forward to. At the age of twenty he was a creature without hope. There was nothing in front of him but a vista of caravans creeping along a road, of rows of glaring show tents and of circles of staring eyes with, at the end, the spectacle of a broken man in a poor law infirmary.

Those who are interested in the evolution of character might speculate as to the effect of this brutish life upon a sensitive and intelligent man. It would be reasonable to surmise that he would become a spiteful and malignant misanthrope, swollen with venom and filled with hatred of his

213

fellowmen, or, on the other hand, that he would degenerate into a despairing melancholic on the verge of idiocy. Merrick, however, was no such being. He had passed through the fire and had come out unscathed. His troubles had ennobled him. He showed himself to be a gentle, affectionate, and lovable creature, as amiable as a happy woman, free from any trace of cynicism or resentment, without a grievance and without an unkind word for anyone. I have never heard him complain. I have never heard him deplore his ruined life or resent the treatment he had received at the hands of callous keepers. His journey through life had been indeed along a *via dolorosa*, the road had been uphill all the way, and now, when the night was at its blackest and the way most steep, he had suddenly found himself, as it were, in a friendly inn, bright with light and warm with welcome. His gratitude to those about him was pathetic in its sincerity and eloquent in the childlike simplicity with which it was expressed.

As I learnt more of this primitive creature I found that there were two anxieties which were prominent in his mind and which he revealed to me with diffidence. He was in the occupation of the rooms assigned to him and had been assured that he would be cared for to the end of his days. This, however, he found hard to realize, for he often asked me timidly to what place he would next be moved. To understand his attitude it is necessary to remember that he had been moving on and moving on all his life. He knew no other state of existence. To him it was normal. He had passed from the workhouse to the hospital, from the hospital back to the workhouse, then from this town to that town, or from one showman's caravan to another. He had never known a home nor any semblance of one. He had no possessions. His sole belongings, besides his clothes and some books, were the monstrous cap and the cloak. He was a wanderer, a pariah and an outcast. That his quarters at the hospital were his for life he could not understand. He could not rid his mind of the anxiety which had pursued him for so many years—where am I to be taken next?

Another trouble was his dread of his fellowmen, his fear of people's eyes, the dread of being always stared at, the lash of the cruel mutterings of the crowd. In his home in Bedstead Square he was secluded; but now and then a thoughtless porter or a wardmaid would open his door to let curious friends have a peep at the Elephant Man. It therefore seemed to him as if the gaze of the world followed him still.

Influenced by these two obsessions he became, during his first few weeks at the hospital, curiously uneasy. At last, with much hesitation, he said to me one day: "When I am next moved can I go to a blind asylum or to a lighthouse?" He had read about blind asylums in the newspapers and was attracted by the thought of being among people who could not see. The lighthouse had another charm. It meant seclusion from the curious. There at least no one could open a door and peep in at him. There he would forget that he had once been the Elephant Man. There he would escape the vampire showman. He had never seen a lighthouse, but he had come upon a picture of the Eddystone, and it appeared to him that this lonely column of stone in the waste of the sea was such a home as he had longed for.

I had no great difficulty in ridding Merrick's mind of these ideas. I wanted him to get accustomed to his fellowmen, to become a human being himself, and to be admitted to the communion of his kind. He appeared day by day less frightened, less haunted looking, less anxious to hide, less alarmed when he saw his door being opened. He got to know most of the people about the place, to be accustomed to their comings and goings, and to realize that they took no more than a friendly notice of him. He could only go out after dark, and on fine nights ventured to take a walk in Bedstead Square clad in his black cloak and his cap. His greatest adventure was on one moonless evening when he walked alone as far as the hospital garden and back again.

To secure Merrick's recovery and to bring him, as it were, to life once more, it was necessary that he should make the acquaintance of men and women who would treat him as a normal and intelligent young man and not as a monster of deformity. Women I felt to be more important than men in bringing about his transformation. Women were the more frightened of him, the more disgusted at his appearance, and the more apt to give way to irrepressible expressions of aversion when they came into his presence. Moreover, Merrick had an admiration of women of such a kind that it attained almost to adoration. This was not the outcome of his personal experience. They were not real women, but the products of his imagination. Among them was the beautiful mother surrounded, at a respectful distance, by heroines from the many romances he had read.

His first entry to the hospital was attended by a regrettable incident. He had been placed on the bed in the little attic, and a nurse had been instructed to bring him some food. Unfortunately, she had not been fully informed of Merrick's unusual appearance. As she entered the room she saw on the bed, propped up by white pillows, a monstrous figure as hideous as an Indian idol. She at once dropped the tray she was carrying and fled, with a shriek, through the door. Merrick was too weak to notice much, but the experience, I am afraid, was not new to him.

He was looked after by volunteer nurses whose ministrations were somewhat formal and constrained. Merrick, no doubt, was conscious that their service was purely official, that they were merely doing what they were told to do, and that they were acting rather as automatons than as women. They did not help him to feel that he was of their kind. On the contrary, they, without knowing it, made him aware that the gulf of separation was immeasurable.

Feeling this, I asked a friend of mine, a young and pretty widow, if she thought she could enter Merrick's room with a smile, wish him good morning, and shake him by the hand. She said she could, and she did. The effect upon poor Merrick was not quite what I had expected. As he let go her hand he bent his head on his knees and sobbed until I thought he would never cease. The interview was over. He told me afterwards that this was the first woman who had ever smiled at him, and the first woman, in the whole of his life, who had shaken hands with him. From this day the transformation of Merrick commenced and he began to change, little by little, from a hunted thing into a man. It was a wonderful change to witness and one that never ceased to fascinate me.

Merrick's case attracted much attention in the papers, with the result that he had a constant succession of visitors. Everybody wanted to see him. He must have been visited by almost every lady of note in the social world. They were all good enough to welcome him with a smile and to shake hands with him. The Merrick whom I had found shivering behind a rag of a curtain in an empty shop was now conversant with duchesses and countesses and other ladies of high degree. They brought him presents, made his room bright with ornaments and pictures, and, what pleased him more than all, supplied him with books. He soon had a large library, and most of his day was spent in reading. He was not the least spoiled; not the least puffed up; he never asked for anything; never presumed upon the kindness meted out to

216

him, and was always humbly and profoundly grateful. Above all, he lost his shyness. He liked to see his door pushed open and people to look in. He became acquainted with most of the frequenters of Bedstead Square, would chat with them at his window, and show them some of his choicest presents. He improved in his speech, although to the end his utterances were not easy for strangers to understand. He was beginning, moreover, to be less conscious of his unsightliness, a little disposed to think it was, after all, not so very extreme. Possibly this was aided by the circumstance that I would not allow a mirror of any kind in his room.

The height of his social development was reached on an eventful day when Queen Alexandra—then Princess of Wales—came to the hospital to pay him a special visit. With that kindness which has marked every act of her life, the Queen entered Merrick's room smiling and shook him warmly by the hand. Merrick was transported with delight. This was beyond even his most extravagant dream. The Queen has made many people happy, but I think no gracious act of hers has ever caused such happiness as she brought into Merrick's room when she sat by his chair and talked to him as to a person she was glad to see.

Merrick, I may say, was now one of the most contented creatures I have chanced to meet. More than once he said to me: "I am happy every hour of the day." This was good to think upon when I recalled the half-dead heap of miserable humanity I had seen in the corner of the waiting room at Liverpool Street. Most men of Merrick's age would have expressed their joy and sense of contentment by singing or whistling when they were alone. Unfortunately, poor Merrick's mouth was so deformed that he could neither whistle nor sing. He was satisfied to express himself by beating time upon the pillow to some tune that was ringing in his head. I have many times found him so occupied when I have entered his room unexpectedly. One thing that always struck me as sad about Merrick was the fact that he could not smile. Whatever his delight might be, his face remained expressionless. He could weep but he could not smile.

The Queen paid Merrick many visits and sent him every year a Christmas card with a message in her own handwriting. On one occasion she sent him a signed photograph of herself. Merrick, quite overcome, regarded it as a sacred object and would hardly allow me to touch it. He cried over it, and after it was framed, had it put up in his room as a

217

kind of icon. I told him that he must write to Her Royal Highness to thank her for her goodness. This he was pleased to do, as he was very fond of writing letters, never before in his life having had anyone to write to. I allowed the letter to be dispatched unedited. It began, "My dear Princess," and ended, "Yours very sincerely." Unorthodox as it was, it was expressed in terms any courtier would have envied.

Other ladies followed the Queen's gracious example and sent their photographs to this delighted creature who had been all his life despised and rejected of men. His mantelpiece and table became so covered with photographs of handsome ladies, with dainty knickknacks and pretty trifles, that they may almost have befitted the apartment of an Adonis-like actor or of a famous tenor.

Through all these bewildering incidents, and through the glamor of this great change, Merrick still remained in many ways a mere child. He had all the invention of an imaginative boy or girl, the same love of "make-believe," the same instinct of "dressing up," and of personating heroic and impressive characters. This attitude of mind was illustrated by the following incident. Benevolent visitors had given me, from time to time, sums of money to be expended for the comfort of the *ci-devant* Elephant Man. When one Christmas was approaching I asked Merrick what he would like me to purchase as a Christmas present. He rather startled me by saying shyly that he would like a dressing-bag with silver fittings. He had seen a picture of such an article in an advertisement which he had furtively preserved.

The association of a silver-fitted dressing-bag with the poor wretch wrapped up in a dirty blanket in an empty shop was hard to comprehend. I fathomed the mystery in time, for Merrick made little secret of the fancies that haunted his boyish brain. Just as a small girl with a tinsel coronet and a window curtain for a train will realize the conception of a countess on her way to court, so Merrick loved to imagine himself a dandy and a young man about town. Mentally, no doubt, he had frequently "dressed up" for the part. He could "make-believe" with great effect, but he wanted something to render his fancied character more realistic. Hence the jaunty bag which was to assume the function of the toy coronet and the window curtain that could transform a mite with a pigtail into a countess.

As a theatrical "property" the dressing-bag was ingenious, since there was little else to give substance to the transformation. Merrick could not wear the silk hat of the dandy, nor, indeed, any kind of hat. He could not adapt his body to the trimly cut coat. His deformity was such that he could wear neither collar nor tie, while in association with his bulbous feet, the young blood's patent leather shoe was unthinkable. What was there left to make up the character? A lady had given him a ring to wear on his undeformed hand, and a noble lord had presented him with a very stylish walking stick. But these things, helpful as they were, were hardly sufficing.

The dressing-bag, however, was distinctive, was explanatory, and entirely characteristic. So the bag was obtained, and Merrick the Elephant Man became, in the seclusion of his chamber, the Piccadilly exquisite, the young spark, the gallant, the "nut." When I purchased the article I realized that, as Merrick could never travel, he could hardly want a dressing-bag. He could not use the silver-backed brushes and the comb because he had no hair to brush. The ivory-handled razors were useless because he could not shave. The deformity of his mouth rendered an ordinary toothbrush of no avail, and as his monstrous lips could not hold a cigarette, the cigarette case was a mockery. The silver shoehorn would be of no service in the putting on of his ungainly slippers, while the hat brush was quite unsuited to the peaked cap with its visor.

Still, the bag was an emblem of the real swell and of the knockabout Don Juan of whom he had read. So every day Merrick laid out upon his table, with proud precision, the silver brushes, the razors, the shoehorn, and the silver cigarette case, which I had taken care to fill with cigarettes. The contemplation of these gave him great pleasure, and such is the power of self-deception that they convinced him he was the "real thing."

I think there was just one shadow in Merrick's life. As I have already said, he had a lively imagination; he was romantic; he cherished an emotional regard for women, and his favourite pursuit was the reading of love stories. He fell in love—in a humble and devotional way—with, I think, every attractive lady he saw. He, no doubt, pictured himself the hero of many a passionate incident. His bodily deformity had left unmarred the instincts and feelings of his years. He was amorous. He would like to have been a lover, to have walked with the beloved object in the languorous shades of some beautiful garden, and to have poured into her ear all the glowing utterances that he had rehearsed in his heart. And yet—the pity of it!—imagine the feelings of such a youth when he saw nothing but a look of horror creep over the face of every girl whose eyes met his. I fancy when he talked of life among the blind there was a half-formed idea in his mind that he might be able to win the affection of a woman if only she were without eyes to see.

As Merrick developed he began to display certain modest ambitions in the direction of improving his mind and enlarging his knowledge of the world. He was as curious as a child and as eager to learn. There were so many things he wanted to know and to see. In the first place, he was anxious to view the interior of what he called "a real house," such a house as figured in many of the tales he knew, a house with a hall, a drawing room where guests were received, and a dining room with plates on the sideboard and with easy chairs into which the hero could "fling himself." The workhouse, the common lodging house, and a variety of mean garrets were all the residences he knew. To satisfy this wish I drove him up to my small house in Wimpole Street. He was absurdly interested, and examined everything in detail and with untiring curiosity. I could not show him the pampered menials and the powdered footmen of whom he had read, nor could I produce the white marble staircase of the mansion of romance nor the gilded mirrors and the brocaded divans which belong to that style of residence. I explained that the house was a modest dwelling of the Jane Austen type, and as he had read *Emma* he was content.

A more burning ambition of his was to go to the theater. It was a project very difficult to satisfy. A popular pantomime was then in progress at Drury Lane Theatre, but the problem was how so conspicuous a being as the Elephant Man could be got there, and how he was to see the performance without attracting the notice of the audience and causing a panic or, at least, an unpleasant diversion. The whole matter was most ingeniously carried through by that kindest of women and most able of actresses—Mrs. Kendal. She made the necessary arrangements with the lessee of the theater. A box was obtained. Merrick was brought up in a carriage with drawn blinds and was allowed to make use of the royal entrance so as to reach the box by a private stair. I had begged three of the hospital sisters to don evening dress and to sit in the front row in order to "dress" the box, on the one hand, and to form a screen for Merrick on the other.

220

Merrick and I occupied the back of the box, which was kept in shadow. All went well, and no one saw a figure, more monstrous than any on the stage, mount the staircase or cross the corridor.

One has often witnessed the unconstrained delight of a child at its first pantomime, but Merrick's rapture was much more intense as well as much more solemn. Here was a being with the brain of a man, the fancies of a youth, and the imagination of a child. His attitude was not so much that of delight as of wonder and amazement. He was awed. He was enthralled. The spectacle left him speechless, so that if he were spoken to he took no heed. He often seemed to be panting for breath. I could not help comparing him with a man of his own age in the stalls. This satiated individual was bored to distraction, would look wearily at the stage from time to time, and then yawn as if he had not slept for nights; while at the same time Merrick was thrilled by a vision that was almost beyond his comprehension. Merrick talked of this pantomime for weeks and weeks. To him, as to a child with the faculty of make-believe, everything was real; the palace was the home of kings, the princess was of royal blood, the fairies were as undoubted as the children in the street, while the dishes at the banquet were of unquestionable gold. He did not like to discuss it as a play but rather as a vision of some actual world. When this mood possessed him, he would say: "I wonder what the prince did after we left," or "Do you think that poor man is still in the dungeon?" and so on and so on.

The splendor and display impressed him, but, I think, the ladies of the ballet took a still greater hold upon his fancy. He did not like the ogres and the giants, while the funny men impressed him as irreverent. Having no experience as a boy of romping and ragging, of practical jokes or of "larks," he had little sympathy with the doings of the clown, but, I think (moved by some mischievous instinct in his subconscious mind), he was pleased when the policeman was smacked in the face, knocked down, and generally rendered undignified.

Later on another longing stirred the depths of Merrick's mind. It was a desire to see the country, a desire to live in some green secluded spot and there learn something about flowers and the ways of animals and birds. The country as viewed from a wagon on a dusty high road was all the country he knew. He had never wandered among the fields nor followed the windings of a wood. He had never climbed to the brow of a breezy down. He had never gathered flowers in a meadow. Since so much of his reading dealt with country life he was possessed by the wish to see the wonders of that life himself.

This involved a difficulty greater than that presented by a visit to the theater. The project was, however, made possible on this occasion also by the kindness and generosity of a lady—Lady Knightley—who offered Merrick a holiday home in a cottage on her estate. Merrick was conveyed to the railway station in the usual way, but as he could hardly venture to appear on the platform the railway authorities were good enough to run a second-class carriage into a distant siding. To this point Merrick was driven and was placed in the carriage unobserved. The carriage, with the curtains drawn, was then attached to the mainline train.

He duly arrived at the cottage, but the housewife (like the nurse at the hospital) had not been made clearly aware of the unfortunate man's appearance. Thus it happened that when Merrick presented himself, his hostess, throwing her apron over her head, fled, gasping, to the fields. She affirmed that such a guest was beyond her powers of endurance, for, when she saw him, she was "that took" as to be in danger of being permanently "all of a tremble."

Merrick was then conveyed to a gamekeeper's cottage which was hidden from view and was close to the margin of a wood. The man and his wife were able to tolerate his presence. They treated him with the greatest kindness, and with them he spent the one supreme holiday of his life. He could roam where he pleased. He met no one on his wanderings, for the wood was preserved and denied to all but the gamekeeper and the forester.

There is no doubt that Merrick passed in this retreat the happiest time he had as yet experienced. He was alone in a land of wonders. The breath of the country passed over him like a healing wind. Into the silence of the wood the fearsome voice of the showman could never penetrate. No cruel eyes could peep at him through the friendly undergrowth. It seemed as if in this place of peace all stain had been wiped away from his sullied past. The Merrick who had once crouched terrified in the filthy shadows of a Mile End shop was now sitting in the sun, in a clearing among the trees, arranging a bunch of violets he had gathered.

His letters to me were the letters of a delighted and enthusiastic child. He gave an account of his trivial adventures, of the amazing things he had seen, and of the beautiful sounds he had heard. He had met with strange birds, had startled a hare from her form, had made friends with a fierce dog, and had watched the trout darting in a stream. He sent me some of the wild flowers he had picked. They were of the commonest and most familiar kind, but they were evidently regarded by him as rare and precious specimens.

He came back to London, to his quarters in Bedstead Square, much improved in health, pleased to be "home" again, and to be once more among his books, his treasures, and his many friends.

Some six months after Merrick's return from the country he was found dead in bed. This was in April 1890. He was lying on his back as if asleep, and had evidently died suddenly and without a struggle, since not even the coverlet of the bed was disturbed. The method of his death was peculiar. So large and so heavy was his head that he could not sleep lying down. When he assumed the recumbent position the massive skull was inclined to drop backwards, with the result that he experienced no little distress. The attitude he was compelled to assume when he slept was very strange. He sat up in bed with his back supported by pillows, his knees were drawn up, and his arms clasped round his legs, while his head rested on the points of his bent knees.

He often said to me that he wished he could lie down to sleep "like other people." I think on this last night he must, with some determination, have made the experiment. The pillow was soft, and the head, when placed on it, must have fallen backwards and caused a dislocation of the neck. Thus it came about that his death was due to the desire that had dominated his life—the pathetic but hopeless desire to be "like other people."

As a specimen of humanity, Merrick was ignoble and repulsive; but the spirit of Merrick, if it could be seen in the form of the living, would assume the figure of an upstanding and heroic man, smooth browed and clean of limb, and with eyes that flashed undaunted courage.

His tortured journey had come to an end. All the way he, like another, had borne on his back a burden almost too grievous to bear. He had been plunged into the Slough of Despond, but with manly steps had gained the farther shore. He had been made "a spectacle to all men" in the heartless

223

streets of Vanity Fair. He had been ill-treated and reviled and bespattered with the mud of Disdain. He had escaped the clutches of the Giant Despair, and at last had reached the "Place of Deliverance," where "his burden loosed from off his shoulders and fell from off his back, so that he saw it no more."